AT THE HEART OF MURDER

In all the years of reporting to crime scenes
and viewing murdered human beings, Vince
had never really gotten used to the sheer
violence of it. He was no longer squeamish
about seeing broken and mutilated corpses;
they were the stuff of homicides and homicide
detectives soon hardened themselves to the
mechanics of killing. What was hard for him,
and for all cops, was bridging the gap between
accepting random violence and understanding it. A successful homicide investigation
hinged on the investigator's ability to climb
inside a killer's head and reconstruct his
motives. He had to finally arrive at a point
where the murder made as much sense to him
as it did to the murderer. Most killings were
senseless, and Vince knew that a lot of homicide detectives went as bonkers as their quarry trying to get into that frame of mind . . .

Bill Kelly, NYPD
and Dolph Le Moult

CHARTER BOOKS, NEW YORK

STREET DANCE

A Charter Book/published by arrangement with
the authors

PRINTING HISTORY
Charter edition/December 1987

ISBN: 0-441-79033-X

Charter Books are published by The Berkley Publishing Group,
200 Madison Avenue, New York, New York 10016.

The name "Charter" and the "C" logo
are trademarks belonging to Charter Communications, Inc.

PRINTED IN THE UNITED STATES OF AMERICA

10 9 8 7 6 5 4 3 2 1

The following is a work of fiction. The incidents and characters portrayed are based on real persons and events in the twenty-year career of Homicide Detective Bill Kelly, Police Department of the City of New York.

1

IN MID-MARCH THE streets and alleyways surrounding Macy Futterman's store in the East Bronx take on the appearance of death. The last pale remnants of sooty snow reveal the ravages of winter, the random refuse of a beleaguered and uncaring citizenry: papers, bits of food and aluminum cans, a dog's rotting carcass, a baby carriage stripped of all but its metal frame, broken glass everywhere, a discarded typewriter, one black high-top basketball sneaker, a Christmas wreath.

During the day the population carries on with grim purpose. They are men and women with barely concealed fear and anger; mostly old, wrapped and corseted against the rage of weather and circumstance. They walk faster than in spring or summer, partly to flee the freezing streets, partly to escape muggers and panhandlers, their eyes cast downward, not wanting to see more than is absolutely necessary to reach their destination.

At night broken concrete and worn cobblestones flatten to the howl of icy winds from the East River. I-beams groan; ancient wooden joists crack; families huddle in their beds or around makeshift gasoline heaters, finding whatever warmth they can in unheated apartments abandoned by the

1

landlords. The streets are almost empty. Here and there isolated bands of vagrants hover over burning garbage cans; young blacks argue over the price of a bag of heroin; an aging prostitute slouches in a urine-soaked doorway. Above all is the incessant wail of the siren: a police patrol car speeding toward an armed robbery in progress, a disturbed teenage mother of four teetering on the edge of a rooftop, a domestic disturbance, or a homicide. Sometimes it is simply a warning—the cop's way of telling the felon that he is at the end of his shift and heading in, that criminal activity should be suspended at least until the car passes. No more busts tonight. No more paperwork . . .

Macy Futterman knows all the sounds, all the signs. He has been operating his store at this location since 1942. Like the area around it, the store has changed over the years. When he bought it, it was a soda fountain and magazine store. The neighborhood was mostly Jewish then, with a smattering of Irish and Italians mixed in. The store was a gathering place where a richly ethnic potpourri of gossip and debate was held daily over frosty seltzers, glasses of hot tea, and generous slabs of raisin pumpernickel bread baked fresh daily by his wife Sarah in their small apartment upstairs.

Now the fountain has been replaced by a row of electronic video games: Pac-Man, Donkey Kong, Centipede—the mindless amusement of bored neighborhood youths. *Time, Collier's,* and *Harper's Bazaar* have been replaced by the *National Enquirer*. The face of the store has changed reluctantly over the years with the changing population of the street. Macy's old friends, those who are still alive and have stayed in the neighborhood, no longer come to the store for conversation and companionship. Like the Futtermans, they triple-lock their doors at night and cower in their remembrances, venturing out only on "Shabbas," and then only in groups of six or more.

*   *   *

"You there, in the leather pants . . . either you buy it or put it back on the rack. This ain't no library!"

The figure in the tight leather pants paused awkwardly before the magazine rack, unsure of how to respond. He despised confrontations, dreaded them in his dreams. He would buy the magazine if he had the money, but he was practically flat broke, his last twenty dollars spent on two dime bags of smack just three hours ago.

"It's a piece of shit anyway," he snarled, shoving the magazine back in the rack upside down. "Who needs it?"

"They're all shit," Macy concurred. "Garbage, every one of them."

"Well you can keep your garbage, garbage man, cause I already seen it all."

"I'm sure you have." Macy followed him to the door with his eyes and replaced the magazine right side up on the rack. It was almost six-thirty, close enough to closing time. Upstairs, Sarah would be waiting, looking forward to seeing him for the first time since early that morning. She never came down into the store anymore. They never even discussed it. He locked the door and turned off the lights. For a moment, the mirror of his mind caught the faint smell of raisin pumpernickel.

Outside, the figure in the leather leotards lit a reefer and inhaled deeply. He was Miguel Ramos, a transsexual prostitute who had adopted the street name of Marguerita. Transplanted from Cuba in the freedom flotilla of 1980, he spoke heavily accentuated English with an almost comical feminine lilt. His voice was high and scratchy, a partial result of the massive doses of the female hormones estrogen and progesterone he had been taking for more than three years. When he worked he was a waiter, but alcoholism and drug addiction had rendered him unemployable in that trade. Now, he did the best he could, turning tricks and dealing drugs when the opportunity presented itself.

Tonight he had been unable to score, and time was

running out. He had to make a connection—another quarter load, better still a half, to get him through the night. That meant turning a trick as soon as possible, but nothing had worked for him so far; not the men's room at the bus station, not the park, not the head shop. More than likely, anyone in the market for a little action was snug in some bar by now. He took a last deep drag on the reefer, clipped the end, and headed for the river.

The Blue Parrot was an illegal after-hours drinking spot frequented by male homosexuals, two flights below street level at the rear of an abandoned small-appliance factory overlooking the East River. Marguerita shifted his weight uneasily on the freezing stairwell as an unseen eye behind the sliding door panel scrutinized him. After what seemed an eternity, the door slowly opened and he was admitted by Shampoo, the maître d', matchmaker, bouncer, and sergeant at arms.

"It's early," Shampoo grunted. "Nobody's here yet."

Marguerita surveyed the darkened room. A few scattered early arrivals were sipping drinks amid the crush of chairs and tables crowded into the small space. The bar was empty except for Rickyanne, the bartender, who was slicing fruit for the evening's mixed drinks. Raoul, the owner, was preparing the stage for the night's show: pink and yellow pillows, some oversized peacock feathers, nothing too exotic. Probably just a couple of fairies grunting and sucking, Marguerita thought as he headed for the club's only bathroom. Raoul was too cheap to spring for anything more imaginative.

Inside, the bathroom was cramped and smelly, the walls crusted with slime and graffiti. Two oversize turds clung tenaciously to the sides of the waterless toilet bowl, surrounded by mounds of fetid, sopping paper. Gingerly, he released the flush handle with his foot. Nothing happened. A class joint, the Blue Parrot.

The milky, pockmarked mirror over the sink reflected his

face, beardless now as a result of the hormone treatments. Somehow softer than it once had been. Still, there were too many wrinkles, the eyes too bulgy and bloodshot. His hair seemed stringy and lifeless. How long since he'd had a permanent—a month, two? Things had been moving too fast lately for that kind of simple indulgence. Besides, a fancy hairdo would be too good for the pigs he'd been tricking lately. They couldn't have cared less whether he had hair or not.

He turned sideways to the mirror and noted his profile. The breasts were becoming round and firm, peaking to erect nipples that strained the fabric of the flimsy cotton blouse he was wearing. Each day Miguel was becoming more and more Marguerita. The hormone treatments were smoothing out the hard edges, molding his body into the woman it had always yearned to be.

With effort, he wriggled the tight leather leotards down over his hips and pissed into the reeking bowl. Seven thirty-five; if he was going to score, it would have to be soon, before the butches and bikers swaggered in and muscled all the choice meat. Whatever was out there now would have to do. There was no time to be choosy. That was an option he had abandoned long ago.

Outside, Raoul was testing strobe lighting for tonight's performance, bouncing beams of blinding color off the walls and ceiling, bracketing the scattered patrons in hard silhouette. Marguerita squinted through the unaccustomed glare, faces assaulting him like kidney punches, grins and death masks like faces in a Fellini film. They were flaccid and jowly, hard and catlike, ancient and innocent, drawn together to this place in common need, mutual desperation. They were the ghouls and hobgoblins of his dreams, the grim routine of his daily existence.

"Hi, bitch!" Rickyanne greeted him at the bar. "You look positively dreadful."

He ignored it. "Anything interesting here tonight?"

Rickyanne grimaced. "Hog slop. The absolute depths. You better check yourself into a clinic and get some meth, darling. There's no way you're gonna score enough to get yourself fixed in this cesspool."

Marguerita peered into the blackness, spotted a solitary figure in the flickering half-light reflected by the strobes. "Who's that over by the post?"

"Dunno, darling. Never saw the bitch before. Probably some friend of Raoul's."

He made his way through the maze of tightly packed tables to where the stranger was seated. "Hi, I'm Marguerita."

The face was bland, not handsome, but seemingly alert. The stranger stared for a moment, and then motioned to the empty chair beside him. "My name is Robin. I'm looking for someone to have sex with."

Marguerita was startled and somewhat pleased at this directness. He sat and softly touched the stranger's knee. "Will you buy me a drink first?"

The knee jerked away. "How much?"

Marguerita swallowed hard. "Fifty for the night, another ten for the room . . ."

"Thirty dollars for two hours. We'll use my place."

The money was too little, and an unfamiliar place could be dangerous. Still, it was only two hours. He could hold it together for that long, bargain for a quarter load in the neighborhood, then get fixed and return in time to pick up any straggles that might be left over in the Blue Parrot. Time was critical and haggling for a few extra bucks would only get him more strung out. He smiled, took the stranger by the hand, and accompanied him out into the street.

2

BILLY WHALEN WAS asleep, frail now, almost birdlike, hunched forward in the hospital wheelchair and drooling on the cold linoleum floor. Vince Crowley took a handkerchief from his pocket and wiped away some of the yellow mucus that had accumulated at the corners of Billy's mouth. He adjusted the green hospital blanket around Billy's shoulders and brushed a strand of greasy black hair from his face. "Doesn't anybody ever give him a bath?" He glared across the dining room at Ricco, the male nurse.

Ricco acknowledged with a disinterested shrug. Faggot, Vince thought. He doesn't know and he doesn't care. Most of the staff were that way. He guessed it was a defense mechanism, a way of not getting too close. The ones who allowed themselves to become involved with the patients usually burned out early. Most of them only lasted a few months, a year tops. It was depressing work and the pay was lousy. Only Ricco stayed. He alone had been there when Billy was first admitted back in 1980. Ricco seemed to like the work. He was growing old in the place.

Four years . . . Billy was growing old, too, even if you couldn't tell it. His face remained unlined, as fresh and youthful as it had ever been. With the exception of a drooping left eyelid that had crusted shut, it seemed an alert face. At rest, maybe; catching a couple of hard-earned Z's between shifts, or just pondering. Billy was a great one for pondering. He did more thinking asleep than most cops did when they were awake.

The hospital dining room was almost empty; a few patients spread randomly, staring, smoking, shuffling around. The far end of the room was a blackboard, streaky, with a few crude drawings: flowers, birds, an airplane. Someone had written a poem:

> *And we went picnicking*
> *marshmallow sky thick enveloping*
> *festooning the catafalque*
> *where we lay . . .*

Always the drawings were about freedom, Vince thought. Freedom and death. A young girl, fifteen or sixteen, had started to play the piano in the corner of the room. She was wearing a quilted, flowery bathrobe, her hair wrapped in oversize curlers. Vince remembered Sister Mary Dominick, the old nun at Our Lady of Lourdes Grammar School in Queens Village who had tried to teach him to play the piano. She'd carried a wooden ruler and used it on his knuckles when he messed up a chord or hit a sour note. How many piano lessons had there been? Ten, twelve? Sister Mary Dominick had given up on him somewhere along the way, he remembered. She would sit him down and make him listen to her play. Sometimes she played show tunes or lullabies he could recognize, but most of the time she just sat and repeated the same mournful set of chords over and over, crying for the entire hour he was there. It was an odd memory, but it stuck.

Brownsville and the Seventy-third Precinct. His first foot post as a probationary patrolman for the police department. There was music there, too. More frantic, more discordant, but somehow more alive. He remembered his fear and amazement at the horde of black humanity cramming the neglected streets. Nothing in his background had prepared him for the awful sense of isolation he felt, the dread certainty that all of them, every man, woman, and child, would stick a knife in his ribs if they only got the chance.

The music came from portable radios and phonographs set on sidewalks and fire escapes; groups of truant teenagers and unemployed men harmonizing, bopping, jiving, investing black soul into the tormented streets. Later on it would be salsa in the South Bronx and tight young Puerto Rican girls writhing to the haunting beat of ghetto blasters. It was their music and, like the streets, there was a part of it he could never share. He was the outsider, peering warily at the ceremonial, unable to partake of the sacrament.

Everywhere along the way there was music, and Billy had been the sweetest. In his own way he'd brought soul to the singing wherever he went. He was an Irish tenor at wakes and weddings when he wasn't being a cop. The songs were the same ones everybody had known since childhood: "O Danny Boy," "Mother Macree." There was nothing different about the words, only the way Billy sang them. He could focus a thousand years of Irish pain into a few lyrical sentences. There was never a dry eye in the crowd.

"When was the last time you gave him a bath?" he demanded of Ricco.

"I don't give baths. The hospital has orderlies for that."

"His hair is filthy. There are bugs crawling in it."

"There are bugs all over this place."

"He stinks."

Ricco eyed him coldly. "I don't make the rules around here. You oughta know that by now."

Vince made his way to the men's room, retrieved a pile of paper towels and a cupful of warm water. He washed Billy's face and neck as best he could, discarding the soiled

towels on the table until he'd used them all. Billy remained
impassive through it all, like a limp rag doll showing no
sign of appreciation or displeasure. Billy probably didn't
know or care whether he was dirty, Vince thought. He was
doing this for himself, for what Billy used to be.

Outside the partially open window he could see the
hospital parking lot three stories below, rimmed with
freshly planted maples. Spring was on its way, breathing
magnetic life into the dormant landscape of Long Island.
Green was beginning to appear everywhere, renewing itself
as it did each year. Each year the land renewed itself, and
Billy stayed the same. Each year the city of New York paid
Queens Hospital enough money to assure that Billy Whal-
en, hero cop, was given three squares a day, a bed, and an
orderly to change his shitty drawers a couple of times a
week whether he needed it or not. His badge had earned
him that.

Vince unwrapped the package he'd brought with him and
placed a faded, framed photograph on the table. "I found
this when I was cleaning the closet, Billy. Can you believe
you and me ever looked that young?" The picture was of
the two of them, taken in the summer of '69 when they'd
vacationed with their wives in Far Rockaway. "How old
were we then bro, thirty, thirty-one? Jeez, that was some
time, wasn't it? We were a couple of fucking iron men then.
There wasn't anything we wouldn't try."

The young men in the photograph smiled out at him with
easy familiarity. Vince mugging for the camera and Billy,
more contained as always, grinning behind an oversize pair
of aviator glasses. Behind them was the water, spread flat
against a cloudless sky. It was evening, five or six P.M.,
Vince guessed. The sun was in their faces, judging from the
trailing shadows . . . cocktail time.

There had been a lot of drinking, he remembered, a lot of
unforced laughter. Swimming, water skiing, picnics, endless nights of bridge and Monopoly, nobody seemed in a

hurry to break the magic by getting serious about life. It just wasn't time for that yet. Billy had come closest to it when the two of them were alone together fishing. He talked about being a cop, about how it was just a means to a larger end for him. He talked about going to school, about getting a law degree, about writing a book; things that might never have happened but it really didn't seem to matter. Billy had shared them, that was what counted.

"How's chances of getting this hung in his room?" He held the photograph high for Ricco to see.

"I guess nobody'd mind. Have to take the glass out of the frame though."

"What the hell for?"

"Regulations."

"You think he's gonna slash his wrists? He hasn't moved in four years, for chrissake!"

Ricco shrugged.

"I know. You don't make the rules, just carry them out." He laughed darkly. "Just like on the force, right Billy? It's always some other asshole who's responsible. What you and me oughta do when you're out of this place is hunt down the guy who's really responsible for making up all these rules that nobody gives a shit about. How about it, buddy, it'll be our first assignment when we're back together, when we're partners again . . ." He paused, felt his throat go dry. "Better hurry, Billy. I'm just not sure how much longer I can last. Eleven months to go for my pension and I wake up every morning knowing I'm not gonna make it." He removed the glass from the frame and placed it on the table. The youthful, confident faces stared up at him and grinned.

3

EVERYONE AT THE Thirty-seventh Precinct knew that Squad Commander Art Boyle was an asshole. The homicide detectives under his immediate command knew he was an asshole. The plainclothes division knew he was an asshole. The uniformed cops, from captain to the rawest probationary patrolmen, knew he was an asshole. The civilian employees, telephone operators, meter maids, and cleaning personnel knew he was an asshole. Even Moustache Augie Bruno, who had been shining shoes at the precinct since 1946, knew he was an asshole, and nobody was about to argue with Augie. It was generally known that he had put four sons through Ivy League colleges on his shoeshine earnings and had managed to invest in Manhattan condominiums with what was left over. Moustache Augie was a very smart man. If he said Art Boyle was an asshole, Art Boyle was an asshole.

Vince Crowley didn't disagree. Art Boyle had been his boss at Homicide for almost three years and in all that time he'd managed to pull every stupid mistake in the book. He was the kind of cop other cops really didn't dislike; they just felt deeply embarrassed by him. He was the kind of human being other humans couldn't simply ignore, only try to avoid whenever possible.

Vince had been on the force long enough to know that there were two kinds of men who made good cops. There were the guys who considered the job a noble, almost patriotic calling. For them, police work was a moral duty, a social imperative for separating the criminals from the solid citizenry, the city's last thin line of defense against anarchy and total chaos. They believed their work was necessary and important. They accepted as an article of faith that they were needed by a vulnerable and unwary public who were incapable of understanding or appreciating their mission.

Then there were the guys who were simply fascinated by police work, procedures, and criminality. Their passion was the job itself, the intrigue and excitement of investigation, the sifting, sorting, and unraveling of clues, the thrill of the hunt, the gratification of success. They were good cops because their instincts rather than their consciences led them there. They were good cops because they had a knack for it, not a vocation.

Art Boyle was neither of these. His overriding talent was an uncanny ability to remain unobtrusive in the intricate but not always subtle politics of the New York City Police Force. To the hierarchy he was an unknown quantity. He created no ripples by being bold or adventurous. His command was spotless, if somewhat undistinguished. He posed no threat to men of greater ability and ambition. The most complimentary thing most people could find to say about Art Boyle was that he kept his nose clean.

His men did not consider this an admirable achievement. Most of them believed that being a cop meant walking a tightrope between what was technically legal and illegal. They believed that while criminals were free to operate outside of society's rules and regulations, policemen were bound by a mystifying set of prohibitions that were designed by politicians for political reasons. It was understood that any cop who adhered strictly to these senseless prohibitions was a bad cop. To do the job the way it was supposed to be done, the rules had to be skirted, reinterpreted, forgotten, and sometimes disregarded in order to bring criminals to justice. Politicians were usually willing to look the other way if the infraction was discreet and professional. Politicians weren't interested in protecting the citizenry; they were interested in getting elected, avoiding public scandal, and lining their pockets. Every cop in every precinct of the city of New York knew this to be true.

Except Art Boyle. While his infertile mind was too limited to grasp the political or social implications of the rules, he believed passionately that it was his duty to enforce them. If he understood anything at all, it was that a large portion of the politicians and the public wanted desperately to find cops with their noses in the trough. To him, a cop who accepted a free cup of coffee from a local luncheonette operator was worse than a murderer. Murderers could be caught and jailed and that would be it. If a cop was caught accepting favors and he happened to be from the Thirty-seventh Precinct, he could cost Art Boyle his job. That kind of simple equation was not lost on him.

He immersed himself in technicalities as only men of limited vision can. If a homicide was solved he would scrutinize the records, searching for the instances where the suspect's rights might have been abused. Better to kick a murderer free, he reasoned, than let some smart-assed downtown lawyer catch his command in a procedural slipup. His men resented this. To them, suspects' rights simply got in the way of efficient justice.

What Art Boyle failed to realize was that good cops have an instinctive ability to tell the guilty from the innocent. Perps looked guilty, acted guilty, smelled guilty. Every pore of their bodies gave off an aura, a kind of musk that made them sitting ducks for any trained investigator worth his salt. Years of living with the guilty had honed the homicide detective's senses to a point where bureaucratic meddling only got in the way. The suspects he collared were guilty and, for the most part, they were slime. The cops Vince knew thought they should be shot, then read their rights.

Some days were harder than others. Vince had learned to dread the slow times when Boyle had nothing better to do than pore over the DD-5 forms looking for errors or prowling around the stationhouse, trying to stir up trouble. Day tours were the worst because very little happened during the day. Murderers preferred the anonymity of night. Darkness shielded them, much as heat fueled them. Cold weather seemed to numb their murderous instincts. They did their best work in summer. Almost seventy percent of the homicides handled by the Thirty-seventh Precinct took place during July and August.

March was a swing month. Vince knew that he would be as busy, or as bored, as the weather allowed. Warm weather and an early thaw usually meant that the precinct could look forward to a lot of domestic violence once the inevitable cold reappeared. Men stretched to the limits of their endurance by the interminable winds of winter would allow their brittle hopes to soar as the warm weather arrived, then carve up their wives and lovers when the cold came back again. The approaching spring whetted the appetites of burglars and muggers, seducing them, drawing them out of their burrows and onto the streets. Summer was just around the corner and the pickings would once again be easy.

If the weather remained cold, there was the likelihood of dreaded days and nights of tedium and languor, of Art Boyle carrying on endlessly about dress codes and demeanor and illegal precinct parking and improperly filed records and any one of a thousand other real or imagined slights and bureaucratic errors. It was Boyle's time to howl and Vince's time to lie low and cringe. Every detective in the division prayed for warm weather. Short of that, they prayed for an ax murder to ease the tension.

March 11 was one of those days; cold and gray and interminably routine. The bad guys were still hibernating so the detectives of the Thirty-seventh had only Art Boyle, boredom, and bad attitudes to combat. It was the turnaround tour, eight A.M. to four P.M., and Vince had the duty with Walt Cuzak and Tommy Ippollito, grinding out the time with paperwork, playing gin, drinking coffee and beer, doing crosswork puzzles—anything to break the monotony. Tommy Ippollito was writing the great American novel; his fourth that week. Walt Cuzak was inspecting the bottom of his left foot where a cluster of angry, red blisters had begun to appear. Vince was writing a letter to his daughters, Kelly and Katie, explaining for the ten thousandth time why he and their mother hadn't been able to make a go of their marriage. The letter would be thrown away, same as all the others. It was a way of passing the time.

"How's about some food?" The voice was brittle, demanding, and came from the occupant of the brown-barred holding cell that ran halfway along the length of the homicide room.

"How's about fucking yourself?" Cuzak replied.

"You gotta feed me. The law says you can't hold me without feeding me!"

Vince stared at Cuzak and shrugged. He had no idea what the law was on the matter and couldn't have cared less. As a matter of fact, he had no idea who the occupant of the holding cell was. The man had been there at the start of his tour and hadn't said a word until now.

"How's this," Ippollito interrupted. "The sky was a finger of purple smeared across the tawdry landscape of the Bronx . . ." He grinned broadly. "Doesn't that just tear you up?"

"What's it supposed to mean?" Vince asked.

Ippollito stared at his newly begun manuscript. "It doesn't fucking *mean* anything, you ignorant bastard. It's allusion!"

"What kind of an illusion?"

"Ay-lusion, you asshole. It's a word picture. It means the sky was dark and angry."

"Why not just say the sky was dark and angry?"

"I don't fucking believe this . . ." Ippollito returned sullenly to his writing.

Vince smiled at Walt Cuzak. Busting Tommy's balls was a favorite pastime when things got slow in the squad room. Tommy always reacted, even when he knew they were just kidding around. Writing was his latest passion and he was too involved in it to see the humor in their remarks. He was taking a creative writing course at the College of New Rochelle and he was taking it seriously. Apparently his instructor had told him that he had some talent, and there had been no talking to him since. In his mind, he was a budding Hemingway and anybody who made jokes about it was an asshole, plain and simple.

"How's about some of that pizza?" The guy in the holding pen pointed through the bars at a grease-smeared pizza carton on the floor near Vince's desk.

"Who the hell is this guy anyway?" Vince asked.

"Beats me," Cuzak replied. Tommy just shrugged.

"Who arrested you?" Vince asked the prisoner.

The man stood languidly at the bars, staring at the pizza carton. "I dunno, some cop. I'll give you a dollar for some of that pizza. I ain't had nothing to eat since yesterday."

Vince eyed him quizzically. He was young, twenty or twenty-one, slightly built and short, probably Hispanic, and a drug user, judging from the involuntary twitching of his facial muscles. There was a tattoo on his left wrist, a crest of some sort, that had been covered over by a series of inexpertly rendered black bars—a sure sign the guy had done hard time somewhere. Already, his teeth had begun to rot, and above his sore-infested lips a wispy moustache sprouted irregularly like a poorly seeded lawn. Whoever he was, he bore the unmistakable signs of life on the streets.

Vince pegged him as another one of the floating fragments of human garbage that regularly passed through the doors of the Thirty-seventh.

"What'd you get busted for?" he asked.

"I didn't do nothin' man. This fuckin' cop hit me over the fuckin' head and hauled my ass in here when I was minding my own fuckin' business . . ." He parted some strands of greasy, black hair and exhibited a wound on his scalp. Vince walked over to the bars and examined it briefly. "Doesn't anybody know why this guy is here?" No response.

He walked to Robbery in the adjoining room. Detectives Steve Appelbaum and Snuffy Quade were the only ones on duty. "Either of you two collar that guy in the pen?" Appelbaum and Quade looked at each other and shook their heads.

"Doesn't anyone know who this poor bastard is?" he barked back into the Homicide room. There was no response. He retrieved the pizza carton, passed it through the bars, and returned to his desk. Inside the cell, the young prisoner began tearing at the hardened crust ravenously. Vince felt a twinge of revulsion but stifled it. The pizza had to be a week or more old but it was probably better than the guy was used to eating. He returned to his letter.

The harsh ring of the telephone interrupted him. He answered and recorded the message and the time in his notebook. "It's a floater in the Bronx River," he said, replacing the receiver. "Anybody up for a picnic in the park?"

Cuzak and Ippollito grimaced, pretended to become busy at their desks. Floaters were usually bad news; stiffs who got killed somewhere else and were dumped in the relative obscurity of the Bronx. The killings were usually professional, mob-related, and as surgically clean as murder can be. There was never a fingerprint, rarely a clue, and the killings almost always went unsolved. The files were filled with floaters who had never even been identified. Once a year, somebody would routinely go over the cases and mark them still open. Homicides were never closed but nobody kidded themselves that the floaters' killers would ever be brought to justice. Nobody ever won a medal or a commendation from a floater. They were no more than a royal pain in the ass.

"Ippollito, you go with Crowley." It was Boyle, standing in the open doorway of the squad room.

"It's a *floater*, Lieutenant," Tommy moaned.

"It's a body. Get your ass in gear."

Vince made his second entry in the notebook, underneath the time and manner of his first notification. "A.H. assigns Det. Ippollito to assist investigation . . . 9:40." If his notes were ever called into question, the letters "A.H." would conveniently be changed to "A.B." For now they stood for asshole.

NYPD FORM UF61   MARCH 11, 1984
INITIAL REPORT OF CRIME

DET. V. CROWLEY   COMPLAINT #9892

HOMICIDE/   UNIDENTIFIED M/H   VISIT TO SCENE
EMASCULATION.

1.   AT 0934 HOURS, THIS DATE NOTIFIED BY 37 PA-
TROL SUPERVISOR SGT. GARRITY, SHIELD #956, OF A
POSSIBLE DOA (FLOATER) AT BRONX BLVD. AND
EAST GUN HILL RD., IN THE BRONX RIVER. (SECTOR
X-RAY).

2.   AT 0952 HOURS, ACCOMPANIED BY DET. IPPOLLITO OF
37 PDU, ARRIVED AT ABOVE LOCATION AND OBSERVED
A HUMAN BODY IN PLAIN VIEW, APPARENTLY DOA, IN
THE WATER OF THE BRONX RIVER FLOATING FACE-
DOWN.

3.   FIRST OFFICER ON THE SCENE, P.O. JOSEPH STERNS,
SHIELD #5684, STATED THAT HE HAD RESPONDED TO A

20

RADIO CALL FROM 911 CENTRAL AND THAT UPON
REACHING PLACE OF OCCURENCE, HE WAS MET BY
REPORTEE, CALVIN STREET OF 814 WILLOW AVE., WHO
DIRECTED HIM TO BODY IN WATER . . .

The trip from the stationhouse took little more than ten
minutes, with Tommy chattering into a hand-held tape
recorder the entire way: ". . . Lagana's Funeral Parlor . . .
an empty lot filled with debris . . . several homes in need
of painting and repair . . . an unused schoolyard with grass
and weeds growing up between the cracks in the
pavement . . ."

"Would you mind telling me just what the hell you're
doing?" Vince asked finally.

"Getting the flavor of the neighborhood," Tommy answered, shutting off the recorder. "Good writers have to
keep track of their life experiences."

"You were born six blocks from here for chrissakes,
what do you need that thing for?"

Tommy moaned. "Jesus H. Christ. Don't you know
anything? People see stuff every day of their lives but they
never really *see* it, you know what I mean?"

"I guess so," Vince conceded.

"I mean, shit . . . everybody's got experiences. What
separates the writer from your average schmuck is that he
stores stuff up in his mind so he can use it later on in a book.
I mean, it can be years old but when he writes it, it's just
like it happened that minute, you know?"

"So you're gonna write a book about this neighborhood?"

"Shit no. Nothing ever happens around here . . ."

"So what're you recording all that stuff for?"

Tommy shook his head hopelessly. "I can't talk to you,
man. You just don't have a creative bone in your body.
You're just another dumb cop, that's all."

Vince let it pass. Cops called one another dumb all the

time and it never meant anything. As for Tommy, he was angry and frustrated because he had a dream and he hadn't figured out how to go about making it come true. Vince understood that. Plenty of his own dreams had gone by the boards over the years and the pain was always the same. Vince didn't know a cop who hadn't sacrificed one dream or another during his career and all of them felt that same pain. The older guys just didn't show it as much, that was all.

Tommy was still young enough to think that maybe it was all going to come true for him, and who was to say it wouldn't? Cops had become writers before, and artists and musicians and politicians. Maybe it would happen for Tommy. Deep down, Vince admired him for his enthusiasm and his stamina. For all his bullshit, he was a pretty good writer and a pretty good cop, too. It was just that he was a rookie detective and nobody told rookies they were good. They took the shit until they'd been around long enough to start dishing it out themselves. Nobody gave them respect until they'd earned it. If Tommy Ippollito was going to become the Hemingway of the Thirty-seventh, he'd have to become a good detective in the bargain. Nobody would put up with him otherwise.

Several blue-and-whites had already arrived at the crime scene by the time they got there, and uniformed policemen were busy cordoning off the area from curious passersby. From the top of a stone overpass, Vince could see a body floating facedown in a few feet of murky water at the bottom of a steep embankment. The body appeared to be that of a woman, nude from the waist down, a shock of abundant black hair matted across her shoulders and back. There were no apparent signs of violence; no scars, contusions, or open wounds that he could see. No blood, no twisted or torn limbs to indicate a struggle. She was resting almost peacefully, her legs drawn up under her like a napping child. If there had been a homicide it had happened somewhere else, he concluded. The place was too serene for murder.

The immediate area was a remote part of Bronx Park known to be frequented by illicit lovers, drug dealers, and minor mob functionaries who depended on isolation to conduct their business. Vince had recovered murder victims there before, lots of them, but they had always been killed at another location. They were shot, knifed, beaten, or garroted in Manhattan or Brooklyn or Staten Island and transported to the leafy solitude of the Bronx River for dispostion by the Thirty-seventh Precinct. There was a bizarre but logical continuity in the metabolism of murder. It was never routine but it was almost always predictable.

Vince questioned the reporting officer, who verified that the area had been secured and that the Crime Scene Unit, the Emergency Services Unit, and the Medical Examiner's office had all been contacted and were on their way, then descended the slippery embankment to the river's edge. Around him, the shrill of sirens penetrated the stiff morning mist as more vehicles arrived, disgorging their hurried occupants in the general melee of confusion that always attended the scene of violent death.

He could see from the shore that the victim was dark skinned, tall and angular for a woman, and bore several tattoos on her upper left bicep. Her head was resting in the crook of her elbow, eyes and mouth partially open. He made a note of the position and attitude of the body as well as his initial impression of the surrounding area. These could later be verified or contradicted by on-the-scene photographs taken by the Crime Scene Unit. Even the most insignificant detail was important. From this point on, Vince was in charge of the investigation. From here, it would be his job to reconstruct a life from the floating body in the water, to establish a timetable for murder out of the meaningless shreds of information in the drizzly park.

At 1024 hours, the District Attorney's Video Unit

arrived and recorded the scene from several angles. Members of the Crime Scene Unit waded out into the shallow water, removed strands of loose hair, crusted mud, blood, and other unidentifiable debris from the body and sealed them in plastic bags for delivery to the ME's office. They wrapped the victim's hands in plastic and stood aside while the Emergency Services Unit lifted the body and carried it to shore, where it was placed on a rubber sheet.

What had seemed so tranquil in the water erupted into savagery on land. The victim had been disemboweled, a deep meandering slash from the lower left rib cage to the groin laying bare a jumble of auburn entrails that had popped free from the body when it was lifted from the water. The genital area had been mutilated and the nipples of both breasts removed. It seemed almost as if the killer had placed his victim in a position of repose to disguise these horrors until the last minute. As if in a ghoulish game of show-and-tell, he had prolonged his final presentation for maximum impact.

In all the years of reporting to crime scenes and viewing murdered human beings, Vince had never really gotten used to the sheer violence of it. He was no longer squeamish about seeing broken and mutilated corpses; they were the stuff of homicides, and homicide detectives soon hardened themselves to the mechanics of killing. What was hard for him, and for all cops, was bridging the gap between accepting random violence and understanding it. A successful homicide investigation hinged on the investigator's ability to climb inside a killer's head and reconstruct his motives. He had to finally arrive at the point where the murder made as much sense to him as it did to the murderer. Most killings were senseless, and Vince knew that a lot of homicide detectives went as bonkers as their quarry trying to get into that frame of mind. It wasn't the kind of livelihood that made for restful nights.

The Assistant Medical Examiner from Jacobi Hospital,

Shem Wiesen, arrived and removed the canvas blanket that had been placed over the corpse. He felt the pelvis, poked around in the entrails and the open mouth. "You got yourself a castrated male here," he said unemotionally. "See here . . . some traces of seminal vesicle . . . a piece of vas duct . . ."

"What about the tits?"

"Probably a transsexual. They take hormones to promote mammary growth and retard facial hair."

"How long's he—she, whatever it is—been dead?"

"Preliminary guess . . . six to eight hours, judging from the pooling of the blood in the extremities. Been in the water only about two or three hours though."

"It figures," Vince nodded. "Any probable cause?"

Wiesen shrugged. "Stabbing's most probable. I'll let you know as soon as I've completed my work-up." He rinsed his hands in the murky water. "You guys got anything for me?"

Vince retrieved the plastic evidence bags from the Crime Scene detectives and handed them over to Wiesen, then retraced his steps up the embankment to the bridge where Tommy Ippollito was directing a foot-by-foot search of the immediate area. "Find anything yet?" he asked.

"Uh-uh. What did you get?"

"A castrated male homosexual with tits."

"A transsexual?"

"Whatever. Been in the water two or three hours. That'd mean he was put here seven or eight this morning, while it was light out . . ." He surveyed the surrounding landscape for any homes or structures. "Somebody in the area might have seen something. Send a team out to canvass the neighborhood . . . You know, any suspicious sounds, vehicles, the usual shit." He returned to the car and radioed headquarters with his preliminary report, then settled back in the seat and lit a cigarette. It was the first he'd had since arriving at the crime scene. Smoking was forbidden until the area had been swept for clues. A cigarette butt could be an important lead.

Outside the car, the Emergency Services Unit was depositing the canvas-wrapped body in a dark blue van marked "CORONER" in large block letters. From here it would be transported downtown to the morgue at 520 First Avenue for autopsy, then buried at the city's expense, barring the unlikely possibility that someone might claim it. All in all, hundreds of people and thousands of dollars would be used in the disposition of an unnamed transwhatchamacallit piece of garbage that nobody gave a rat's ass about. The investigation would proceed by the book with nobody apprehended until everybody at headquarters was satisfied that they could put it to bed without raising a stink from downtown. Then, all that would be left to do, was examine the open file once a year or so, mark the case unsolved but active, and get on with the business of processing other hunks of human garbage through the system until it was time to take the pension and run. There would be no heroes on this one.

5

NYPD FORM DD-5   MARCH 12, 1984
COMPLAINT FOLLOW-UP

DET. V. CROWLEY   COMPLAINT #9892

HOMICIDE/EMASCULATION
MIGUEL RAMOS/AKA MARGUERITA   VISIT TO M.E.

1. AT 1045 HOURS THIS DATE, I RESPONDED TO MEDICAL
    EXAMINER'S OFFICE FOR INFORMATION AND FINGER-
    PRINTS OF DECEASED.

2. I RECEIVED AUTOPSY REPORT FROM ASST. M.E. WIESEN
    AND ENTERED SAME INTO RECORD.

3. DET. WIGGAND OF M.E.'S OFFICE PRINTED DECEASED
    AND TURNED SAID PRINTS OVER TO ME FOR IDENTIFICA-
    TION AT B.C.I.

4. AT 1230 HOURS, SAME DATE, I RESPONDED TO B.C.I.

WHERE P.O. MASSET PROCESSED PRINTS OF DECEASED.

5. FINGERPRINTS DISCLOSED THAT DECEASED WAS AR-
   RESTED ON TWO PRIOR OCCASIONS AS FOLLOWS:

   1/29/81 MIGUEL RAMOS #27603214
   7/17/82 MARGUERITA (NLN) #27603214

6. AT 1330 HOURS I PICKED UP PHOTOS ON ABOVE-LISTED
   ARRESTS FOR THE DECEASED.

7. INVESTIGATION CONTINUES. CASE ACTIVE.

Walt Cuzak peered gloomily at the sole of his left foot,
which was being eaten away by an unidentified fungus.
"Hey Tommy, take a look at this for me, willya?"

Tommy Ippollito grimaced. "You gotta be kidding.
There's more shit growing between those toes than there is
in the botanical garden."

"I'm not kidding," Cuzak insisted. "This is getting bad.
What does ringworm look like anyway?"

Tommy grinned. "It's probably some alien life form you
picked up from the floor at Sodom and Gomorrah," he
said, referring to the Throg's Neck Health and Racquet
Club, where Walt was a lifetime member.

"You're full of shit," Cuzak protested. "The only
reason you don't like the place is because I whipped your
ass at racquetball . . ."

"You never seen anything like it," Tommy said to
Vince, who was scanning Marguerita's rap sheet. "Cuzak
took me there once and there was an inch of water on the
locker-room floor that looked like it'd been there since they
built the place . . ."

". . . Thirty years old and he was sitting on the floor,
panting like he was gonna die any minute," Walt interrupted.

"I swear to God, you could see things moving around in it. It was fucking disgusting."

"Hey man, I'm damn near fifty and I ran his ass into the ground," Walt bellowed.

"Who the hell can play in a pigsty like that . . ."

Vince returned to the arrest records for Miguel Ramos/ aka Marguerita. There were two busts, one in January of '81 and the other in July '82, both for soliciting and prostitution. The arrests were routine, defendant pleading guilty on both occasions, paying a small fine and being released on his own recognizance. There were mug shots taken more than a year apart, showing the effects of drugs and hormone treatments over that period of time. The first: a slight, handsome young man in his late teens or early twenties, his face frightened but determined, dark eyes set deeply over a flawless aquiline nose, mouth curled in a faint smile. He might have been any one of a thousand young men Vince had known in the army or on the force. With the exception of the numbers emblazoned across his chest, he might have been Vince himself, twenty or so years ago.

The second photograph showed a sickly, wasted queen, looking at least forty, less frightened and defiant than bored with the whole process. The dark eyes were dead, a blank mirror of indifference and decay. He scanned the Medical Examiner's report:

THE VICTIM IS A MALE CAUCASIAN, APPROX. 22-25 YRS., OF PROBABLE HISPANIC ORIGIN WHO IS A CHRONIC HERO-IN ABUSER. (NOTE: MULTIPLE PUNCTURE MARKS ON ARMS, LEGS, AND TORSO AS A RESULT OF SYRINGE INJECTION. LARGE QUANTITIES OF THAT SUBSTANCE FOUND IN VICTIM'S BLOOD AND PERTINENT ORGANS.)

OTHER CHEMICAL SUBSTANCES FOUND IN BLOOD SAM-PLING INCLUDE HORMONES ESTROGEN AND PROGESTER-

ONE, QUANTITIES OF METHAQUALONE, DEXEDRINE, AND
ALCOHOL IN THE AMOUNT OF .27%.

CAUSE OF DEATH IS ASPHYXIA BY STRANGULATION WITH
PENETRATION OF VISCERA BY A SHARP OBJECT CAUSING
DISEMBOWELMENT AFTER DEATH. EXCISION OF PENIS
AND TESTICLES AS WELL AS MUTILATION OF BREAST
TISSUE OCCURRING SOME TIME BEFORE DEATH . . .

Shem Wiesen had explained it all to him at the autopsy,
and what it boiled down to was that Miguel Ramos had been
tortured and castrated while he was still alive. Not pretty;
homicides never were.

While it was not technically required for an investigating
officer to attend an autopsy, Vince made it a practice to do
so over the years. He felt it gave him an insight that the dry,
medically crafted reports were missing. Medical examiners
were a strange breed, as hardened to the gruesome realities
of death as anyone Vince had known, but they were only
mortal. Working day after day in a penetrating reservoir of
gore and human waste, they developed a kind of reflective
gallows humor to mask their revulsion. Their reports, while
clinically precise, often omitted poignant, human elements
that might provide an important clue. Vince had learned
enough about them to read between the lines.

The autopsy of Miguel Ramos/aka Marguerita was not
substantially different than a hundred others Vince had
attended over the years. The square, windowless city
morgue at 520 First Avenue in Manhattan seemed as
innocuous as ever when he entered. The unmistakable smell
of alcohol, formaldehyde, and decay penetrated his nostrils
as he descended one flight of cement steps to the basement
where he was met with the same hollow, antiseptic corridors lined floor to ceiling with stainless steel vaults filled
with corpses. It reminded him of a catacomb, like the ones

he had seen in pictures of ancient Rome back at Our Lady of Lourdes.

Inside the operating theater, Shem Wiesen had already begun cutting when he arrived. Shem was at table number three, directly in the middle of the huge, high-ceilinged room, flanked with five identical tables occupied by other corpses in various stages of evisceration. As often as he'd been there, Vince had never quite gotten comfortable with the sight: two bodies on adjacent tables, split neck to crotch, purplish mounds of entrails hanging limply over the sides, dripping blood and running water into the ever-present drain in the brown tile floor. A black male, his face surgically peeled away like the skin of a banana and dangling limply from the back of his head, his auburn dreadlocks sweeping the slippery tiles, two perfectly rounded eyeballs staring sightlessly from an unrecognizable hunk of muscles, tendons, and bone. A Japanese intern placidly sawing the top of a woman's head off while the waiting surgeon nonchalantly gnawed a salami sandwich. It all seemed too random and casual to be scientific.

Shem Wiesen was examining a spleen and speaking into a running tape recorder as Vince moved to the side of the table. "Anything interesting so far?"

"Spleen's shot," Wiesen answered unemotionally. "Liver, too. Look at this . . ." He lifted an organ out of the gaping body cavity and pointed to some hard, brown splotches. "That's cirrhosis, probably from alcohol, but could be from all the progesterone this bird's taken. If it's taken orally, it breaks down in the liver and causes scarring."

"Any way of telling?"

"Maybe, but it'd be a lot of work. Why? This guy special or something?"

Vince shrugged. "Probably not. You know what killed him yet?"

"We're working on it, gotta eliminate the obvious first. So far I've eliminated old age." His assistant guffawed.

"Anything out of the ordinary?"

"Not really, unless you consider a bilateral orchidectomy out of the ordinary."

"What's that?"

"Castration," Wiesen said, pointing to the yawning brown chasm between Marguerita's legs. "Whoever did this was pretty methodical about it; might've known something about what he was doing."

"Like a doctor?"

"Possibly. Could've been anybody with a little anatomical knowledge though; a sculptor, a butcher . . . anybody trained to cut meat."

"He been printed yet?"

"About ten minutes ago. See Wiggand in the property room."

Vince retreated from the operating theater and climbed the stairs to the lobby. Instinctively, he gulped the relatively clean air as he headed down the hall. It would be hours before the smell of putrefaction left his lungs completely. The memory would take longer.

By comparison, the written Medical Examiner's report was a sterile, unfeeling document. Reading it in the comfortable surroundings of the squad room, Vince was almost able to remove himself from the grizzly events he'd witnessed a day earlier. The report opened some doors, found evidence in the victim's wounds that established a fundamental timetable to his death. It explained that blood drained away and pooled in the extremities of dead bodies. Wounds inflicted after death were paler, and the wounds found on this victim's genitals and breasts were of a deeper, more purple hue. That meant the heart was still pumping at the time they were inflicted. Rope burns on the wrists, ankles, and neck indicated he was tied during the procedure. What they were dealing with, the report concluded, was probably a sexual psychopath.

The report placed the time of death at roughly 0230 hours on the morning of March 11. That meant every scrap of evidence found at the crime scene that could be traced to that approximate time period might be a direct link to the killer. One piece of recovered evidence was a Merit cigarette butt that had burned down to its filter tip. That was significant, since the Hunt's Point weather station verified it was raining heavily in the park prior to 2:00 A.M. If the cigarette had been discarded before that time, it would have been drenched through. There was a good possibility it belonged to the killer, or someone who may have seen what went down.

Saliva tests on the cigarette butt had come up with a number of facts: The smoker was a male, in the second quadrant of age (eighteen to thirty-five years), had O Negative blood, and was suffering from a respiratory ailment at the time he smoked the cigarette. Outside of that, there was little else to go on. Other scraps of evidence found in the park—a pale blue plastic button, tire tracks on the bridge, cloth fibers from the victim's fingernails—could all be important if they were linked to a particular suspect. For now, they were just data to be filed and remembered.

Pete Yorio entered the squad room with his nine-year-old adopted son, Mikey. Mikey was Korean, short for his age, and full of mischief. Pete adored him. "Hey guys. We were on our way to the zoo and thought we'd stop in to see how the working class is doing."

Pete was on vacation and that meant he was spending every minute doing things with Mikey and his wife, Marianne. In a way, Vince resented that. Pete had one of the few really good marriages he'd ever seen in the department. He and Marianne had been married for twenty-five years and raised three kids of their own. Now they were starting all over again with this little Korean waif Pete had found starving in some tenement in the South Bronx. When people asked him how he and Marianne managed to cope with another brat at their advanced ages, he just smiled and told them that love keeps you feeling young. Pete was just too fucking good to be true.

"Hey partner." Vince ran a hand through Mikey's straight black hair. "How're things going?"

"Good." Mikey grinned. "When you coming to our house again?"

Vince remembered the day he'd spent at Pete and Marianne's house in Rockland County last summer, a month or so into his enforced bachelorhood. He remembered how kind and considerate they had been, never mentioning Jessy or the girls but treating him with a sort of pitying deference, like he'd lost a leg or something. He'd loved them but was uncomfortable with the pity. He supposed that people who really had their lives together treated everyone who didn't just like that.

"I'll be out one of these days."

Art Boyle appeared in the doorway of his office to see what all the fuss was about. "What's this?" he asked, approaching Mikey stiffly.

"This is my son Mikey, Lieutenant. Mikey, say hello to Lieutenant Boyle."

"Hi!" Mikey extended a small hand.

"Well, hi to you, young man." Boyle shook his hand. "Do you want to be a detective like your old man?"

Mikey scowled. "Nah. Cops don't make no bread. I'm gonna be a big-league ballplayer."

Boyle stared at him idiotically. One round of dialogue was all he was up to. "Well, good to see you, young man." He retreated to his office.

"How about it Vince?" Pete said. "Marianne and I would love to have you up again. How about this weekend, got a day off?"

"Thanks buddy, but I've got a million things . . . you know how it is."

"Sure . . ." Pete hesitated. "Hear anything from Jessy?"

"Funny you should mention that. I'm driving up to Connecticut tomorrow. Be able to tell you more after that."

"Good enough." Pete wrapped a massive arm around his son and headed him for the door. "And look, you guys . . . if you get in trouble, call somebody else, okay? We're gonna spend some serious father-and-son time at the seal pond."

The seal pond . . . Jeezus! Vince wanted to cry. It had been years since he'd taken his girls to the zoo. Now they were probably too old for that sort of thing. He stared sullenly at the report and tried to concentrate on the case. Miguel/Marguerita had been a prostitute. That was the point of departure. From here on in, it would be his job to build a character, a personality, an individual with tastes and habits, quirks and passions, out of the evidence available to him. The ME's report was just the beginning.

To create an individual, he would have to establish some sort of routine and that would be difficult in this case. Prostitutes were notoriously unpredictable because they were in an unpredictable occupation. A good hooker knew that routine could be as damaging for her as a fingerprint. Prostitutes who followed a routine were prostitutes who got busted. The veterans knew that to survive on the streets was to keep one step ahead of the vice cops, the social workers, and the psychos. They kept on the move and they kept their schedules strictly secret. It wasn't likely that an old pro like Marguerita would leave an easy trail to follow.

He replaced the records in the case folder and signed his report. Art Boyle would read it in the morning and find at least ten things wrong with it. That was okay; Vince was off for the next two days, and by the time he returned, Boyle would have found something else to piss him off. The precinct's Annual Integrity Report was due soon and that always got a rise out of him. Damned if he didn't always discover his men were not all squeaky clean all of the time. It flabbergasted him, sent him into brooding bouts of deep depression and outpourings of violent rage. Vince knew it was all bullshit, so did everybody else, but it rankled just the same. If nothing else, Vince had two days to get away from that.

6

MARION, CONNECTICUT OPENED before him like a multidimensional slide in a New England travelogue: streets and houses, lush expanses of green lawn and rolling hills, the sawmill and the pungent smell of fresh-cut pine drifting up from the mist-shrouded valley, the country store, painted brown now where it had once been white. Something new: a shopping mall where the old waterworks had been, a gas station, a 7-11 store, a laundromat, a pharmacy . . .

Vince drove past the mall toward the center of town. Marion itself had changed little from the way he remembered it. Main Street was one-way now, but the buildings and shops remained pretty much the same. The Courier Building was still the dominant structure fronting the picture-book green, its neat white facade forming the town's center.

There was a new Holiday Inn here someplace. Jessy had told him about it when they'd spoken on the phone. He could stay there, she said, if he planned on being in Marion longer than one day. It would have been pointless for her to add that he was unwelcome to stay at her parents' home; he already knew that. He'd known it from the first day he met them, from the very first time they realized an Irish cop from Queens was about to snatch their debutante daughter from the roots of her Connecticut squirearchy.

So be it. Nothing had changed over the years as far as the Dennis Sloans of Marion, Connecticut and Naples, Florida were concerned, and nothing would ever change. There were certain things a decent, well-brought-up girl just didn't do, and running off with a lowlife rookie patrolman from the bowels of New York City headed the list. From the Sloans' point of view, the only good thing their daughter had managed to do in the past twenty years was to pack up the girls and move back to Marion one rainy April night when Vince was away on stakeout.

That was almost a year ago, a year of hurt and confusion and fury. The anger had come to him first, sometimes desperate and uncontrolled, sometimes seething just below the surface; propelling him up unfamiliar vistas and driving him into fits of titanic, raging gloom. He pampered it, nurtured it alone at home and on the job, in saloons and whorehouses, in his own unrelenting thoughts. It took everything he had to give until it had run its course and left him limp; then he'd begun to look for reasons.

Always, they were the same and always they were unsatisfactory. Cops didn't marry above their station and live happily ever after, those things only happened in movies. Young ladies born to the incubated ease of limitless wealth soon tire of having to cope with day-to-day survival. They have no stomach for it, no antibodies to combat the fear. Love wasn't enough. Commitment wasn't enough. Having kids only seemed to deepen the chasm between them. No cop could provide Jessy's daughters with a suitable birthright. It was a matter of class, as simple as that.

1969: Spring Valley, New York, and their first house together. Vince had reluctantly agreed to accept a five-thousand-dollar loan from Jessy's father for the down payment after months of brooding over whether he was compromising his independence. Jessy pleaded, threatened, sank into fits of sulking until he agreed to take the money, only on the condition that it would be paid back, whether the old man needed it or not.

It was a common-sense decision, he had reasoned. Kelly was almost three, bouncy and curious, rapidly outgrowing their tiny, one-bedroom apartment in Yonkers. Jessy had announced she was again pregnant. Getting a larger apartment was like throwing money down the drain, she told him. Houses were an investment and their children would be healthier and happier living in the country. Her reasons were as compelling as her moods. He relented more out of exhaustion than conviction.

The house was split-level colonial; "Hi-Ranch," the builder called it—four bedrooms, a den, a fireplace, a two-car garage, and almost a half acre of land for thirty thousand dollars. It meant a two-hour drive to the precinct but it was worth it. He was a landowner, a member of the gentry. Maybe it wasn't Marion, Connecticut, but it was a beginning. Jessy could be happy there . . .

Katie had been born the following spring, and Dennis Sloan had let it slip at her christening party that he was putting the monthly payments Vince was sending him into a trust fund he'd established for the two girls. Vince had been furious, practically thrown the Sloans out of his house. He'd felt wounded, robbed of his dignity and his manhood. He hadn't asked for charity. He and Jessy and their daughters would get along just fine on what he made as a cop, nothing more. The Sloans had never forgiven him for that. From their point of view, the only thing worse than being poor was not hating it a lot. It was like being a Communist or something.

He thought of the girls: Kelly, nineteen now, and Katie approaching her sixteenth birthday. How had they gotten along this past year of living without want? Had they become gracious and considerate like their mother had once been or had they turned cold and brittle like the rest of the Sloans? Kelly would have an easier time of it, he thought. She was away at college most of the time. She could reap the benefits of wealth without having to live with its pinching dicipline. Katie would feel the brunt of that. There would be riding classes and etiquette classes and junior assemblies; things her mother had once hated, then remembered wistfully as she found herself mired in the middle class.

Katie Crowley with hair the color of corn and a laugh as big as the sky. She was named after her grandmother, his father's mother, whom he had never known. She'd been a large woman, he was told, uneducated and moody but possessed of a lusty peasant beauty and a lyric sense of living that remained long after she was gone. Katie had some of that, and a flavoring of haughtiness she'd inherited from the Marion aristocracy. She could be zesty and she could be cool, depending on her needs, but even her aloofness was fleshed with mischief. She could be poised but never wooden. Deep down she was Irish, and nothing her mother or grandparents did could change that. No matter what happened she was Vince Crowley's kid.

He hoped she was as certain of it as he was. Winding past the sentry rows of overhanging Elms that lined the half-mile-long driveway leading to the Sloans' home, he wondered whether they had tried to poison her and Kelly against him. There was plenty of ammunition they could use if they cared to. They could talk about his crudity, his bullheadedness, his drinking. There was enough bad stuff for them to keep it lively without getting messy. The Sloans hated messes. Everyone in Marion did.

He reached the end of the driveway, parked behind a brand-new Ferrari, and climbed the stone steps to the massive front door. Stanley, the Sloans' houseboy, greeted him stiffly and led him to the den where Dennis Sloan was poring over his stamp collection. "Vincent, it's been a long time," he said too earnestly to be sincere.

Vince accepted his lukewarm handshake. "Where are Jessy and the girls?"

"I'm afraid it's going to be just the two of us for a while, Vincent. Everyone's away so we'll have a chance to discuss a few things . . ."

He felt his collar tighten. Speaking to the old man in the best of times was a chore. Now he felt as if he was about to be grilled by the high school principal. He followed Sloan to the bar and accepted a scotch and water. Sloan settled into an overstuffed sofa, took a long draft of his drink, and peered at Vince over rimless glasses. "I don't think it would be helpful or fair to either of us for me to beat around the bush. Jessica wants a divorce and I'd like to see it happen as painlessly as possible for everyone involved."

Vince drained his glass. "Why doesn't she tell me herself?"

"She will of course, in time. She was concerned about how you might react. We all know you can be . . . strident."

"What the hell did she think I was going to do, tear the place up?"

"Apparently she wasn't sure you wouldn't. At any rate, everyone felt it would be better handled this way, at least in the beginning."

Vince felt his grip tighten on the arm of the chair. "Would you mind telling me who 'we' is, sir? Are Kelly and Katie part of this decision?"

"Both girls are aware of their mother's wishes."

"What about *their* wishes?"

Sloan eyed him evenly. "This is a matter between Jessica and yourself, Vincent. I see no reason to drag them into it."

"You're goddamn right it's between Jessy and me," Vince fumed. "And when she's ready to talk to me face-to-face she knows where she can find me!" He slammed his glass on the coffee table and stood to leave.

"Vincent, please, hear me out." Sloan stood and took him by the elbow. "This isn't easy for me. I truly had hoped you and Jessy might have worked things out. I know you don't believe that but it's the truth. All I've ever wanted is my daughter's happiness . . ."

"Don't give me that crap, Sloan," Vince snarled. "You and Jessy's mother tried to sabotage our marriage from day one. It was always just a matter of time."

"That just isn't true," Sloan protested. "You never gave us a chance. You started out with a chip on your shoulder and no matter what we did you refused to lose it." He took a deep breath. "None of this is going to change anything, Vincent. You can walk out of that door and it won't alter a thing. Jessica wants out and that's what she will get. You can make it as easy or as difficult as you choose."

"I want to see my daughters."

Sloan backed off and went to the bar. "For once in your life, take a minute to hear what I have to say. When I'm finished you can do anything you want, but I hope you'll take time to consider what's at stake here . . ." He took Vince's glass and refilled it. "You see Vincent, despite what you may think, I've always respected you in my own way. I may not have always agreed with your point of view, your inflexibility, even your manners, but I always sensed a kind of nobility in you . . . an atavistic sort of straight-on John Wayne morality that was rather appealing, if somewhat naive.

"What I'm getting to, is that you never impressed me as the sort of man who would deliberately set out to harm anybody. Oh, you might bluster and pose . . . throw a tantrum or two to appease your manhood, but in the long run you would always end up doing the right thing. I think you'll be man enough to do that now."

Vince felt the air go out of him. "And what's your idea of the right thing?"

"It's time to end it, Vincent. There's been too much

hurt, too much bitterness on both sides. Keeping up the facade is only adding to everyone's unhappiness . . . preventing you both from getting on with your lives . . . causing your daughters undue anxiety . . ." He paused and sipped his drink. "I'm prepared to offer you a substantial settlement in return for your goodwill in this matter; one which I'm certain you'll agree is more than fair."

"Money?" Vince heard himself ask. "You're offering me money . . . ?"

"In return for your legal assurances that my grandchildren will be allowed to remain here in Marion, yes."

"Let me get this straight. You're offering to pay me to give up my own children?"

Sloan stared at him. "How does a hundred thousand sound to you, Vincent? Cash, bonds, debentures . . . any way you want it. I can have my people help you soften the tax impact if you like . . . see to it you have liberal visiting rights. The girls can even spend vacations with you if they choose to do so. All I'm asking is that you allow your daughters the opportunity of experiencing the kind of life you could never hope to provide them. If you really loved them, you could hardly deny them that."

Vince steadied himself. "Sloan . . . I know I've always had a problem communicating with you. Maybe it's the way I talk. I know they teach better grammar at Groton and Princeton than they do at Our Lady of Lourdes. But that's my problem. I just want to make sure that we understand each other before I leave here, so now that I've heard you out, I want you to hear me out . . . and please watch my lips so you don't misread my message. Go fuck yourself!"

7

THE SPRING MAN sat by the front window of Finger's Luncheonette and stared across the street at the Wellington Armored Car Company with all the longing of a dirty old man inspecting a pubescent teenage girl. He had been sitting in that same corner booth, staring out the same front window, drinking the same sour coffee and eating the same stale bagels every day for the past two and a half years, patiently waiting for the day when he would transfer a sizeable portion of Wellington's assets to his own accounts. It was no longer a question of whether the money would be his, or even how it would be his . . . only when it would be his.

The Spring Man was Vito "Tony Clams" Prestipino, a fifty-year-old, 335-pound lieutenant in the Carlo Madalena crime family. He did not like being called the Spring Man; that was a name hung on him by the police because of his ability to bounce mob functionaries all over the city. Drugs, prostitutes, policy—he was involved in every facet of the family's business.

If things got too hot for a particular operation in any one of the five boroughs, it was Vito's job to see that it was relocated with speed and a minimum of hassle. He was

44

good at what he did, respected by men of stature and substance.

Today, Vito was a troubled man. His troubles had nothing to do with family operations, nothing to do with his plans for the Wellington Armored Car Company. Those were business matters and business was just fine. There was no reason for it to be otherwise. It was a political off year and he didn't have to worry about frenzied office-seekers developing a political conscience over his activities. That only happened in election years when candidates for office discovered it was good politics. Today, almost everyone who wanted a job had one and they were all happy. Business was profitable and the only heat came from an occasional rookie cop who was too green to understand how the system worked.

As for the Wellington Armored Car Company, everything was right on schedule. His cousin Franco had been installed as a dispatcher for the company and had been on the job for almost a year. He had furnished Vito with a complete dossier on Wellington's operation, including a customer list, pickup and delivery schedules, a personnel file, and complete blueprints of their telephone and communications apparatus. Timetables had been approved and money allocated. The operation was looking more and more like a lead-pipe cinch.

What was troubling Vito was a personal matter . . . the matter of his wife, Delores, and a black pimp called Ball-Bearings. It was a sword thrust deep into his heart, a point of extreme personal shame that he had been unable to keep her faithful to him. He knew now that he had been wrong to disregard the warnings. Delores was far too young; she was undisciplined and wild; she was from outside the family; she was unfamiliar with their ways. Now they were snickering behind his back over her infidelities. It would be only a matter of time before younger, more ambitious soldiers in the family would press the point that anyone who could not keep his own wife in line could hardly be trusted to negotiate sensitive family business. Punks barely out of their teens who knew nothing of his years with the organization would extend the sign of the horns with their fingers when his name was mentioned. They would call him cuckold.

These thoughts preyed on his mind as he stared through the plate-glass window, and the sight of Vince Crowley entering the luncheonette did little to raise his spirits. He sommoned a halfhearted smile as Vince approached his booth. "Vince, my good friend. How you been?"

Vince shook his hand. "Real good, Vito. How about you?"

"You know, Vincenzo . . . win a few, lose a few. I get by. How's your family?"

"Everybody's okay, Vito. You put on some weight since the last time I saw you?"

Vito guffawed. "Who the hell knows? I ain't weighed myself since I was sixteen." He shifted his massive bulk and patted his stomach. "What's a guy like me gotta do but eat? I ain't got no other vices. You had lunch yet? They make a pretty good Reuben here . . ."

"Just a cup of coffee for me."

"A Reuben for my friend Detective Crowley," Vito bellowed to the counterman, "and a piece of that pie, whaddayacallit, Boston cream." He turned back to Vince. "You hear anything about Billy?"

"Saw him a couple of days ago. He's about the same."

Vito shook his head sadly. "That's a real shame. Billy was a real good boy. Whatever happened to that nigger that shot him?"

"He's up in Attica, using up his appeals."

"I hope they fry the son of a bitch," Vito snorted. "Too bad you couldn'ta turned him over to me first, Vince. There wouldn't of been no goddamn appeals, eh?"

Vince leaned back in his seat as a papery-thin waitress put a runny Reuben sandwich and a cup of coffee in front of him. He waited until she had mopped up, rearranged the silverware, and left before he leaned across the table. "Vito, what can you tell me about the floater we pulled out of the river last week?"

"Floater? How should I know? Some kinda faggot, wasn't it?"

"Transsexual. Somebody opened him up like a side of beef. You must've heard something."

"Hey Vince, that's none of my action, you know that. I don't mess around with that shit."

"Everything's your action Vito," Vince said evenly. "Nobody gets dumped in my river without you knowing about it."

Vito assumed a pose of hurt innocence. "Why is it I know everything that goes on in the city of New York? Come on, Vince, you know me better than that. I got more important things on my mind than blowing away fags. If you want, I'll ask a few questions around for old times' sake . . ."

"That'd be good, Vito. I'd hate to have to run some of your boys in on this one."

"Hey, no threats," Vito protested. "I do this because I owe you, Vince . . . because you and me got history together. You want a name, I'll see what I can do, but no threats, okay?"

"Okay, but I need something soon."

"No promises, eat your sandwich."

Threatening Vito was a bluff and they both knew it. There was really no chance that he or any of his people were involved in this killing. It just wasn't their style. Also, Vito would never have allowed the body to be dumped in plain view in his own backyard. Local mob victims were brought to outlying areas of the city, like the Jersey meadowlands, or deposited at one of the local Italian-run funeral parlors for dismemberment and burial in the false bottom of some other stiff's casket. They were too disciplined and efficient to have anything to do with this sloppy mess.

What Vince wanted to accomplish by talking to the Spring Man was to get word out on the street that the mob was asking questions about the killing. That kind of pressure could cause the killer to panic, make a dumb mistake. It was a long shot but it was as good as anything else he had going for him at this point.

Back at the precinct, Tommy Ippollito reported that BCI had traced the victim's last known address to a vacant lot in lower Manhattan. Back to square one. Vince entered the information in his notebook and hustled Tommy out of the building for a trip across town to the Bronx Criminal Courts Building and a visit to Nathan the Fag.

"Ever see a hundred grand?" he asked Tommy as they pulled onto the Bruckner Expressway.

"You gotta be kidding."

"Let me give you a hypothetical instance," Vince went on. "Suppose somebody was to tell you they would give you a hundred thousand dollars if you would just compromise your principles. Would you take it?"

Tommy eyed him quizzically. "What's this all about? You got something going?"

"Just answer my question. Nobody'd get hurt, nobody'd get in any trouble. All you'd have to do would be swallow your pride . . . eat a little crow."

Tommy gulped hard. "Nobody's invented the clock that could measure the speed with which I would grab that dough. Why?"

"Just something I've been thinking about."

"Sounds like a good plot for a novel." Tommy began scribbling in his notebook.

"I thought you already had a plot for your novel."

"Not the right one," Tommy said. "You know, just writing about everyday life doesn't make it. I mean, all the really great books were about really great things. Look at Herman Melville. He wrote about a fucking white whale. Jeez, a white whale, for chrissakes. You can't hardly get greater than that . . ."

"I guess not," Vince conceded.

"I'm bouncing a couple of ideas around," Tommy said. "How does this one sound to you? The unexpurgated diary of Jack the Ripper's girl friend?"

"Jack the Ripper had a girl friend?"

"How the hell should I know? I told you, it's just an idea."

They parked at a bus stop in front of the Bronx Criminal Courts Building and climbed three flights of stairs to the records room where Nathan worked as a clerk-typist. Nathan was Vince's court snitch, an inside ear on the judges and prosecutors who could sabotage good detective work by making politically expedient deals. Sometimes it was possible to head them off if you knew their plans in advance. Nathan the Fag gave him that edge.

Vince had met Nathan in 1979, when he and Billy were still partners. Nathan had come to the precinct with a complaint against his landlord, an Albanian bookie named Peshloff. Nathan told them Peshloff had harassed him to get him to move from his apartment. He insisted Nathan leave because he was a homosexual and homosexuals were a blot on the earth. In the old country, homosexuals were slowly strangled while the skin was peeled from their bodies, he said. Nathan the Fag could expect nothing less if he decided to stay.

Peshloff's message was clear to Nathan and he left in a hurry, without taking his expensive stereo equipment with him. When he returned for it later, Peshloff had again threatened to fillet him. There was nothing Nathan could do

but report the incident to the police and hope they were
better disposed toward homosexuals than the Albanians. All
he wanted was his stereo back.

Vince and Billy visited Peshloff in his Bronx apartment
and invited him up on the roof to discuss the complaint
against him. There, surrounded by TV antennas festooned
with drying laundry, they explained that threats of the sort
he had made to Nathan the Fag were illegal and improper in
this country. They explained that coercion and violence
could not be tolerated in a civilized and democratic society,
especially that part of it known as the Thirty-seventh
Precinct in the Bronx. Then, for emphasis, they hung him
by his ankles six stories above the flagstone courtyard until
they were convinced he understood the workings of partici-
patory democracy. Nathan the Fag got his stereo back, his
apartment, too.

Nathan ogled Tommy hungrily when they arrived. "Vincent, you've brought me a birthday present!"

Vince grinned at his reddening partner. "I didn't even
know it was your birthday Nathan."

"It isn't, but who gives a shit. Where did you find this
one?"

Vince introduced Tommy, who shuffled like an embarrassed schoolgirl, then handed Marguerita's mug shots to
Nathan. "Ever see this queen before?"

"She's really frowzy," Nathan clucked. "What'd you
bust her for—pros?"

"Not this time. We pulled her out of the Bronx River."

Nathan winced. "It's nobody I ever saw but I could ask
around . . ."

Vince took the photos back. "I could use some names,
Nathan . . . somebody who can give me a line on this
thing. Maybe a couple of places he was likely to hang out."

"Could be anywhere." Nathan shrugged. "It really
depends on what she was into . . ." He paused. "Try

Sylvia. If a fruit's been through this town in the last ten years, she knows all about it. You'll probably find her at Cruise Control in Manhattan; Twelfth and Second.''

"This Sylvia have a last name?"

Nathan scowled. "Come on, Vincent. There are no last names in fairyland!''

8

NYPD FORM DD-5   MARCH 16, 1984
COMPLAINT FOLLOW-UP   COMPLAINT #9892

DET. V. CROWLEY

HOMICIDE/EMASCULATION
MIGUEL RAMOS/AKA MARGUERITA

SUBJECT:
INTERVIEW WITH CARLO MARTINEZ/AKA CHARLENE

1. ON MARCH 16, AT APPROX. 0130 HOURS, THE UNDER-
   SIGNED INTERVIEWED CARLO MARTINEZ. M/H, 27
   (TRANSSEXUAL), OF 20 W. 25 ST. (ELSINOR HOTEL),
   ROOM 600, TELEPHONE 555-7780.

2. INTERVIEWEE STATED THAT SHE MET THE DECEASED AT
   CRUISE CONTROL, (BAR-DISCO), LOCATED AT 275 E. 12
   ST., NYC. TELEPHONE 847-9820. DETAILS ARE AS
   FOLLOWS:

3. RAMOS (THE DECEASED) ENTERED THE BAR AT APPROX.

0245 HRS, WITH A WHITE MALE COMPANION AND
ENGAGED CHARLENE IN A BRIEF CONVERSATION.
INTERVIEWEE STATED THAT BOTH INDIVIDUALS SEEMED
HIGH (DRINKS AND QUAALUDES), AND THAT THE
DECEASED HAD AGREED TO MEET HER LATER ON THAT
NIGHT AT THE PM-AM. (AFTER-HOURS CLUB LOCATED IN
THE VILLAGE.) THE INTERVIEWEE STATED THAT SHE
EXITED THE PREMISES LEAVING BOTH THE DECEASED
AND COMPANION INSIDE AND THAT SHE NEVER AGAIN
SAW RAMOS ALIVE.

4. DESCRIPTION OF MALE COMPANION OF RAMOS:
    M/WHITE, APPROX. 25-28 YRS., 5'8-5'9, STRONGLY
    BUILT, (NOT MUSCULAR). CLEAN SHAVEN,
    MEDIUM-LENGTH WAVY BROWN HAIR COMBED TO THE
    REAR, WEARING A BLACK SHIRT, DARK TROUSERS, AND
    A GOLD CHAIN.

5. INVESTIGATION CONTINUES. CASE ACTIVE.

The street was a sea of sensory overload: shapes, colors,
sweat, perfume; bodies moving unrhythmically, pushing,
shoving, snaking along the teeming sidewalk, trying to get
around one another. The warmth of the evening had brought
them out of their burrows, freed them from their tiny
carved-up flats over the delicatessens, their hollow lofts,
their chained and padlocked cells; and delivered them
sprawling on the sidewalks, carrying their belongings with
them for sale or barter, for safekeeping, for public viewing.

Vince walked among them: fussy, erect young men
wearing sleeveless body shirts, arm in arm in balletic
lockstep; middle-aged men and women, bearded and
braided, their meager harvest of possessions set lovingly on
one of the hundreds of blankets lining the sidewalk; couples
in dashikis and beads fondling one another on doorsteps;

winos sprawled ingloriously amid a profusion of overflowing garbage cans, the piercing, discordant wail of music,
mingled smells and conversations, the press of the street,
the celebration of another springtime.

It was almost eleven P.M. on a Friday night and things
were just getting started in the East Village. Vince was
working alone, four to one, his favorite shift, picking his
way through the throng of massed humanity, past the street
vendors and derelicts, past the mincing faggots, the overage
hippies and drag queens that inhabited the neighborhood.
By contrast, he stood out like a sore thumb. Straight and
conservative in slacks, blue blazer, shirt and tie, he was
immediately identified by every experienced felon on the
street. He could sense their nervousness as he approached,
feel their relief as he passed them undisturbed.

Cruise Control, a shabby reconverted storefront at the
corner of Second Avenue and Twelfth Street, was bracketed
by a phalanx of hookers patrolling the sidewalks outside,
lounging on all four corners of the intersection. Vince's
sudden appearance roused them out of their lethargy long
enough to determine that he was no threat. "Let the *man*
through," they chirped playfully as he made his way past
them toward the door. "You're cute honey, even if you are
the heat . . ."

Inside he readjusted his eyes to the dark and surveyed the
room. It was small, no more than ten by thirty feet, and
crammed with more fags than he cared to count: gay,
bisexual, transvestite, transsexual. Who the hell could
figure out who was what, who was doing what to who, and
how they did it. He was convinced they weren't really sure
themselves, that they rolled the dice night after night and
whatever came up was it. It was better than nothing at all.

The only illumination came from a black light in the
middle of the ceiling, setting whites apart in sharp fluores-
cence; disembodied shirts and teeth and headbands sailing
through the blackness leaving eerie vapor trails, highlight-

ing the comic assemblage of circus faces lining the bar and
pressed onto the tiny floor. The music blared from a
loudspeaker above the bar, a couple of decibels above
deafening. Above it, a row of incongruous posters in black
and white: Fred MacMurry, Edgar Bergen and Charlie
McCarthy, June Allyson, Judy Garland as Dorothy in *The
Wizard of Oz*, the Three Stooges. There were some hand-
lettered signs: NO CREDIT, NO CHECKS CASHED, NO FIRE-
ARMS. A poster from the Gay Activists' Alliance: a picnic,
concert, and demonstration to raise money for AIDS
research. Someone had scrawled a caveat across it in
magenta lipstick: *No homos allowed*.

An aging queen billowing over a corner barstool ap-
praised him through a jeweled, hand-held lorgnette. "You
looking for someone, honey?" The voice was deep and
silky.

"Sylvia." He flashed his badge.

"Oh God, that piss-queen. I think she fled the country,
darling . . . something about a violation of public morals,
or maybe it was *pubic* morals. How on earth did you hear
about her?"

"My friend Nathan from the Criminal Courts Building
told me she could help me out."

"In what way, darling?" The mascara fluttered.

"I'm investigating a homicide." He reached into his
jacket pocket and removed the manila envelope containing
Miguel Ramos's mug shots. "I was hoping she could give
me a lead."

The queen hesitated. "I'm Sylvia."

"Can you answer a couple of questions?"

Sylvia slid ponderously off the stool. "Not in here. Too
much noise for conversation." She led Vince outside and
down the street to the light of an open-air fruit stand.
"Okay, what is it you want to know?"

He handed over the mug shots. "Ever see this individual
before?"

Sylvia studied the photos. "Maybe. What's she wanted for?"

"She was murdered."

"How ghastly!" She grimaced and returned the photos. "She came around to the club a few times."

Vince put the mug shots in his pocket. "Can you remember when you saw her last?"

She rolled her eyes. "Who knows? A week ago maybe."

"Could it have been Saturday the tenth?"

"It might have been. One night's just like another in this place."

"Can you remember whether she was with anyone?"

"Probably Charlene. That's who she usually cruised with."

Vince entered the name in his notebook. "You know where I can find this Charlene?"

"Try the Elsinor Hotel—Twenty-fifth and Broadway. She should still be there."

"She's a hooker?"

Sylvia squinted through the jeweled lorgnette. "Do cops have flat feet?"

They walked back to the club, passing the gauntlet of prostitutes that lined the street. "You come back and see us again, hon . . . Next time bring your partner. Bring the whole precinct. There's plenty to go around."

"How do you think they made me so fast?" he joked. "I walk funny or something?"

Sylvia sniffed. "Maybe it's the white socks and loafers darling . . . not exactly 'de rigueur' in this neighborhood."

He slipped her a dime, crossed the street to his car, and drove across town to the Elsinor Hotel. Broadway at Twenty-fifth Street was a lot different from the Village, its streets empty and deathly still, its shops and lofts manacled behind steel grillwork. The hotel was one of those sagging, decaying structures common to that part of town, brutalized over the years to feed the greed of transient landlords, the need of the transient poor.

The towering barrel-vaulted ceiling of the lobby bore the faint remains of what had once been ornate metal relief work, now barely visible beneath countless layers of peeling, yellow paint. The furniture was threadbare and insect infested; the floor was uncarpeted, stained with blood and urine; decades of old newspapers and magazines lay strewn everywhere; an out-of-order Coca-Cola vending machine stood, shattered and disembowled by local predators; the lingering smell of marijuana, of stale beer, of human excrement hung in the air.

The night manager scowled at him from behind a clear plastic barricade affixed to the front desk. "Yeah?"

Vince flashed his badge. "I'm looking for Charlene."

"What for?"

"Charlene," he said firmly.

The manager extracted a small amount of matter from his left nostril, rolled it into a ball with his fingertips, and flicked it into the corner of his cubicle. "Use the red phone behind you. Ring six hundred."

The voice on the other end was tentative. Vince introduced himself, stated his business, and waited the five minutes she requested to clear her room of her current customer before taking the elevator to the sixth floor. He passed the john in one of the beehivelike corridors, a middle-aged white male who kept his eyes diverted to the floor as he elbowed by, found room 600, and knocked loudly on the door.

"Who's there?" a husky feminine voice demanded.

"Crowley—police. I talked to you on the phone."

"Just a minute." There was a fumbling of locks and chains before the door swung slowly open, revealing a solitary figure dressed in a halter top and a pair of orange gym shorts. She was short, no more than five feet two, dark skinned and heavily made up, her blond hair stiff and artificial looking from countless bleachings, coming in

black at the roots. It was difficult to tell just how old she
was, the usual sight references concealed behind chalky
layers of cosmetics. She could have been a child or she
could have been an old lady. He supposed it made little
difference to the johns.

She stepped back and ushered him inside the tiny
apartment. It was oppressively hot; beige bare walls and
again the painted-over bas-relief ceiling. There was a large
waterbed covered with a pink embroidered afghan; a
cemented-up fireplace, a glowing red bulb hidden inexpertly among a stack of artificial logs; a peeling wicker table
and two black beanbag chairs set randomly against the
windowless wall. Above the bed was a crucifix, and several
weathered palm leaves tucked behind. Above all, the mixed
aromas of food and drugs, of cheap penetrating cologne and
incense, of mildew and unwashed bodies; the smells of sex,
the smells of decay . . .

Charlene sat on the edge of the waterbed and motioned
for Vince to sit in one of the chairs. She seemed subdued,
strangely compliant. Vince assumed she was on something:
'ludes maybe, or a heavy dose of Valium. "Can we get this
over with quick?" she asked. "I have a customer in twenty
minutes."

"That depends." He handed her the photographs. "You
know this individual?"

"Sure, that's Marguerita. She in some kinda trouble?"

"The worst. She got herself killed last week."

"Oh God." She began sobbing softly. Vince waited until
she'd composed herself. "I understand you and Marguerita
were friends."

Charlene nodded. "I told her . . ."

"Told her what?"

"She was getting wild . . . you know, into too many
things."

"What kinds of things?"

She buried her head in her hands. "I don't know, I don't

know. Who would kill her?''

"That's what we're trying to find out. Can you tell me when was the last time you saw Marguerita?''

"Last week—Saturday night. We were supposed to meet later at the PM-AM, but she never showed up.''

"Is that a bar?''

"An after-hours club. We used to meet there sometimes after we were finished with all our tricks.''

"And she didn't show up that night?''

"Like I said, I waited, but . . .'' Her voice trailed off.

"Were there other people at the PM-AM that night?''

"Oh sure. That place is always jumping . . . all people like us, you know.''

"Transvestites?''

"Transsexuals. There's a difference.''

"Like what?''

"Like transvestites dress up like girls . . . you know, like a female impersonator. Transsexuals take female hormones, sometimes get operations—''

"Sorta like Christene Jorgensen?''

She stared at him disgustedly. "Man, I ain't heard that name since I was a kid. Where you been for the last twenty years, in a monastery or something?''

He reddened. "But that's the general idea, right?''

"Sort of. Marguerita was transsexual. So am I.''

"Were you lovers?''

"No. Friends is all.'' She wiped her eyes with a Kleenex.

"No sex . . . even casual?''

"We were like sisters,'' Charlene protested. "We shared everything, clothes, makeup . . . you know.''

"Did she have her own place or did she live here with you?''

"She stayed here sometimes. She useta have an apartment on Twenty-ninth but the building was condemned in January.''

"So where was she staying?''

Charlene shrugged. "Around mostly."

"Where did she keep her stuff?"

She shook her head. "I dunno where her clothes are. She just left some makeup and stuff in my medicine cabinet."

"Can I see it? It might be important."

She slid off the waterbed, went to the bathroom, and returned with an assortment of bottles and tubes. Vince inspected each and placed them in his jacket pocket. The last, an almost-empty container of Valium, was dated less than a month ago and was written by a Dr. Zeitlin. Vince made a note of the name and placed the container with the others. "This Dr. Zeitlin, do you go to him, too?"

She scowled. "There's only two doctors in the whole city who'll see transsexuals and he ain't one of them."

"So how did Marguerita get these?"

"I dunno." She shrugged.

"Was she seeing him regularly?"

"I think she was getting shots from him but I'm not sure. She wasn't making no money so I don't know how she could afford them anyway."

"Are they expensive?"

She rolled her eyes. "Oh man, you said it. Five years ago you could get one for a yard. Now they're thirty bucks a pop."

Vince let out a long, low whistle. "And on top of all the other drugs she was taking she must have been spending a lot of money—"

"I didn't say she was taking drugs," Charlene interrupted.

"She was on heroin, wasn't she?"

She shook her head. "I don't know about none of that."

"She took some kind of drugs, didn't she?"

"Everybody takes drugs. She didn't take no more than nobody else."

Vince paused and collected his thoughts. "Just how long did you know Marguerita?"

"I dunno. A couple of years."

"Do you remember when you first met her?"

She gazed skyward. "Eighty, eighty-one—somewhere around there. I think it was Christmastime."

"And where was that?"

"The old Carioca Club. She was working there . . . doing an act."

"What kind of act?"

"You know . . ."

"No I don't. Tell me."

Charlene let out an exasperated sigh. "You know, a sex act . . . with another guy."

"Was she Marguerita then?"

"No. She was still Miguel; a real handsome boy, like in that picture you showed me. She'd just started taking the injections and she was a little scared about what was happening to her body. I told her some things about it and we just kinda fell in, you know what I mean?"

"This Carioca Club, where's it located?"

"It ain't no more. They shut it down a couple of years ago."

"You remember who the owner was?"

She thought about it. "It might have been a guy named Raoul. I think he runs the Blue Parrot up in the Bronx now."

"Any last name?"

"Sanchez, I think. All I know is he's a real pig. He uses people like us to make money and then throws us away."

Vince entered the name in his notebook. "You said Marguerita was into some wild things. What kind of things were you talking about?"

"Between you and me, she was into a lot of bad shit." She leaned forward on the waterbed, her voice becoming conspiratorial. "She met some people . . . rich people, at a restaurant she was bussing at uptown. I don't know what kind of people they were but they were into kinky stuff

. . . like they got it off goofing on fairies, shit like that—''

"What's that mean, 'goofing on fairies'?" he inter-rupted.

"You know . . . taking transsexual people like me up-town to their parties and having weird sex with them."

"Did you ever go to any of these parties?" he asked.

"No," she answered emphatically. "Those people were bad, man. They filled Marguerita's head with all kind of phony shit; like they were gonna take her to Hollywood—make her a big star."

"And Marguerita believed these people?"

Charlene was becoming more agitated. "She believed them! She started getting uppity . . . like she was better than everyone else. You know what I mean?"

Vince nodded. "Did she ever give you any of their names?"

"Uh-uh . . . I don't remember . . ."

Vince could see she was slipping away. "We're just about finished here, Charlene. I'll want you to come to headquarters and give our artist a description of the man you saw with Marguerita that night . . ." He slipped her five dollars. "Do you think you can do that for me?"

"I guess so . . ."

"We can nail this guy with your help."

"Sure." She stared at him with empty eyes.

9

ART BOYLE THOUGHT of the Annual Integrity Report spread on his desk and winced; partly because of the unfinished task before him and partly from the trenchant stabbing in his gut, a sure omen that another bout with the runs was imminent. It was inevitable, the inescapable result of years of job-related stress, thousands of meals on the run: cold pizza, greasy cheeseburgers, unidentifiable lumps of fried chicken. He was a victim of fast foods, and the quart or more of sour mash bourbon he'd been putting away daily for the last couple of years.

He closed his eyes, applied a small amount of pressure to his abdomen, and waited for something to happen. Nothing. He was spending half his life sitting on the crapper and his output for a week wouldn't fill a Dixie cup. For all his pain and effort, he produced nothing more than pitiful, mucoid strands and booming, spasmodic eruptions of gas that left him limp and exhausted. There was no way he would be able to complete the report, no way he would be able to concentrate on anything as long as the scourge persisted.

He pulled himself to his feet and walked into the squad

room where Detective Cuzak was making a fresh pot of coffee. "Where is everybody?" he asked.

"Beats me, Lieutenant. I just got here myself. You feeling all right?"

"Whattaya mean?"

Cuzak shrugged. "Forget it, sir. It's probably nothing."

"What's nothing?"

"I dunno . . . You just look a little pale, that's all."

"Pale?" He felt himself beginning to get queasy again. Around him, the familiar sights of the squad room loomed menacingly, magnifying his discomfort: the chipped and rusting metal desks along the wall . . . unmatched swivel chairs torn and taped at the seams . . . teletype, typewriters of a vintage seen only in police stations and antique shops . . . bulletins and handmade signs covering the walls: ATTENTION ALL PBA RETIREES . . . A sales pitch for additional insurance to supplement pension benefits . . . ARRESTING OFFICERS. MAKE SURE ALL PRISONERS ARE PRINTED AND PHOTOGRAPHED BEFORE LOCK-UP! . . . ORDER YOUR TICKETS NOW FOR PBA BENEFIT SOFTBALL CHAMPIONSHIP AND CLAMBAKE AT RANDALL'S ISLAND MAY 1. SIGN UP BELOW TO WORK ON COMMITTEES . . . The space provided was blank.

He reached behind him and steadied himself against the wall. Cuzak knew he was slipping . . . they all knew. It would only be a matter of time before word got to Division and they sent someone to evaluate his fitness to command.

"Can I get you anything, Lieutenant?" Cuzak asked.

"Maybe some of that coffee . . ."

Cuzak lifted the glass coffeepot from the machine and replaced it with a styrofoam cup. "It's this lousy weather, Lieutenant. One day it's freezing, next day it's like summer. Everybody's feeling like shit." He handed Boyle the cup, brimming to the top.

Boyle accepted it with shaking hands and got it to his lips without spilling any on his shirtfront. "Yeah, that's probably it . . . some kind of allergies maybe . . ."

There was something he should be doing, he knew. Some element of police work that would make him feel important, needed; something that would take his mind off the unrelenting Integrity Report that had dominated his time and sapped his energy these past weeks. The charts were almost empty; a few minor investigations in progress but nothing out of the ordinary, nothing he should be involved with at this point. "What's happening with this Miguel Ramos homicide?" he asked Cuzak.

"Crowley's on that, and Ippollito."

"Well, what're you on?" he demanded.

"It's on the chart, Lieutenant. I'm ninety-eight."

That was the code number for any officer who was free to accept a new assignment. To Art Boyle it meant an officer who was sitting on his ass wasting time and the taxpayers' money. He would have to find something for Cuzak to do. A detective sitting around was a bored detective, and bored detectives had time to think up ways of getting into trouble. "When's Crowley due in?" he asked.

"He phoned in a couple of minutes ago, said he'd be here by three."

Boyle glanced at the yellowing Seth Thomas on the wall: two forty-two. "Send him in to see me as soon as he gets here." He returned to his office and slammed the door shut. The noise almost took his head off.

Vince arrived at 1525 hours and found a handwritten message from Walt Cuzak on his desk. He went to Boyle's office, knocked lightly, and opened the door. "You wanted to see me, Lieutenant?"

Boyle eyed him suspiciously. He'd forgotten what he'd wanted to see Crowley about. He shifted his glance to the Integrity Report on his desk. "Uh . . . do you think this officer would be likely to accept an offer from a merchant in return for favors . . . ?"

"Which officer, Lieutenant?"

"Cuzak."

Vince cleared his throat. "Detective Cuzak's an upstanding police officer, sir."

"Of course he is . . ." It was coming back to him now. "I really wanted to see you about this floater homicide . . . that transfaggot or whatever."

"Transsexual, Lieutenant."

"Whatever. Where are you on it?"

Vince took his notebook from his jacket pocket. "Not a helluva lot more since my last DD-5, Lieutenant. I interviewed the deceased's girl friend, Carlo Martinez . . . calls himself Charlene. He states he last saw Ramos at an East Village club called Cruise Control at approximately two forty-five the morning of the murder in the company of a white male . . . no ID yet."

"You get a description?"

"Yeah. Nothing out of the ordinary. Charlene's gonna talk to the artist. We'll try to get a sketch on the street by the end of the week."

Boyle looked exasperated. "What the hell is it, Crowley, Carlo or Charlene?"

Vince shrugged. "Take your pick, Lieutenant."

"Jeezus. What kind of people are they anyway?"

"Transsexuals, sir . . ."

"I know that!" He was becoming agitated. "What else?"

"The deceased worked in a club called the Carioca for a while. I've got the owner, a guy named Raoul Sanchez, coming in this afternoon to answer some questions." He referred to his notes. "Deceased was on drugs. I'm checking out a prescription for Valium found in the girl friend's apartment; a Dr. Zeitlin. That's pretty much it."

"No solid suspect?"

"Maybe the girl friend. She admits she saw Ramos the night of the murder with another guy. She coulda carved him up out of jealousy . . ."

Boyle nodded. "Sounds like a plausible theory . . . work on that."

"I will, Lieutenant."

There was an awkward silence. "Maybe we ought to put Cuzak on this one, too."

Vince shrugged. "There's already two of us, Lieutenant. This is a routine case."

"Um . . . I guess so. Keep me informed though."

"Soon as I know something, you will."

"Very good . . ." He waved Vince away with his hand.

Outside, Walt Cuzak was inspecting his armpit with a hand-held mirror. "Hey Vince, take a look at this, willya?"

Vince ignored him. "Why don't you quit that goddamn health club. It's ruining your health, for chrissakes."

Cuzak buttoned his shirt. "What's with Boyle?"

"Who the hell knows? I think he's got the GI shits again. He asked me for an evaluation of your honesty."

"What'd you tell him?"

"You know . . . that you never take from little old ladies and cripples—just from the other 'goniffs' like yourself."

Cuzak nodded. "Yeah, I told him pretty much the same thing about you."

A short, swarthy figure appeared in the doorway. "I'm looking for Detective Crowley."

"Who're you?"

"Ronnie Sanchez . . . Raoul . . . you phoned me yesterday."

Vince pointed to a chair by his desk. "Why the hell does everybody on this case have a half a dozen names?"

Sanchez was about forty, squat, pasty complexioned, and sullen. He was there reluctantly, only because he felt it was better than having the heat nosing around his business establishment. "Can we make this quick? I have an appointment downtown."

Vince nodded noncommittally. "Okay, Raoul. Just a couple of questions and we'll try and get you out of here."

"Call me Ronnie. The 'Raoul' is for the clientele."

"Okay, Ronnie. Tell me when you last saw Miguel Ramos."

He shrugged. "Who the fuck knows; last week, last month. I don't keep records about that sort of thing."

"You did know Ramos, didn't you?"

"No, I didn't *know* him. He was just another fag who hung around the club, that's all."

"The Carioca?"

He bristled. "The Blue Parrot."

"What about the Carioca . . . he worked there for you, didn't he?"

"That club's been closed for a couple of years now."

"Yeah, but when it was open, Ramos worked there, right?" Vince persisted.

"How should I know? I can't keep track of every queen I've hired over the years . . ."

"This one did some performing for you . . . live sex, that sort of thing."

Sanchez sat back in the chair and gazed skyward. "Look, Detective Crowley. I run a legit operation and I'm straight with the cops—"

"Ramos worked for you in the Carioca," Vince interrupted. "I don't care who you're straight with. We're gonna be here all day if I don't get some answers."

"Okay, maybe he did. What's the big fuckin' deal anyway?"

"And he performed live sex in your club?"

Sanchez groaned. "All the clubs do it, for chrissakes. That's what the fags want."

"What kind of acts did he perform and who did he perform them with?" Vince asked.

Sanchez held up his hands. "Whaddaya want from me? That was two . . . maybe three years ago. I seen a thousand of those acts since then. They all do the same thing. It don't make no difference who they're doing it with or how they do it. It all comes out the same. I don't understand what the hell's going on here anyhow. I'm a legitimate businessman, for chrissake; just trying to make a buck like everybody else . . ."

"Did you and Ramos ever argue over money?"

"I don't fuckin' believe this!" Sanchez howled. "Ramos is a piece of dirt, same as all of them. He didn't get paid no salary for that shit . . . whatever tips the fags in the audience stuffed in his drawers is all. These scumbags *like* doing that sort of stuff. I provide them a safe place to do it. What's wrong with that?"

"That kind of public spirit gets me right here." Vince held a hand to his heart. "Try to remember the night of March tenth. It was a Saturday. Was Ramos in the Blue Parrot that night?"

"I dunno."

"Was his girl friend Charlene with him?"

"I told you, I don't know nothing about that night."

"What night is that?"

Sanchez stood. "Look copper, you got any more questions, you call my lawyer. His name's Grossman, it's in the book."

"You're making a mistake," Vince said evenly. "You'd be a lot better off if you cooperated."

"Look pal. This ain't the first time I've been around with the cops. I'll take my chances."

Vince shrugged. "Have it your way."

"I always do." Sanchez headed for the door.

Vince waited until he'd left the squad room before phoning the "Mosquito" at Public Morals. Wally Fry was an old friend from his first tour in Brooklyn, a tough, unrelenting interrogator who'd earned his nickname with an unerring ability to get under a suspect's skin. Among his memories, Vince cherished a visit he'd made with the Mosquito to Misericordia Hospital back in '68. The witness was a Jamaican who'd been slit belly to brisket and somehow managed to survive, his prostrate body a snarl of tubes, wires, and valves connected to a mass of artificial life-support systems set in the Intensive Care Unit wall.

"Who did this, man?" Mosquito had asked.

"Dunno," the Jamaican had answered weakly.

"You don't know who cut you?" Mosquito asked again.

"That's right, man."

It was then that the Mosquito had invented in a flash of inspiration what was to become in police vernacular "SHIT"—an acronym for the Standard Hospital Interrogation Technique: He began deliberately to close the valves leading from the Jamaican to his life-support systems in the wall.

"What you doing, man?" the wide-eyed Jamaican had asked.

"Turning off the tubes, man," Mosquito answered.

"What's gonna happen, man?"

"You're gonna die, man."

That day, they had gotten everything from the witness they could possibly hope for.

Mosquito sounded chipper when he answered the phone. "Vince, how you doing, bro?"

"Real good, Wally. I got a favor to ask."

"Name it, bro."

"I got a club in the East Bronx; the Blue Parrot, run by a scuzzball named Sanchez. It caters to homos, live sex . . . all that crap. Can you close 'em down for a couple of days?"

"No problem, baby. I send a guy in undercover, let him get himself propositioned and we bust them for soliciting. He issues a summons on the spot and the Alcoholic Beverage Commission puts a padlock on the door. When you want it done?"

"Sooner the better. Tomorrow if that's okay. One more thing; can you have the guy who issues the summons deliver a message to Sanchez? Just tell him 'Crowley says hello.' "

10

NYPD FORM DD-5   MARCH 17, 1984
COMPLAINT FOLLOW-UP

DET. V. CROWLEY   COMPLAINT #9892

SUBJECT: INTERVIEW OF STEWART ZEITLIN, M.D.

1. ON MARCH 17, AT APPROX. 1645 HOURS, I INTER-
    VIEWED DR. STEWART ZEITLIN (ENDOCRINOLOGIST) AT
    HIS OFFICES AT 260 PARK AVENUE, MANHATTAN, N.Y.,
    SUITE #1812, TELEPHONE 555-3260.

2. INTERVIEWEE STATED TO UNDERSIGNED THAT THE
    DECEASED HAD VISITED HIS OFFICES ON TWO OCCA-
    SIONS IN 1983 (3/12/83 AND 5/2/83) AND THAT HE DID
    NOT REMEMBER THE METHOD OF TREATMENT OR MEDI-
    CATION PRESCRIBED.

3. FILES SHOWED THAT THE DECEASED WAS ISSUED TWO
    PRESCRIPTIONS FOR VALIUM (25 MG).

4. INTERVIEWEE WAS GENERALLY UNCOOPERATIVE AND
   OF A SUSPICIOUS NATURE.

5. CASE ACTIVE PENDING FURTHER INVESTIGATION. HAPPY
   ST. PATRICK'S DAY!!!

260 Park Avenue was a thirty-story steel-and-glass structure on the corner of Forty-eighth Street in the heart of
midtown Manhattan. Vince rode the elevator to the eigh-
teenth floor and the office of Dr. Stewart Zeitlin. The
receptionist was prim, attractive, in her early thirties. She
smiled mechanically as Vince entered. "May I help you?"

He displayed his shield. "Detective Crowley. Is the
doctor in?"

She seemed momentarily flustered. "Can you tell me
what this is in reference to . . . ?"

"I have a few questions. It'll only take a minute."

She pressed a button on the telephone console and lifted
the phone to her ear. "There's a Detective Crowley from
the police out here . . ." She waited a moment and
replaced the receiver. "Dr. Zeitlin has a patient. If you'll
take a seat he'll be with you shortly."

Vince moved to an ornate wood watered-silk love seat in
the corner of the waiting room and began leafing through a
copy of the *New Yorker*. The place was ultrachic, from the
French Provincial antique chairs, to the original oil paintings on the wall, to the delicate porcelain figurines on the
occasional tables set strategically about the room. Hardly
the sort of setup somebody like Ramos would be visiting.

He was alone in the room except for the receptionist; Jan
Webster, according to the brass nameplate on her desk. She
was pretending to ignore him, busying herself with paperwork on her desk, trying unsuccessfully to appear disinterested. Her body language said she was nervous, the way
most civilians are when they're paid an unexpected visit by
the police. Vince noticed she was also posing; sitting more

erect in a way that emphasized her figure and called attention to her left facial profile, the view she obviously considered most flattering.

The desk console buzzed. She answered it and relayed the doctor's message that he was free to see Vince. He entered the office through a carved mahogany door at the end of the reception room and was met by a tall, middle-aged man with a mid-August tan and oversized shoulders that strained the resilience of his custom-tailored suit jacket. He smiled amiably and extended his hand. "I'm Stewart Zeitlin. How can I be of help?"

Vince surveyed the spacious office: walls, tables, and bookcases covered with plaques and trophies; sailing, football, soccer . . . It seemed almost every sport was represented. "I see you're a sportsman."

Zeitlin smiled. "Used to be. I'm getting too old for it now." He patted what looked to Vince like a rock-hard stomach. "Too much good food."

Vince realized he was sucking in his own gut unconsciously. "I'm investigating a homicide, Doctor. Some prescription medicine taken by the victim prior to death has been traced back to this office. I'm hoping you'll let me see your records so I can clarify a couple of things."

Zeitlin shook his head. "Our records are confidential. I'll be glad to help in any other way if I can."

"The name is Miguel Ramos, a transsexual prostitute. Does that ring a bell?"

"A prostitute?" He seemed shocked. "Are you sure you have the right Dr. Zeitlin? There are several practicing in New York . . . none of them related."

"No mistake about it, sir."

"A prostitute, you say?"

"Transsexual, Doctor. Not exactly your normal clientele. I wouldn't think you'd have any trouble remembering him."

"Hardly . . . It just doesn't ring a bell."

"Can't you check your files?"

Zeitlin eyed him coldly. "I will, Detective, after you've gone. If you'll leave your telephone number with my receptionist I'll get back to you."

Vince stood his ground. "I'd appreciate it if you could do it now, Doctor. This is a homicide we're talking about here . . . kinda important."

"I'm sure it is, but my files are privileged."

"So is my investigation, Dr. Zeitlin. Now I can get a subpoena ordering you to open up your files but that would make us both angry and unpleasant; or you can tell me what I need to know and I'll leave you alone. I don't want any trouble from you and I'm sure you don't want any trouble from the police."

Reluctantly, Zeitlin opened the door to the reception room. "Jan, will you run a file on the computer for Detective Crowley? That's all I can do, Detective, I hope you appreciate that." He allowed Vince to pass and shut the door behind him.

"Jan, that's a pretty name," Vince said.

She ignored the compliment and activated a computer terminal at the side of her desk. "Name, please?"

"Ramos, first name Miguel."

She punched it in on the keyboard and the unit's TV screen came alive with information. "Miguel Ramos was here on two occasions," she said. "March twelve and May two of 1983. He was treated for hypertension."

"What was the treatment?"

"Outpatient therapy. He was given a prescription for Valium."

"That's it?"

"That's it. At least that's all I can tell you from this . . ." She turned off the computer and stood. "And if that's all, it's quitting time. I've had a long day."

"Me, too. Can I buy you a drink?"

She seemed startled at the offer. "This in your official capacity, Detective?"

He grinned. "It's Saint Patrick's Day. Aren't you Irish?"

"Scotch-German, but I could use a drink anyway. Give me a few minutes to freshen up, okay?" She locked her desk and strapped her pocketbook across her arm. "No questions, promise?"

"Promise."

She was back in less than five minutes and they rode the elevator to the ground floor together. Outside, the streets were filled with frenzied teenagers in band uniforms, guzzling green beer, indulging in adolescent high jinks and puberty rituals. The midtown bars were overflowing and Vince steered them through a half dozen before they found one that seemed reasonably subdued, halfway across town.

"How long you worked for Zeitlin?" he asked, once they'd found a table and ordered their drinks.

She frowned. "I thought you promised there'd be no questions."

"Hey, that's unfair. You can't get to know somebody without asking questions," he protested.

"Well, suppose you let me answer all the important ones right off and that'll free us both to enjoy ourselves. I'm twenty-eight, divorced, I live in Jackson Heights, like quiet nights, lots of laughs, and modern jazz. I had my tonsils and appendix taken out by the time I was ten, have all my own teeth, and I don't ascribe to the theory that marriage is a dead institution. What about you?"

"Let's just say we have more in common than meets the eye." He hoisted his glass. "To Queens!"

"To freedom," she toasted him back.

"To Saint Patrick and the Irish."

"To getting together," she said.

* * *

There was an angry flow of water, cresting, ebbing, moving swiftly past an open window. He watched it with a curious detachment, as if it were happening on a television newscast. He could hear rumbling in the distance, a low, menacing growl that grew with each labored breath he took. A tidal wave coming toward him, carrying foundationless houses and uprooted trees in its swirling currents. He wanted to run but his legs had become entangled in ropes and coils of metal at his feet. He struggled until the wave was almost on him, then allowed his body to go limp, awaiting the inevitable impact. It was on him with a deafening roar, carrying him upward with it, tumbling, turning, riding the giant crest of the wave out over the countryside. He could see towns below, streets and homes nestled in the arms of gently sloping hills. Beyond them was Rockaway Beach, where his father had taken him to wander endless stretches of sand, collecting shells and pebbles in a small metal pail.

Around him the contours of the wave began to dip and sputter, forming frothy white flecks that lapped his head and shoulders. The wave was cresting, building to an awful climax, dropping into the black abyss below. He was fighting, struggling against the force of onrushing water . . . screaming at the top of his lungs . . .

"Vince, you're having a dream." Jan was massaging his forehead.

He opened his eyes to an unfamiliar room; a narrow shaft of yellow light streamed through the venetian blind. Jan leaned toward him and kissed him lightly on the lips. "It's all right. I get nightmares, too."

"It's not exactly a nightmare . . ."

She smiled. "I know, you're too tough to have bad dreams, right?"

He accustomed his eyes to the semidarkness. "Funny, it's always about water. When I was a kid my family had a summer place out in Rockaway Beach—the Irish Riviera, we called it. I had no problem with water then. I never really learned how to swim very well, just enough to get by . . .''

"Everyone's afraid of something," she said.

He was beginning to feel embarrassed. "How much did I drink last night, anyway?"

"Too much; we both did."

"Well, I guess you gotta get loaded on Saint Patrick's Day," he said.

She laughed. "Where's it written?"

"Hey, I'm a cop, remember? Who knows more about the law than cops? NYPD is arresting sober people all over the city this very minute . . ." He drew her toward him and buried his face in the soft folds of her neck, inhaling the musky aroma of her skin. "Morning sex is a law, too . . ."

She was breathing heavier, stretching and relaxing, gliding her hands down the length of his back, forming delicate patterns on his skin with her fingertips. Instinctively, he allowed his hand to slip into the still-moist recesses of her thighs. He could see the glimmer of her even, white teeth as she set her jaw in anticipation. He judged her response waiting for the right moment, then slid gently inside. They fumbled momentarily, like musicians tuning their instruments, before settling into the rhythm. Jan stiffened, exhaled a long, hoarse gasp, and went limp as he knew she would. He corrected the pace; slower now, concentrating on his own needs. He pictured her body beneath him, pumping, writhing, drawing him deeper and deeper into her, until he felt his own pulsating release.

He lay quietly, breathing heavily into the scented skin of her shoulder. "That was good."

She pushed him gently away and looked directly into his eyes. "I lied to you yesterday. I'm thirty-five years old."

He rolled away and lay on his back. "I know, it's okay."

"Well thanks a lot!" she huffed.

He would never understand women. They wanted to hear

what they wanted to hear even when they knew it was a lie. "I didn't know how old you really were, only that you weren't telling the truth. Cops have a sixth sense about that sort of thing. It used to drive my wife crazy."

"What's she like, your ex?" Jan asked.

"As long as we're telling the truth here, I guess you could say I'm not technically divorced."

She nodded. "I know. Single women in Manhattan have sixth senses, too."

"We've been separated for about a year. She's living in Connecticut with the kids."

Jan walked to the window and raised the blind. "Want some breakfast?"

"Uh-uh." He propped the pillow behind his head and sat. "How long have you lived in this place?"

"Six years. Stewart owns the building. I'd be ashamed to tell you how little he charges me for rent."

He nodded. "I thought the place was a little swanky for a receptionist. You and the doctor good friends?"

Jan stiffened. "You just can't stop being a cop, can you?" She turned abruptly from the window and disappeared into the kitchen.

"Hey, I'm not trying to get personal," he yelled after her.

"Sure you are. That's your job, isn't it?"

Vince lit a cigarette, placed it in the ashtray beside the bed, and began to dress. "You know, you're all wrong . . . okay, maybe partly right. I am interested in your boss but I don't have to use you to get to him." He slipped into his loafers and walked to the kitchen where she was sitting at a small Formica table. "Last night was good for me . . . important for me. It's the first time since Jessy left that I've felt anything for a woman. I'm sorry if I screwed it up. I didn't want to."

"Stewart Zeitlin is a good man," she said slowly. "A considerate employer, nothing more. I've never pried into his private life, and as far as I know, he's never pried into mine. That's all I can tell you. That's all I'll ever be able to tell you, so you might as well go and pick up your investigation somewhere else."

He touched her on the shoulder and felt her muscles tighten. "There won't be any more cop stuff, I promise. Can I call you again?"

She shrugged. "Why not?"

"It would mean a lot to me."

"Sure. See you around."

11

THERE WERE TWO messages on his desk when he got to the precinct. The first was expected: a call from Raoul Sanchez and a telephone number where he could be reached. Mosquito had done his job well. It was remarkable how the prospect of financial ruin could turn a dirtball like Sanchez into a public-spirited citizen. The second message was entirely unexpected and left him unnerved: *Call your daughter Kelly . . . 555-7100, Extension 406.*

It was a New York exchange; probably a hotel in Manhattan. What the hell was Kelly doing in Manhattan? He lifted the phone and dialed. "Hello?" Her voice sounded different, more mature than he remembered.

"Kelly, it's me . . . Daddy."

"Hi Daddy. How are you?" She was as breezy as ever, as if they'd seen each other only yesterday.

"I'm fine, honey, how about you? How's college?"

"Okay, I guess . . . boring mostly."

"How's Katie . . . and your mom?"

"They're okay. I'm here in New York. A bunch of us came down from school for the parade yesterday so I thought I'd give you a call and say hello."

"Well I'm glad you did. How long are you staying?"

"Just today. We're leaving for MOMA in about fifteen minutes and we'll drive back after that."

"Any chance we can see each other while you're here?"

"Uh . . . you know where MOMA is?"

"I don't know *what* MOMA is," he admitted.

She laughed. "It's the Museum of Modern Art. I think it's on Fifty-third Street."

"I know where it is. If I get there in time for lunch will you miss your ride back home?"

"I don't think so."

"Twelve noon okay?"

"Great. There's a garden out back. I'll be there."

"See you then, honey. Bye."

He dialed Ronnie Sanchez.

"Crowley!" Sanchez screamed into the phone. "What the fuck are you trying to do to me?"

"Whaddaya mean, Raoul?"

"You know what I mean. Your goons were here last night and put me out of business!" He was hyperventilating, each labored breath coming across the lines like a mortar volley. "Now you listen to me and you get this straight. You stop humping me around and get offa my back or I'm gonna see that a lot of people in your department take a fall . . . including that fat fuck Fry. I'll nail both your badges over my bar, you hear me?"

"Hold it a minute!" Vince interrupted him. "Is that a threat? Am I hearing this right . . . ?"

There was dead silence on the other end.

"Because if you want to do business with me, that's one thing . . . but if you threaten me, you're dog meat. Kapish?"

"Whaddaya want, Crowley . . . ?" His tone became more conciliatory. "I already told you everything I know."

"Now you see? That's what I mean . . . it's like you're underestimating my intelligence . . . like you think I'm stupid or something."

Sanchez groaned. "Do me a favor, Crowley. Just tell me what it is you want me to say and I'll say it. I don't want no more shit with you guys. I just want to run my club and make a living. What's wrong with that?"

"All I want is a little cooperation, that's all. Now we both know Miguel Ramos was in your place the night of March tenth. What I want from you is what time he left and who he left with. Is that so hard?"

There was a pause. "I'll have to check around."

"Take all the time you want. There'll be somebody down at the club in an hour to take your statement. Get all the facts together and tell him the truth." He hung up.

It was a minor break, one of those openings that comes from playing hunches. Nobody had placed Ramos at the Blue Parrot the night of the murder but he could as easily have been there as anyplace else. If Sanchez really didn't know anything, it was a good bet he knew somebody who did. It was simply a question of getting him into a helpful frame of mind.

Eleven oh-five. He would have to leave or he'd be late for his date with Kelly. He left a note on Tommy Ippollito's desk, telling him to go to the Blue Parrot as soon as he returned, checked out a short-wave radio at the desk, and headed for Manhattan. It was raining on and off along the way, gentle spring showers that did little more than dampen the parched pavement and slow the already heavy traffic along the Bruckner Expressway and FDR Drive. He exited onto Sixty-first Street, inched through midtown, and arrived at the museum fifteen minutes late.

He was still too early. Kelly was late, as he should have known she would be. In that, she was more like her mother than he cared to think. Jessy was late as a matter of principle; she was late as a matter of style. It was as if she feared showing up on time; as if she would be humiliated for seeming overly anxious to please, for being an eager beaver.

He wandered into the garden, which was still damp from the recent rain, and surveyed the various pieces of sculpture set along the walkways: an enormous, out-of-proportion figure of a nude woman by someone named Jacques Lipchitz . . . an unidentifiable mass of twisted metal by Duchamp-Villon called *The Horse* . . . a soaring monolith called *Bird in Space* by a guy named Brancusi. Vince wanted to understand them but they left him cold. Across the courtyard was a massive bronze figure more to his liking: *Monument to Balzac* by Auguste Rodin. At least he could tell what was going on; everything looked about the way it was supposed to look. He found a seat on one of the marble benches along the walkway, making sure it wasn't a piece of art before he sat, and waited. Kelly showed up at twelve-thirty.

"Daddy!" She returned his hug and kissed him on the cheek.

"Hi honey, how've you been?"

"Great, just great. Come with me, I want you to meet somebody." She hustled him out of the garden, through the cavernous lobby, and out onto the street. "Daddy, this is Armand."

Vince reached out and shook the hand of a male, approximately six feet tall, approaching thirty, and urbanely handsome. He was immediately unlikable.

"Armand is my *patron*," Kelly gushed. "He's showing me practically everything about art and culture."

"Nice to meet you," Vince mumbled.

"Mr. Crowley. This is a pleasure. Your lovely daughter has already told me all about you," Armand said with a silky, European accent. "I've been looking forward to meeting you."

There was an awkward moment when nobody was sure what came next. "Have you known each other long?" Vince asked finally.

"We met this winter at Stowe," Kelly said. "Armand

was my ski instructor.''

A ski instructor. It was like the plot of a bad soap opera. "Was she a good student?" he asked.

Armand laughed. "Your daughter is a quick study, Mr. Crowley. She gave me no trouble at all."

He was afraid of that. "Will Armand be joining us for lunch?" he asked coolly.

"I only wish I could, but I must return to business," Armand said. "I'm afraid I used up all of my lunch hour at the museum." He clasped Vince's hand and blew Kelly a kiss. "Ciao, *cara mia.*"

Vince waited until he was out of sight. "Since when do ski instructors have lunch hours?"

"Oh, Daddy. That's only in the winter. The rest of the year he sells Jaguars."

"The car or the animal?"

She giggled. "Where shall we eat?"

"It's your party. You seem to know the neighborhood better than I do."

"Well, it's either quiche and tofu, or pizza. You choose."

"Need you ask?" He took her by the arm.

The pizzeria was on Ninth Avenue, north of Fifty-third street. "How did you find this place?" he asked as they squeezed into one of the tiny booths lining the wall of the ten-feet-wide storefront.

"Armand. He knows every restaurant in Manhattan. He says this is the best pizza in America."

Vince tried to look impressed. "How long have you and Armand been an item, as they say?"

"God, Daddy, we're not an item. Just friends."

He raised an eyebrow. "How old is your *friend* Armand?"

"Daddy!" She was getting exasperated.

"Okay, no more about old Armand. How's school?"

"It's okay, I guess. I'm changing my major to art next semester."

"Sounds like fun. I'll bet you could do a lot better than some of that stuff I saw in the garden."

"Those are *masterpieces!*" she said.

"I still say you could do better. Tell me, how's Katie?"

"Same as always I guess . . . a real airhead."

"You two getting along?"

"Tolerably, I suppose. I'm away at school most of the time so we really don't get a chance to fight a lot."

He shook his head. "You two shouldn't fight. You're sisters . . . family."

"Spare me," she groaned.

"Okay, no more about Katie. Now who does that leave? How about your mom . . . how's she getting along?"

Kelly squirmed. "I guess she's all right. I haven't seen her in a little while."

"Didn't you see her in Marion?"

She eyed him quizzically. "She hasn't been there in a couple of months. Didn't you know?"

"Where is she?" he asked.

"In Silver Hills. She's been there since January."

The name was vaguely familiar; a hospital or sanitarium, maybe a rehab for drunks and drug addicts. "What's she doing there?"

Kelly grimaced. "I'm sorry, Daddy, I just thought you knew."

"It's okay, honey. Just tell me about it."

Kelly paused, lit a cigarette nervously. "There isn't a lot to tell. Grandpa Dennis had her admitted right after New Year's. I guess she had a nervous breakdown."

"That's it?"

"Pretty much . . . at least that's all he told me."

"Have you seen her?"

"We went out there last month and brought her home for

the weekend. She seemed kinda strange . . . like she was
on something . . .''

He tried to collect his thoughts. Sloan obviously knew all
about this last week when he'd been there, and never
mentioned anything. He could feel himself getting angry.
''You haven't had any contact with her since then?''

''Uh-uh.''

They ordered pizza with mushrooms and pepperoni and
ate in relative silence. Vince was trying to sort it out in his
own mind; trying to find a proper target for the fury that
was building inside of him.

''I'm really sorry, Daddy,'' Kelly said finally.

''It's not your fault,'' he reassured her.

''Will you go up there to see her?''

''I dunno, honey . . .''

''I think you should. There's something wrong with her.
I think they're doing something to her in that place.''

''We'll see . . .'' He wiped the grease from his face and
hands with a paper napkin. ''I gotta get back to work,
honey. Can I drop you off someplace?''

''No, you go ahead. I've got an hour to kill . . .'' She
leaned across the table and kissed him. ''Go up there,
Daddy . . . get her out of that snake pit.''

Vince paid the check at the register and phoned the
precinct from a telephone booth just outside the pizzeria.
There was a message that Charlene had called and left a
number where she could be reached. He dialed, received a
busy signal, hung up the phone, and waited.

''Come on, asshole!'' It was a woman of about seventy,
barely five feet tall, banging on the glass door of the booth.
''If you're not gonna use that phone, get the hell outa the
booth and let somebody else use it!''

Vince shrugged and stepped outside to let her in.

''Asshole . . .'' She continued on down the sidewalk.
''. . . City's fulla assholes.''

He returned to the booth and got a connection. ''This is

Crowley, Charlene. You called?''

"Yeah. You know that guy I saw with Marguerita that night? Well, my girl friend Jeanne saw him at the club last night.''

"What club is that?''

"Cruise Control.''

"Were you there?''

"Not me,'' she said emphatically. "I don't go in those places no more. I'm too scared, man.''

"So how do you know it's the same guy you saw?''

"She told me. We were together that night we saw them. She says he's the same guy for sure.''

He took out his notebook. "Where can I find this Jeanne?''

"She's here with me, at the hotel.''

"Don't either of you move. I'll be there in fifteen minutes.'' He made it in ten.

Jeanne was another transsexual, younger than Charlene and more masculine, her short lime-green miniskirt revealing the slim hips and muscles of a teenage boy. It was immediately obvious that she didn't like cops, that she was there only because Charlene had somehow convinced her to stay. He asked a few routine questions and decided to seize the opportunity while it was at hand. He put them both in the car and drove to headquarters at One Police Plaza.

The Police Artist's section was on the seventh floor of the twelve-story, red brick structure on the corner of Madison Street and the Avenue of the Finest, right next to the Latent Prints Division. He introduced them both to Detective Stan Buyniscyk, took the elevator back to the ground floor, and crossed the street to the Metropolitan Improvement Company Bar and Grill, a favorite hangout of cops stationed in the area.

The place was almost empty, a few scattered patrons dispersed among the stools and tables, sipping draft beers, eating cold sandwiches, talking, watching TV—a Mets game in progress, spring training from their camp in Florida. Vince found a convenient stool at the bar and ordered a beer. Around him, the familiar sights and smells of the tavern began to relax him, set him at ease. There was something about taverns that did that. They were unchangeable; the signs, the smells, the people were the same no matter where you were. They were comforting, a recurring nugget of constancy in a world that was moving much too fast.

The Metropolitan Improvement Company was that kind of place: the homely familiarity of the window display— Calvert's and Four Roses in dimly plastic and neon . . . the faint aura of neglect . . . the understatement. Nobody had to overstate the benefits of a tavern, he thought. Its virtue was its sameness, its lack of originality. Nobody came to the Metropolitan Improvement Company for surprises. They came so they could be with cops but not have to *be* cops. They came so they could belch and fart and flex their muscles and arm wrestle and play liar's poker and hang out . . . and kill time . . . escape.

Halfway into his second beer a message on the bar phone told him the artist's composite sketch was ready. Reluctantly, he scooped his change and headed back. Upstairs, Charlene and Jeanne were seated at opposite sides of the room, staring icily at one another. "Lover's quarrel," Stan Buyniscyk muttered. "I couldn't get them to agree on practically anything." He handed Vince a composite likeness. "This is about the best we're going to do."

Vince looked at the sheet, a photomontage of various facial features put together to form a likeness of the subject. It was an average face, unspectacular in any meaningful way: hair, close cropped and wavy; eyes, even set and alert; nose, straight; mouth, full lipped; no identifying scars or growths; no unusual features. It was the kind of face Vince saw every day and hardly noticed. He showed the picture to Charlene. "Is that the man you saw leave Cruise Control the night Marguerita was killed?"

Charlene shrugged. "Looks like him . . . kinda."

"Any major differences?"

"I guess not."

He showed the photo to Jeanne. "Is that the man you saw leave with Marguerita?"

"Uh-huh."

He turned to Buyniscyk. "I thought you said they couldn't agree?"

Buyniscyk shook his head hopelessly. "You can take that shot with you if you want. I have all I need here for reproduction."

Vince drove Charlene and Jeanne back to the West Side and headed in, north on Riverside Drive and across to the Triborough Bridge and the Bronx, absorbed in his own thoughts, struggling to put overlapping events in their proper context. He turned the short-wave radio on loud, trying to involve himself with the familiar sounds of the precinct: *"All units respond to woman in distress . . . Two twenty-fifth and Laconia . . . respond to domestic disturbance, One ninety-seven Howard Avenue . . . respond to automobile accident . . . respond to assault with a knife . . .* It was all routine, stuff he'd heard a thousand times before.

Thoughts of Jessy muscled in under the squawk.

12

NOAH WEINBERG SUCKED nervously on a three-dollar custom corona, exhaled a massive cloud of blue smoke toward the ceiling, and reached into his top desk drawer for the keys to Wellington's vault. Police made him edgy on the best of days and today was far from the best of days. Today he would turn the Wellington Armored Car Company over to a handful of detectives from the Thirty-seventh Precinct who wanted to play gangbusters.

They had arrived four days ago, Detectives Harris and Santanelo from Robbery Division with the unwelcome news that Wellington was about to be hit by a bunch of organized-crime gorillas who had been casing the place for months. No doubt about it, they had assured him. An inside operative had been planted on the premises and the robbery was scheduled for that coming weekend, when close to six million bucks would be held in Wellington's vault for deposit in banks Monday morning. The police understood that Wellington had its own security system, they told him, but these were men of serious intent. There was the possibility of violence and it was better handled by the police.

Amen, Weinberg thought. What Wellington's security force for that weekend actually consisted of was his no-good brother-in-law, Moe, a mindless, cowardly schmuck who couldn't hold down a real job if his life depended on it; and another half-wit named Elmer whose only qualification for the job was that he happened to fit the only available uniform. Between the two of them they couldn't spot a nigger in Harlem, much less handle a full-scale holdup. Any twelve-year-old kid with half a brain and a little chutzpah could knock the place over in five minutes. If the police didn't know this, the mob certainly did. They were better organized than the cops anyway.

The operation would be such a cakewalk, he'd thought more than once of setting it up himself but always changed his mind. What he had at Wellington was just too sweet to take the risk, however small. He'd spent too many years manipulating the records and procedures of the company, too many hours sucking up to the bigshots at Taubman Holding Company, the owners of Wellington, to blow it all by getting too greedy. Now, the day-to-day operation of Wellington was up to him and him alone. Nobody at Taubman ever questioned his methods and that was just as good as a license to rob the place.

A crime would open the company's records to public scrutiny, and the scrutiny of the Taubman Holding Company. While they were undemanding employers, they weren't stupid. Chances were, that if they discovered how much of their profits he'd been socking away for himself these past few years, he would be rewarded with a pair of concrete swim fins and a vacation at the bottom of Jamaica Bay.

Naturally he had called the Thirty-seventh Precinct and checked everything out. Harris and Santanelo were to act as undercover operatives until they learned the exact time the robbery was planned. Once this was known, they would infiltrate additional police onto the premises and set up an ambush. A routine operation, the police called it, as long as he followed orders and stayed out of their way.

Weinberg handed the keys to Detective Harris, seated across from him at his desk. "There's nothing to worry about," Harris reassured him. "As long as you remember that secrecy is the key to this entire operation. You go home and have yourself a good weekend, like nothing out of the ordinary is happening. By the time you come in Monday morning, these guys will be behind bars."

Across the street Vito Prestipino returned from the men's room in Finger's Luncheonette to find Vince Crowley sitting in his favorite booth. He maneuvered his massive bulk onto the opposite seat and reached across the table. "Vincenzo, good to see you. What brings you down to this end of town?"

Vince shook Vito's hand. "Nothing much, paisan. I was wondering if you'd heard anything about that floater."

"I checked into that Vince. All I could get was a name and I figured you already had that."

"Miguel Ramos?"

"Yeah. Called himself Marguerita. Those people are really something."

"Nothing else?"

Vito shrugged. "What else? Just another faggot who got iced. It happens all the time. One fag fucks another fag's boyfriend and before you know it he's fish bait. What's the big deal with this one?"

"No big deal . . . just part of the job." Vince hailed the waitress and ordered a cup of coffee and a piece of strawberry-rhubarb pie.

"I'll bet you came here because you can't find nobody as cultured as me down at the three-seven, right?" Vito joked.

"Something like that, my friend."

"Seriously Vince, you look tired. Maybe you're working too hard, huh? Why not take the wife and kids and go on a vacation for a couple of weeks. You know, put the job behind you for a while . . .''

Vince shrugged. "My kids are off doing their own thing. You know how it is.''

"Kids! You don't have to tell me about it," Vito said. "You bust your hump for them all your life and they end up kicking you in the ass.''

"How many kids you got?" Vince asked.

"Three by my first wife. They're all grown up now.''

"Ever see them?''

"I seen the oldest a couple of years ago. He's in insurance out in Detroit and he don't want nothing to do with his old man." Vito shook his head sadly. "Imagine that; my business put the kid through college and now it's like he don't want to admit where he came from . . . I dunno.''

"That's too bad," Vince said. "What about the others?''

"Same thing. The other boy's out on the coast, in the travel business or something. I ain't talked to him in a couple of years either. My daughter's back in Sardinia with her mother. That's where my first wife is from. My whole family's from there.''

"Were you born there?" Vince asked.

"No, not me. I was born on Mulberry street, in Little Italy. My old man stowed away on a steamer when he was a kid; raised his family here and retired back to the old country back in sixty-four. The doctors told him he had a bum pump . . . only a couple of months to live. You should see the old man now, Vince . . .'' Vito grinned. "He's strong as a mule; still servicing half the widows in Cagliari. If that old man ever dies, they're gonna have to jerk him off before they can close the coffin lid.''

Vince smiled. "You ever go back to see him?''

"Not for a while now. I used to go every year but then I got married and . . . well, you know how it is.'' His voice was sad. "Sardinia's a beautiful country though. I fell in love with it the first time I went there . . . back in fifty-five to find a wife."

"You went all the way to Italy for a wife?" Vince asked.

"It was the thing to do in those days. My family was old-fashioned. They thought American girls were too fast . . . too smart-alecky. Whores, my mother called them. In those days, good Sardinian sons went back to the old village to marry and I respected my parents, respected their ways.

"Kids today don't have respect; for their parents, their elders . . . nobody. When I was coming up we worshiped the older guys, guys who had proved themselves . . . who showed what they were worth. A button man was a real hero, a Don was like a God. I woulda kissed the ground they walked on if they wanted me to, you know what I mean? Today, these punks . . . these *stunads* from the street don't respect nobody. They think they can move in anywhere they want to, without rules, without honor. I ask you, Vincenzo, what good is a man without honor?"

Vito looked embarrassed, as if he had revealed too much. "Hey Vincent, you didn't come in here to hear some *mezzopotzo* old guinea moaning about the way things used to be, did you?"

"It's okay," Vince said. "I know what you're talking about. Lots of things have changed from the old days, and they're not all good, either."

"Changed for the worse Vincenzo . . . for the worse. Honor and respect are dying in this country, my friend; maybe they're already dead. I won't go back to Sardinia now because it hurts too much to leave there. I see what they still have . . . I don't mean money, Vince; it's still a piss-poor country. I mean they still got values, and respect for tradition. When I see that, I realize how much we lost over here. No, I won't go back there unless it's for good. Maybe I'll retire there soon, take life easy for a change."

"No problem moving back where your ex-wife lives?"

"Problem . . . no, she's still the best woman I ever knew."

"So how come you're divorced?"

Vito shrugged. "For all the reasons I been telling you about. Angela was no fat guinea mama who spent all her time in the kitchen cooking pasta for me and the bambinos. She was a spirited woman from a proud family. She had money of her own, too; money she got from a lot of worthless land her father left her when he died . . ." Vito began chuckling. "You know, Vincent, it was always the custom in Sardinia for fathers to leave their sons the good grazing and farming land on the sides of the mountain. The worthless sandy soil down by the water went to the daughters. Well, it worked okay until one day some jet-set developer comes in and builds a hotel on the beach and before you know it half of European society is stabbing one another to get a piece of the place. The Sardinian women all become millionaires and the men are left up on the mountain humping the sheep. Fuckin' beautiful, huh?"

"Poetic justice," Vince agreed.

"The women thought so. Angela hated America from the first day I brought her here. She hated the vulgarity, the ugliness, the dirt and confusion of the city. If she'd been a Sicilian or a Corsican she wouldn't have had any choice; they got nothing to go back to. But she waited until the kids were old enough and gave everybody a choice . . . stay in America or go back to Sardinia with her. I made my choice, they all made theirs. What more can I tell you?"

"Ever wish you'd gone with them?" Vince asked.

Vito paused. "Sometimes maybe, but it's okay here. I done pretty good in this country; made some friends, got some respect. Things used to be a lot better than they are now though. Even the cops had some honor in the old days. No disrespect intended Vince, but you know what I'm talking about. They took only what was right to take, not like these greedy bastards today. They get on the force, they think the badge entitles them to become millionaires. Am I right or am I right?''

He didn't wait for an answer. "Don't get me wrong, my friend. I'm not talking about guys like you . . . never the old-timers. They had too much respect for the system. That's what made it work. The system was good to everybody as long as nobody got too greedy. Now everybody's out to fuck everybody else. It's no good, Vincenzo. The *stunads* fucked it up for all of us . . . you and me both.''

Outside, the sun was rapidly setting behind the Wellington Armored Car Company across the street. Vince shielded his eyes against the glare, drained his coffee cup, and stood to leave. "Oh, by the way Vito—I got a tip that you might be thinking about doing something dumb. I like you, my friend. Do me a favor and don't give me a reason to pull you in.''

Vito remained expressionless. "I like you, too, Vince. Thanks for letting an old man let off some steam.''

13

SEEN BY THE first-time visitor, Silver Hills seemed more a chic country resort than a sanitarium and rehabilitation center. Winding down from the Merritt Parkway, through the tree-lined streets of exclusive New Canaan, Connecticut, Vince felt a tug of resentment at the trappings of privilege surrounding him. They were smug and seclude even in their sicknesses, he thought as he drove across a rustic, white wooden bridge into the main compound. He could see people walking the flagstone pathways, talking, reading, sunning themselves in the unusually warm spring weather. They were probably patients, men and women who were fighting problems with booze or drugs or reality, sick people who had the money and the wherewithall to check themselves in every six months or so for a little genteel therapy. He thought of Billy, of Queens Hospital with its peeling gray-green hallways and padlocked steel doors, its uncaring, brutish attendants, its stench: the legacy of a hero cop with no connections.

He parked in a wooded cul-de-sac and entered the lobby of the main building. A pleasant middle-aged woman smiled at him. "Can I be of help?"

"I'm looking for Jessica Crowley . . . a patient here."

97

She consulted a register of names on her desk. "Crowley? I'm sorry, sir; our records don't show any Crowley as a patient here."

"Tall, good-looking woman, about forty?"

She shook her head. "I'm sorry, there are so many patients here . . ."

"Family name is Sloan . . . from Marion."

She rechecked the register. "Jessy Sloan, would that be it?"

"I guess so. I'd like to see her."

She handed him a printed index card. "If you'll just fill this out, I'll check to see where she is right now."

Vince sat on a velvet-covered love seat near an oversized fieldstone fireplace and studied the form: NAME . . . ADDRESS . . . RELATIONSHIP TO PATIENT . . . PURPOSE OF VISIT. He assumed they were safeguards designed to protect the inmates from outside predators who would invade the premises and try to sell them yachts or mutual funds. He completed it and returned to the desk where the receptionist was talking on the telephone.

She glanced at his card as she talked. "A Mr. Crowley is out here; says he's her husband." She arched an eyebrow.

"Her name is Crowley, too," Vince said emphatically.

The receptionist returned the phone to its cradle. "Mrs. Sloan is in group right now, sir. If you'd care to wait, someone will be with you in a few minutes."

"I'd really like to see Mrs. *Crowley* now." He flashed his badge.

She lifted the phone and punched the keyboard nervously. "The gentleman to see Mrs. Sloan is a policeman of some sort . . ." She paused and replaced it. "I'm sorry, but that's the only name they know her by."

A tall, well-dressed man in his mid-fifties appeared in the reception room and approached Vince. "I'm Dr. Sperry. Is there anything I can do to help?"

"You can let me see my wife."

Dr. Sperry nodded gravely. "Well . . . Mrs. Sloan is in group therapy right now, and we can't disturb her."

"I can wait," Vince said.

Sperry checked his watch. "It may be a while."

"I've got nowhere to go."

"You realize that our normal visiting hours are from two to five on Monday, Wednesday, and Friday."

Vince was starting to get mad. "Look, Doctor, I'll wait around for a half hour and if I don't get to see my wife by then, I'll leave and come back here with a court order and more cops than you've seen in your lifetime . . . got it?"

"There will be no need for that," Sperry said icily. "Mrs. Sloan will be out shortly." He turned abruptly and exited the room.

"Can I get you a cup of coffee?" the receptionist asked sweetly after he'd left.

"No thanks."

"We have a gift shop across the quadrangle if you'd care to browse while you're waiting."

"Gift shop?" He was stunned. "What do you sell there, souvenirs of this place—pennants, sweatshirts?"

"Oh no . . . just the usual things: clothing, toiletries, games, leather goods. The guests feel more at home if they have a nice place to shop."

"Can I get a postcard?" he asked.

"I believe you can." She didn't bat an eye.

"I guess I'll just wait here." He retreated to his seat by the fireplace.

Jessy arrived a few minutes later, trim and sophisticated in a matching tangerine cashmere skirt and sweater, looking less like a patient in a laughing asylum than anyone he'd ever seen. She crossed the room and clasped both of his hands. "Hi stranger. What brings you up here to la-la land?"

"What do you think?" He kissed her softly. "How're you doing?"

"Not too bad now." She sat next to him on the velvet sofa. "How did you know I was here?"

"Kelly told me. We had lunch in the city. She said you had a nervous breakdown."

Jessy laughed silently. "I guess you could charitably call it that."

"What would *you* call it?" he asked.

She shrugged. "I dunno . . . alcoholism, drug dependency, depression, paranoia. Take your pick. Every time I open my mouth around this place, they give me another disease."

He shook his head. "I don't understand. You were never that heavy into booze or drugs."

"Sure I was. You were just never around long enough to notice, that's all."

He winced. "Do we have to start that again?"

"I guess not," she said wearily. "What *are* you here for Vince?"

"I'm concerned. We are still husband and wife, aren't we?"

She nodded. "I'm sorry. I'm just in a bad place these days. I've been scrutinized and analyzed and poked and probed and medicated for so long now that I guess I'm a little gun-shy. I am glad to see you. That's the truth."

"And I'm glad to see you . . ." He was buoyed by her response. "Tell me, what're they doing for you . . . or to you?"

"There's really not much to tell. I got sick. I was drinking out of control and taking pills at the same time. The doctors said they had a synergistic effect on me, and I took a header down the stairs on New Year's Eve. I've been here ever since."

"Are they treating you okay?"

She shrugged. "Sure. I get round-the-clock shrinks who tell me why I'm depressed, AA meetings that tell me how to change my life, Haldol and Thorazine to mellow me out.

What more could a girl want?''

"Jesus . . ." He fell silent.

"It's really not all that bad." She placed a comforting hand on his forearm. "I'm not sure what's happening to me, but I know I'm better off in here than I would be out there, at least for the time being. It's not your fault, none of it; so don't blame yourself if that's what you're doing."

"I'm not blaming myself," he said. "I just want to know what's going on. I was at your father's house last weekend and he didn't even tell me you were here."

She nodded. "That shouldn't surprise you. You were never exactly Daddy's favorite. What were you there for?"

He hesitated. "I went up there to see the girls and ended up hearing you want a divorce."

She stared at the carpet. "Daddy told you that?"

"Uh-huh. Isn't it true?"

"I guess he'd like it to be . . . Maybe it is. I'm just not sure about anything anymore."

Vince was gripping the armrest of the sofa. "I don't understand, Jess. Did you tell him you wanted a divorce or didn't you?"

She raised her eyes to meet his. "I don't know, Vince . . . I'm sure I said a lot of things; I just can't remember. Please try to understand . . ." She began sobbing softly.

He put his arm around her. "Then it's not true."

She pulled away from him. "Vince . . . I have to do this. I have to get my head on straight before I can even think about something like that. I know it sounds selfish, but I have to do this for me. I can't think about you or the girls or Daddy or anybody until I'm better. Maybe then we can talk about your feelings . . . about you and me. For now, I just can't deal with it. I'm sorry."

He wiped a tear from her damp cheek. "Can I come up again?"

"Give me a little while . . ." She kissed his hand. "I know where you are. I'll call when I'm ready."

14

A GRAY MONDAY morning; thick overhanging clouds and air pregnant with moisture. Vince crawled along the barely moving Cross Bronx Expressway toward the precinct, trying to stay awake and keep from losing his temper at the same time. He had slept very little the night before, maybe not at all, thoughts of his visit with Jessy pressing in on him, jarring him awake. Now he was stuck in traffic with what seemed to be every selfish, impatient driver in New York . . . jockeying with one another for better lane positions . . . reviling one another through open windows with hand gestures and shouted threats.

Ahead were blinking lights: an Emergency Services vehicle parked at the side of the busy artery, a black vintage Chevrolet that had lost its right front wheel, the driver sitting forlornly on the concrete dividing wall. A three-car collision, the outraged occupants spilling out into the middle lanes, prepared to do harm to one another. Vince checked the clock on his dashboard: 10:52. Even with clear sailing from here on in, he would be late and Boyle would get to needle him about it for a couple of hours. He lit a cigarette and settled back into the vinyl upholstery. There wasn't a helluva lot he could do about it now.

Closer to the stationhouse there was another traffic snarl, a blue-and-white detouring cars away from Laconia Avenue. An odd assemblage of vehicles and people gathered in front of the precinct: news media and television trucks, reporters with microphones, cameramen with minicams; all corralling anyone who was willing to stand still and answer their questions. Vince pushed through the crush of bodies and equipment and made his way up the brick steps, past the twisted umbilicals of red and black coaxial cable streaming from the television trucks into the building.

Inside, a group of harried brass, including Boyle, were fending off reporters' questions, barking orders to the phalanx of uniformed policemen blocking the stairwells and the elevator. Vince elbowed past them and climbed the stairway to the squad room. "What the hell's going on?" he asked Cuzak, who was standing by the door enjoying the show.

"Somebody knocked over the Wellington Armored Car Company," Cuzak answered.

"No shit? How much did they get?"

"A bundle . . . maybe six million. They had all the weekend receipts from Yonkers Raceway in the vault."

"Jeez!" Vince grinned in admiration. "They know who did it?"

"Not a clue." Cuzak pointed to the open doorway of the Robbery Division, where a crowd of detectives was spilling out into Homicide. "They got Wellington's manager in there, a guy named Weinberg. Seems he knew all about it beforehand."

"An inside job?" Vince asked.

Cuzak laughed. "I don't think so. Ask Snuffy or Bob. I just got in on the end of it."

He walked to the open squad room door and peered through the crowd. Inside, Snuffy Quade and Bob Langonier were listening incredulously as three sweating, slavering male Caucasians screamed uncontrollably at each other. "What's happening?" he asked Detective Steve Appelbaum, who was closest to the door.

"Everyone's blaming everyone else." Appelbaum grinned. "The guy in the open-necked white shirt is Weinberg, the manager. The other two were on guard last night."

"How'd it go down?"

"Smoothest goddamn thing you ever saw. Two guys show up at Wellington one day last weekend, flash some tin, and tell Weinberg they're detectives from the Thirty-seventh. They say they got a tip the place is about to be hit and they want to set up an ambush to collar the perps when they show up . . . only these guys aren't real cops."

Appelbaum was laughing and Vince was beginning to get the drift. "So naturally Weinberg calls the precinct to make sure everything's kosher, but these guys have a splice into his phone line and they intercept the call and tell him everything's cool . . ." His eyes were beginning to water and he wiped them with the back of his hand. "So he puts these guys on the payroll and they start prowling around the place, acting like real G-men until they get the feel of the joint, then they bring in a couple of their buddies, wait until the haul is worthwhile, and clean the vault out in their own sweet time. Beautiful, huh?"

Vince was impressed. "Any idea who these guys are?"

"No, but if you ask me, I think Weinberg was in on it from the beginning. He just doesn't look stupid enough to fall for a scam like this."

Vince shrugged. "It's your case, so you handle it the way you think best. You might want to bring the Spring Man in and ask him a couple of questions though."

"Tony Clams? Why?"

"I dunno. Just a hunch."

"It don't seem like his kind of action."

"Maybe not, but he's been eating lunch at Finger's across the street from Wellington for a couple of years now.

Nobody eats their shit for that long unless they're completely nuts or there's a payoff someplace. Vito Prestipino may be a lot of things but I don't think he's nuts."

He slipped a blank DD-5 into the ancient Smith-Corona on his desk and made his first entry when Tommy Ippollito entered the squad room. "What's all this shit?" he asked.

"Somebody took Wellington; probably the Spring Man. You can bet the farm he was in Miami when it happened, though."

Tommy laughed and checked the messages on his desk. "How'd it go with your uptown society doctor?"

"Zeitlin? Not good. I got a feeling this guy knows a lot more than he's telling me. I mean, here we got a high-class specialist who charges maybe a C-note for an office visit treating a junkie vagrant for nerve problems? Gimme a break! And he prescribes Valium? Come on now . . . Any junkie who needs Valium can get all he wants off the street. What's he need a prescription for? The whole deal smells bad. It just doesn't go down right."

"What about the hormones they found in the pathologist's report? Couldn't he have been supplying those?"

Vince shrugged. "I suppose, but we'd have to subpoena his files to know for sure. He's an uncooperative son of a bitch, I can tell you that. I'm gonna pay him another visit in a day or two just to bust his balls, if nothing else. What'd you get from our friend Ronny Sanchez?"

"More than we had before. I talked to everybody in the Blue Parrot and it seems Ramos was pretty well known there. The bartender's a fag named Rickyanne . . . Knew him practically from the time he blew into town." He laughed. "No pun intended . . . Anyway, he worked for a printing company in New Jersey for a couple of months back in late eighty or early eighty-one until he got himself fucked up on dope and got fired. He was on Jersey welfare for a while, then started showing up as a nude waiter and performer at various sleaze joints around town. Not exactly the great American success story . . .''

"Was he there the night of the murder?"

"Who the hell knows? Everybody all of a sudden develops amnesia . . . You know how it works. I'll tell you this though: They're about as fucked-up a bunch in that place as I've run into since I became a cop."

"Tell me about it." Vince removed a stack of the suspect's photo likenesses from his desk drawer and handed them to Tommy. "Show this to everybody there and see they get spread around to the other joints Ramos frequented. Maybe we'll get lucky."

The telephone rang; a call from 911 Central . . . a double homicide at Gun Hill Road and Laconia Avenue. He noted the time and manner of notification, signaled Tommy to follow him, and headed for his car.

The crime scene was a typical run-down commercial area of two- and three-story shops crammed together behind steel grillwork; puny, inadequate fortresses holding out against the march of crime and decay. Vince parked behind a blue-and-white with its lights flashing and pushed through the crowd of curious onlookers. "What went down?" He passed the patrolman guarding the entrance.

"Robbery and murder. Couple in their late seventies . . . Futterman, I think. Somebody just tied them up and beat the shit out of them. It's really a mess up there."

Vince felt sick. He'd known the old couple almost as long as he'd been with the Thirty-seventh; decent, hard-working people who'd somehow managed to survive the numbing fear they lived with daily, and stick it out in a neighborhood that hadn't deserved them. "Were you first on the scene?" he asked.

"Uh-uh. A rookie named Shannon. He's inside . . . in the back."

Vince walked to the rear of the store where Crime Scene and Emergency Services personnel were gathered at the foot of a stairwell, and found the probationary who'd discovered the bodies. "What happened?"

PO Shannon consulted his hastily scribbled notes. "I entered the premises at approximately eleven hundred hours and noticed that the store was empty. Upon further investigation I came upon two bodies tied together in the living quarters upstairs from the shop; one male and one female Caucasian . . ."

"Okay, Shannon, good work." Vince mounted the narrow stairs and made his way through an unlit hallway to the upstairs apartment, past a kitchen and sitting room to the bedroom, where CSU was photographing the bodies and dusting for prints. The room was a canvas of splattered blood, carpeting, walls, woodwork, windows smeared and dripping like a surrealistic set design. The bodies were in the center of the bedroom floor, trussed together back-to-back like slabs of beef, lying on their sides in a pool of gore. "Find any weapon?" he asked.

"You name it," one of the CSU detectives said. "Whoever did this hit them with everything that wasn't nailed down . . . fireplace poker, frying pans, lamps . . . sloppiest piece of work I've ever seen. Prints all over the place. They've been here for twenty or thirty years . . . robbed a dozen times but they stuck it out. You wonder what the hell could make somebody do a thing like this . . ."

Vince shook his head. "It's the times, bro . . . the times we live in." He went downstairs where two uniformed patrolmen were questioning a couple of Hasidic Jews in black caftans and broad-brimmed black felt hats. "Whaddaya got?" he asked.

"These men saw about six black youths exiting the premises around a half hour ago . . . say they were carrying items from the shop . . ."

"How could a thing like this happen?" one of the Hasids wailed. "They were poor people, just like everybody else. Why did they have to kill them?"

"I don't know, sir," Vince answered. "Can you give us a description of the youths you saw?"

"Who knows?" He shrugged. "They were *schwartzes*, one is like another . . ."

"This used to be a good place to live before they ruined it," the other chimed in. "Look at this . . ." He swept his arm in a wide arc, indicating the debris of the street. "They don't care about anything, cut your throat as soon as look at you."

"Yes sir." Vince turned to the uniformed patrolmen. "See that these gentlemen give you a description of whoever they saw, then escort them home. I'll want them available for ID when we pick up some suspects."

The dark blue coroner's van arrived from Jacobi Hospital and Shem Wiesen walked through the crowd to where Vince was standing. "What do you have?" he asked.

"Double homicide. An old man and his wife beaten to death."

Wiesen shook his head. "Robbery?"

"Yeah. They probably got all of fifty bucks, if they were lucky."

"Christ. It never stops, does it?"

"Not on my tour," Vince said.

15

A RITUAL WHIRRING from the digital clock on the nightstand signified a change in the hour column. What time was it? There were no visual signs, no clues. The room was medium dark, suspended that way from dull brown walls and too much familiarity. Vince groped along the length of the nightstand, felt the cold, familiar shape of his steel-rimmed glasses and adjusted them to his ears. The glasses were a necessary encumbrance, an accommodation to age he still resisted. To the guys at the division, they were for reading only. In truth, the sharp edges disappeared from every part of his world without them.

Five forty-seven. Practically time to get up and he felt like he had hardly slept. Part of the reason was that he was still dressed; sprawled across the unmade bed in his street clothes. The television set was still going, one of those medical melodramas scheduled by the networks for insomniacs: *"Doctor, are you telling us that our daughter is a dwarf?"* He moved to the foot of the bed, turned the set off, and tried to clear his head.

Another one of those nights, and the persistent dream. There had been a lot of them lately, more than he cared to count; nights when he would arrive home dead-tired, fix a sandwich or a frozen dinner, open a cold beer, and fall asleep in front of the portable TV in the bedroom before he'd finished any of it. It was a tolerable life, he supposed; not much different from the way a lot of unmarried cops lived, but then they didn't have to put up with the dream.

It was always of water, dripping gently at first from moss-encrusted rocks. High above were ferns and jack-in-the-pulpits, etched dreamily against a cloudless sky. It was a quiet place, a peaceful place, a place where a kid could go to be by himself. The rocks were sharp and cool, forming a precipice that dwarfed him in its immensity. It surrounded him, engulfed him, cloaked him in anonymity.

The water trickled slowly in convenient channels, forming a glassy pool at his feet. It was a comfortable feeling, even as the water began to rise, lapping his ankles and shins, creating frothy bubbles that caressed his bare skin. Gradually the surface of the water reached his waist, then his chest. He could feel the current pulling at him, dragging him toward the precipice. He tried to run but his feet were mired in an unseen trammel. There was nowhere to go, no escape from the unstoppable surge. He was trapped in its flows and eddies, being carried to the rim of the precipice and the abyss below . . .

That was where the dream always ended, jarring him back to consciousness, bathed in sweat and trembling. He would lie there, listening to the rhythmic pumping of his heart, trying to put everything into perspective. It was only a dream, a fragmented piece of history that had frozen itself in his brain and refused to let go. That was what the police psychiatrist told him years ago when the dream first surfaced. It would disappear in time . . . once the fear had been confronted.

It had become less frequent as time passed, but never disappeared altogether. It was one of those things people put up with but were too embarrassed to discuss in normal

company, like hemorrhoids or bleeding gums. The shrink
was out. Too many trips to the psych clinic was a sure ticket
to disability retirement. Nightmares weren't the sort of
thing you shared with your fellow officers, even your
partner. What you did was live with them . . . sweat them
out and hope each one was the last.

He went to the kitchen, turned the burner on under the
kettle of water, and poured an indeterminate amount of
instant coffee directly from the jar into a ceramic mug.
WORLD'S BEST FATHER, it was inscribed; a present from the
girls on his fortieth birthday a few years back. He really
hadn't been a very good father, he thought. There were
always too many things that got in the way. Even the times
they'd been most intimately alone he'd found it difficult to
tell them how he really felt. Maybe it was fear, maybe it
was embarrassment. Whatever; he'd always felt there was
something in his makeup that prevented deep, personal
sharing.

August of '64 and the police academy swimming pool;
that was where it all began. There had been thirty hours of
lifesaving instructions, and the final exam was an underwa-
ter struggle designed to terrify the rookies and give the
more sadistic of the instructors a chance to vent their
frustrations in the name of education. Eight of them, each
weighing in at over two hundred pounds, had been chosen
to go man to man with the rookies at the bottom of the pool,
the object being to see whether the rookie could break free
from the instructor's viselike grip and escape to the surface.

Vince's instructor had been a weightlifter named Ed
Straub, who had twice won the title of Mr. NYPD in the
city bodybuilding championships. He'd known before he
started that he had no realistic chance of breaking free, but
he reasoned that the burly veteran would release him before
any real harm was done. He'd been dead wrong. The last
thing he remembered thinking before he blacked out was
that, dying, his last vision on earth was to be the flickering,

diffused image of a coiled snake tattooed on Straub's massive biceps as it closed relentlessly around his throat.

So the fear was addressed and still the dream remained. It only confirmed what Vince already suspected about psychiatrists and therapy: that people who underwent extensive periods of therapy in their lives usually had a pretty good idea what caused them to behave stupidly and irrationally. They didn't change their behavior, just got to the root of it. In his case, the dreams hadn't affected his life or his performance on the job whether he knew what caused them or not. He could live with them if he had to. Lots of cops had worse memories to cope with. He drank his coffee, showered, and drove to the precinct.

"Boyle wants to see you," Tommy said as he entered the squad room. "He's on the rag again."

Vince knocked on his open door. "You wanted to see me, Lieutenant?"

Boyle was studying the charts. "Whaddaya got on this double homicide?" he growled.

Vince braced himself. "It's all on yesterday's Five, Lieutenant. Not much to go on yet. We have a description of some kids seen leaving the building at around the time of the crime. That's about it for now."

Boyle shook his head. "It's not good . . . not good at all."

"Lieutenant?"

"This sort of thing is bad for public relations," he went on. "I've got a delegation of those Hasidic Jews coming in this morning, and they're gonna start screaming about the niggers and more police protection. I tell you, if it isn't one goddamn thing it's another . . ." He belched and took a gulp from the Maalox bottle on the desk.

"Public relations, Lieutenant?" The vision of the Futtermans trussed together like slaughtered hogs flashed before him.

"You're goddamn right, public relations!" Boyle snap-

ped. "These people are just looking for an excuse to nail
our asses to the wall. All it takes is some stupid little
incident like this. The sons of bitches get a little press and
media coverage . . . first thing you know the City Council
passes a resolution, the mayor makes a crime in the
Thirty-seventh a major reelection plank and Art Boyle ends
up taking a bath in the toilet!" He slammed his fist on the
desk.

There was an awkward moment of silence. "Is that all,
Lieutenant?" Vince asked finally.

"I want everybody on this!" he screamed. "I'm gonna
tell those bearded kikes they can expect an arrest within a
week and you're gonna give it to me, understand? One word
of this leaks out to the media and I hold your ass personally
responsible . . . got that?"

Vince cleared his throat. "We're working on it, Lieutenant."

"I don't want to hear you're working on it. I want it
solved. I want a collar and I want it quick. I don't give a
fuck who you bring in. Go over to Saint Raymond's and
clear out a whole goddamn classroom for all I care. Just get
me somebody I can feed to them."

"Yessir." He turned to leave and stopped in the doorway. "By the way, Lieutenant; you *do* know the veins in
your neck and forehead are all discolored, don't you?"

"Discolored?" He fled to a mirror hanging on the wall.
"Whaddaya mean discolored? They look all right to me."

Vince shrugged. "Probably just my imagination, sir."
He exited the office with Boyle staring into the mirror in
abject horror.

There was a note on his desk that Mort Silverman from
the Special Investigations Unit had called. Mort was an old
friend from his days on Narcotics; one of the very few
who'd managed to survive the Knapp Commission
bloodbath and still remain a standup guy with his fellow
officers. Now he was heading up SIU's drug division; a

good guy to know when you needed some information in a hurry. He dialed. "Hey Morty, how you been, brother?"

"Doing good, Vince. Eighty-eight days to my pension and I'm counting the minutes."

"No shit, Mort? That's great. What're you gonna do when you leave?"

"I got a cabin on Lake Champlain and a twenty-eight-year-old girl friend. I'm gonna go up there and spend my declining years fishing and fucking. How bad is that, old buddy? Hey, it must be getting close to that time for you, too, huh?"

"Less than a year now," Vince said. "No cabins and girl friends for me though . . . us Homicide grunts don't get those extra little job benefits you guys on Narcotics do. We're just poor, loyal public servants up here."

"Hey, you're breaking my heart," Morty came back. "Anyway, I get the word out to every precinct in the city that I am to be considered persona non grata for the next eighty-eight days and I make one of my rare visits to the office and see a message from my old friend Crowley who actually wants me to go to work. What're you busting my balls for, Vince?"

He laughed. "No sweat, man. You can do this one standing on your head. I'm trying to get a line on a Dr. Stewart Zeitlin; an uptown gland specialist who I think might be pushing illegal substance. I figured it was a long shot you guys may have some paper on him."

"Zeitlin . . . yeah, I think it's better than a long shot. Lemme check it out . . ." He put Vince on hold.

"Boyle talk to you about that double homicide?" Vince asked Cuzak while he waited.

Cuzak shook his head. "I don't fuckin' believe it, man. I could collar his old lady and he'd be happy. I hope those Hasids get him by the *cojones* and squeeze them good."

"Vince baby . . ." Morty was back on the line. "You got yourself a real live one with the good Dr. Zeitlin. Down here he's code-named 'Dr. High.' Our paper shows he's turning on half the beautiful people in Manhattan.''

"Any priors?"

"Nah . . . you know these guys with connections. We can never get enough on them to make it stick. This hump's had more close scrapes than Evel Knievel but he always comes up smelling like a rose. Last year we came within a cunt's hair of an indictment but somebody missed a plane and somebody else came down with bleeding piles and we never even got to the grand jury. You know how it works. What do you have on him?"

"Nothing yet. I'm running down an ex-patient of his and he's coming up with all the wrong answers. I had a hunch the guy wasn't kosher so I checked with you . . ."

"Hey, if you come up with anything I should know about give me a call, okay, bro?"

"I thought you were persona non grata until your retirement?"

"Always room to bust one more cocksucker."

"You got it, buddy. And thanks." He hung up the phone and turned to Walt Cuzak. "Think you can handle that Futterman homicide without me for a while?"

"No sweat," Cuzak said. "It's local kids, we know that. There's a half a dozen blue-and-whites on the street with their descriptions right now. It's just a matter of time before we nail them."

"Not before Boyle sweats a little more."

Cuzak grinned. "We'll see to that, bro. You can count on it."

Vince phoned the desk downstairs. "Can you loan me two uniforms for a couple of hours? Black guys; big ones if you got em."

"What the hell for?" Sergeant Jim Gavin asked.

"Friendly persuasion." Vince replaced the receiver.

Forty minutes later he entered Stewart Zeitlin's reception room flanked by uniformed officers Hotchkiss and Bines.

"Can I see the doctor?" he asked Jan, who glanced nervously at the roomful of waiting patients.

"Dr. Zeitlin is seeing someone," she answered. "Is there something I can help you with?"

"Police business," he said, louder than necessary.

She rang Zeitlin on the intercom. "Detective Crowley is out here with two policemen, Doctor. I think you'd better see him."

He was there in an instant, ushering Vince into his office like a zealous maître d'. "What the hell do you think you're doing, Crowley?" he hissed through clenched teeth once they were safely out of earshot. "This is a business office."

Vince ignored the query. "Just a couple of questions, Doctor, and I'll be out of here."

Zeitlin glared at him. "I know something about harassment, copper. Now you get those two goons out of my waiting room right now or I pick up the phone and call my lawyer. Is that clear?"

"Perfectly clear, Doctor." Vince remained impassive. "But before you make that call I think it's only fair to tell you that before we leave, my men will have to question everyone out there in your waiting room, get their names, addresses . . . stuff like that."

"That's illegal!" Zeitlin snarled. "You can't get away with that kind of crap around here."

"Try me," Vince said evenly.

Zeitlin lifted the phone on his desk. "This is your last chance, flatfoot. Either they go or I make the call."

"I don't think you want to do that, Doctor." Vince opened the door to the reception room. "Hotchkiss, Bines; come on in here . . ."

"Just a minute!" Zeitlin pushed past him and grabbed the door handle. "You can have two minutes . . . that's it."

Vince signaled the patrolmen to stay where they were. "Now let's get this straight, Dr. Zeitlin. There's a lot of

ways I can get you if I want to. I can put in a call to the
Medical Ethics Board and let them check into who you're
pushing pills to these days. I can pull you out of here in
front of all those people out there and take you downtown
for questioning. I can have my men Hotchkiss and Bines
pay you a visit every day for the next couple of months. I
can just make your life real unpleasant unless you decide to
cooperate with me.''

Zeitlin sat heavily in his chair. "I know this is all a
bluff," he said wearily. "I just don't have the strength to
call it. Send your gorillas downstairs and I'll tell you
whatever I can. I promise you it won't be much.''

"I think you can tell me a lot more than you want to,"
Vince said. "For starters, ask yourself what a penniless,
immigrant, fag prostitute is doing coming to a high-priced
Park Avenue pill-pusher like you in the first place. I did,
and I can't come up with any decent answers. I look in your
waiting room and all I see is fat, indulgent society house-
wives and mistresses waiting for their fix. No faggots . . .
no hookers . . . no downtown sleazeballs. So I ask myself,
what is this greaser Ramos doing in a place like this? Is the
doctor involved with him in some way? Maybe the doctor is
a fag himself . . . maybe he's dating this piece of dirt—''

"That's enough!" Zeitlin said. "You're way off base."

"Am I? It's all pretty logical to me . . .''

"I'm not interested in your primitive thinking processes,
Detective," he interrupted. "Why don't you just ask your
questions and take your dirty little mind somewhere else.''

Vince ignored the insult. "Glad to. Who paid his bill?''

Zeitlin squirmed. "That would be in the files. It will take
a few minutes.''

"I have plenty of time." He folded his arms and waited
while Zeitlin called the front desk and Jan arrived with a
pale blue cardboard folder.

"That invoice was paid by a Ms. Julia Stark," he said,
scanning the file perfunctorily. "My secretary will give you

the address and other pertinent information on your way
out.''

"That wouldn't be Julia *Dexter*-Stark?'' Vince asked.

"I'm afraid I wouldn't know that.''

"Are you asking me to believe you treated Ramos on
credit? Without checking to see who was going to pay the
bill?'' he asked incredulously.

Zeitlin eyed the file nervously. "I believe it is the same
person. Apparently payment was guaranteed before Mr.
Ramos's first visit. I'm afraid that's all the information I
can give you. Can I return to my practice now?''

"One more question and I'm out of here,'' Vince said.
"How large were the doses of progesterone you were giving
him?''

Zeitlin paled. "I have no idea what you're talking about.
Our records show that Mr. Ramos was prescribed Valium.
No other medication is indicated.''

Vince shot a glance at Jan, who was trying to remain
unruffled. "No more questions, Dr. Zeitlin. Thanks for all
your help.'' He headed for the door.

NYPD FORM DD-5
COMPLAINT FOLLOW-UP   MARCH 30, 1984

DET. V. CROWLEY   COMPLAINT #9892

SUBJECT: INTERVIEW OF JULIA DEXTER-STARK

1. ON MARCH 30, AT APPROX. 1530 HOURS, I INTER-
   VIEWED MS. JULIA DEXTER-STARK AT HER APARTMENT
   AT 212 SUTTON PLACE SOUTH, MANHATTAN, N.Y.,
   PENTHOUSE C. TELEPHONE #555-3204.

2. INTERVIEWEE STATED THAT SHE HAD KNOWN DE-
   CEASED AS MICHAEL, A WAITER IN A RESTAURANT SHE
   FREQUENTED.

3. INTERVIEWEE FURTHER STATED THAT SHE HAD RECOM-
   MENDED THE DECEASED SEE DR. STEWART ZEITLIN OF
   420 PARK AVE., MANHATTAN, N.Y., AND THAT SHE
   UNDERSTOOD THE DECEASED TO BE SUFFERING FROM
   MIGRAINE.

4. MS. DEXTER-STARK TERMINATED INTERVIEW AT
    APPROX. 1545 HOURS, STATING THAT SHE WOULD
    ANSWER FURTHER QUESTIONS ONLY WITH HER LAWYER
    PRESENT.

5. INTERVIEWEE WAS UNCOOPERATIVE AND OF A SUSPI-
    CIOUS NATURE. FURTHER INTERVIEWS INDICATED.

    CASE ACTIVE PENDING FURTHER INVESTIGATION.

Where the hell was this investigation taking him? From a
scummy welfare hotel downtown to an exclusive Sutton
Place condominium, the home of Julia Dexter-Stark. It
was the kind of place nobody ever got to see unless they
were delivering something expensive; the kind of place
that existed for most people only in TV serials and
novels.

To Vince, Julia Dexter-Stark seemed like a character out
of one of those stories. What he knew about her was no
more than the average citizen could learn from New York's
scandal sheets and gossip columnists on the nightly news.
Hardly a month went by without a story about her latest
romance; her latest battle with food, drugs, alcohol, mental
instability, and general bad attitudes; her latest scandal,
social indiscretion, legal dispute, or hospitilization; her
latest attempt to find happiness, spiritual fulfillment, self-
expression, serenity, exhilaration, or anything else that
happened to be in vogue or suit her immediate whim.
Whether they found her interesting, amusing, or repulsive,
reporters and photographers knew she was good copy and
that was what paid their salaries.

Vince entered the building and was greeted by his own
foreshortened image on a black-and-white TV monitor hung
directly above the front entrance. There were several others,
and barely concealed video cameras poised like electronic
cobras, their beady, unblinking eyes sweeping the marbled

lobby. A uniformed sentry stood before a bank of perhaps ten more television monitors set in the wall behind the security desk. Every corridor, every elevator, every fire exit and linen closet, every unoccupied area in the building was covered. Nobody could scratch their ass in the place without a security officer knowing about it.

He approached the guard and showed his badge. "I'd like to see Julia Dexter-Stark."

"Are you expected?"

"Just ring upstairs and tell her that Detective Crowley from Homicide wants to ask her a couple of questions."

The guard was about to lift the telephone when a disembodied voice rose from a metal speaker on the desk. "It's okay, Hank. Tell Detective Crowley to wait there. I'll be right out."

The voice materialized from a camouflaged doorway behind the security desk and walked toward him. "Hiya, Crowley. How's things up at the three-seven?"

Vince was stunned. It was Angelo Negri, an ex-detective from the precinct who'd been bounced off the force in '79 for unethical conduct. Vince had never liked him and he suspected the feeling was mutual. Negri had been the kind of cop that gives cops a bad name. He was a greedy, unscrupulous bastard who had his finger in every piece of action he could find. Wherever there was a pie to share, he had a slice. Wherever there was a pad, he was a part of it. Nobody at the Thirty-seventh had shed a tear when he was given the ax.

Vince shook his hand unenthusiastically. "Hello, Negri. What brings you up to this neighborhood?"

Negri returned the handshake. "It's my neighborhood now, brother. I run the security for the whole block."

Vince tried to remain impassive. The last time he'd seen Negri, he was operating a half-assed security operation out of a run-down storefront in the Bronx. "You've come a long way from Laconia Avenue."

"Light years away, man . . . check out this suit I'm wearing: custom-made, silk-worsted blend. Six hundred fifty clams! I got a dozen of them. Check the watch: a Rolex chronograph; eight big ones, man. I mean, no shit Vince . . . with this baby I can tell you the water temperature in fuckin' Tokyo . . ."

Vince nodded. "Not bad, Negri. Someday you gotta tell me how you did it."

Negri beamed. "It's no big fuckin' secret man. These people want to feel safe, that's all. It don't make no difference whether they really *are* safe . . . as long as they feel that way; know what I mean? They know the cops ain't good for diddly-squat . . . just for picking up the pieces after the bad guys done cleaned them out. Shit man, what they want is peace of mind and that's what I give them."

Vince surveyed the lobby. "I gotta admit it's pretty impressive."

"Fuckin' A." Negri nodded. "It beats being a cop ten ways to Sunday. I shit you not, man."

Vince shrugged. "Hey, it's your thing, brother. I wish you all the luck in the world."

"Luck ain't got nothing to do with it," Negri said. "All it takes is balls, plain and simple. A cop with a pair of balls can do all right for himself in this city, Vince. Ain't no reason anybody should have to do without . . ."

"If that's your thing . . ." Vince was beginning to feel uneasy.

"Come on, Crowley, don't give me that squeaky-clean routine," Negri hissed. "Ain't nobody any different than I am. Everybody in this city's getting shtupped for something. The only difference between me and you is that I do it right. None of this penny-ante crap for me. I know who takes and I know who gives. While you schmucks in the three-seven are glomming half-priced cheeseburgers at the diner, I'm down here socking away convertible CDs so fast it'd make your head swim. It's a gold mine down here,

Vince, I swear to you, a standup guy like you could make some real money with this operation.''

"That an offer?"

"You might want to think about it." He handed Vince a business card. "If you ever get tired of being poor, call this number. I can always use a guy with brains."

Vince stuffed the card into his pocket. "Yeah, I'll get back to you. Now how about Julia Dexter-Stark?"

"What do you want with her?" Negri asked.

"Just some questions. I think she might know something about a transsexual who got himself dumped in the Bronx River last week."

"Transsexual, huh?" Negri shook his head. "Don't sound like her kind of action, but you never can tell with her. From what I can see, she's humping anything she can get to stand still long enough: delivery boys, taxi drivers, parking-lot attendants, judges, senators, you name it."

"Homicide detectives?"

Negri laughed. "Who the hell knows? You might just get lucky." He telephoned her apartment and announced that Vince was on his way up. "If I was you I'd keep my pants on though. This cunt's sent more men to the bottom than the *Titanic*."

The ever-present television cameras monitored his climb to the twenty-seventh floor, his exit into the spacious hallway, and his approach to the penthouse apartment. Vince surveyed the massive wooden doors, found what appeared to be a buzzer amid a profusion of embossed flowers decorating the wallpaper, and pressed it several times before Julia Dexter-Stark appeared.

She was gushing and breathless, a pose he imagined was designed to add legitimacy to the fact that she was still dressed in a nightgown at three-thirty in the afternoon. The nightgown was pink, as was most of the apartment, floor-length, and sheer, revealing fleshy contours through the gauzelike fabric and reinforced cleavage bursting from a neckline cut almost to her navel. She was fifty or more but wearing it well, a tribute to carefully invested time and tenacious self-involvement. Her hair was blond, as natural as the process would allow, hanging loosely around her shoulders in soft curls. Her skin was drawn tight against the heightened bone structure of her cheeks, vaguely waxen but flawless, from her pencil-thin eyebrows to her full, sensuous lips.

"You've caught me at a perfectly horrid time." She pouted. "I hope this won't take too long."

"I don't think so, ma'am. I just have a few questions . . ."

She stood in the doorway, not inviting him in. "Well, I have an appointment downtown in less than an hour and I have to get dressed. Can't we do this some other time?"

"I'm afraid that won't be possible. Mind if I come in?"

She stepped aside reluctantly and allowed him to enter. "I can't imagine how I can possibly help you but go ahead and ask your questions if you must. Just be quick about it, please."

Vince opened his notebook. "Do you know an individual named Miguel Ramos?"

There was a slight, involuntary twitch to her mouth. "I don't believe so, no."

"Also known as Marguerita; a transsexual prostitute."

She stiffened. "What makes you think I'd know anybody like that?"

"Because you paid medical bills for him on two occasions, both times to a Dr. Stewart Zeitlin—"

"I'm afraid you're wasting your time, Detective. I have no idea who gets paid and who doesn't. My accountant takes care of that sort of thing for me," she interrupted.

"But you do know Dr. Zeitlin."

"I never said any such thing!"

"Then you don't know him . . ."

She was becoming edgy. "I don't know what you're

getting at, but I can't see how I can possibly be of help to you.''

He waited deliberately, enjoying her discomfort. "My records show that you referred Miguel Ramos to Dr. Zeitlin and that you guaranteed payment for his treatment. Does that square with your recollection?" he asked finally.

She shook her head. "That hardly seems likely—"

"It seemed strange to me, too, ma'am, but Dr. Zeitlin seemed pretty sure about it. He even saved photostatic records of the checks you issued, complete with your signature on them.''

She began to flutter around the apartment like a wounded butterfly looking for a place to settle. "You'll have to speak to my accountant about all of this. I sign hundreds of checks every month. How can I be expected to keep track of all of them?" She made a show of fluffing up the pillows on the sofa. "Good Lord, you certainly can't think I'd have anything to do with a person like that, can you?"

Vince shrugged. "To tell you the truth, I don't know what to think at this point, ma'am. You seem like a sincere person but your answers just don't make any sense. People just don't pay medical bills for total strangers, at least not where I come from.'' He removed the mug shots from his pocket and handed them to her. "Please look at these carefully and tell me whether you've ever seen this individual before.''

"There are two people here," she said.

"They're both Miguel Ramos, taken about a year apart."

She shook her head and handed him the photos. "I'm afraid I can't help you, Detective.''

"Think about what you're saying," he urged her. "This is somebody you dug down into your pocketbook to help.''

She remained firm. "I've told you all I can; now if you'll excuse me . . .''

Vince stood his ground. "You know, ma'am, this is a homicide investigation I'm conducting here; not an interview for some local tabloid. I can check all of this easily and it can go hard on you if I find out you're not telling me the truth. I wish you'd think about that before I leave. I don't think you want trouble with the police, do you?''

She sat heavily on the sofa and arranged the nightgown around her. ''Mind you, I can't be sure, but he looks like Michael, a young man who worked in a restaurant I go to occasionally. That's really all I know.''

''And you referred this Michael to Dr. Zeitlin?''

''I never said that!''

''It can be easily checked out,'' Vince said.

She lit a cigarette nervously. ''As I recall, he told me he was troubled with migraine. I just took pity on him, that's all. I don't see how you can construct anything sinister out of that.''

''I'm sure there's nothing sinister about it,'' Vince said. ''I'd just like you to tell me whether or not you referred Miguel Ramos to Dr. Stewart Zeitlin. It's a straightforward question. A simple yes or no will do.''

She stared across the room. ''I don't think I'm going to answer any more of your questions without my lawyer being present. That *is* my right, isn't it?''

Vince nodded. ''Yes it is, ma'am, but I'm sure we can clear everything up without all that—''

''Not without my lawyer,'' she interrupted.

''Can you give me his name?''

She eyed him coldly. ''You seem to have all the answers. Figure it out for yourself.''

17

Dear Jessy,
It's 10:20 P.M. I'm alone in the squad room and nothing much is going on so I thought I'd drop a line and see how you're doing . . .

Vince looked at what he had written and crumpled it in the wastebasket under his desk. He began again:

Dear Jessy,
This is the fourth time I've started this letter and everything I write seems stupid and insincere. I don't know why. I don't even know what it is I want to say but I'm not saying it well . . . at least not so far.
I guess I want to know how you are. I don't know very much about what you're going through but I know it can't be easy. I meant it when I told you I never knew you were having a problem with booze and pills. I really didn't, and I don't think it's because I wasn't paying attention. Whether you know it or not Jess, I noticed every little thing about you, all the years we lived together. I guess I just didn't do a lot of talking about what I saw.
That's always been a problem with me but I guess I don't

127

have to tell you that. I don't want to make excuses but I've thought about it and it seems to me part of the reason was that I really never felt like I had anything worthwhile to say to you. Somehow, for reasons I really can't explain, I think I always felt you might laugh at me.

I think I'm sounding dumb. Am I sounding dumb, Jess? If I am, it's not surprising. After almost twenty years on this job, most guys end up talking to themselves or being led around by the hand. I know you've heard this before but the truth is that it gets to all of us sooner or later. You can't live with what we live with day after day and remain like other people. You have to change just to keep your sanity.

I remember a night a few years back when we were spending a weekend at your father's house in Marion. We were sitting at the dinner table and everyone was talking small talk like they always do . . . you know, about the kids and the weather and how your old man was fighting to keep two-acre zoning in the town to keep out the riffraff. Well, I remember your mother asking me why I was so quiet . . . why I wasn't getting into the spirit of this conversation you all were having . . .

Well, I have to tell you, Jess. That afternoon, before we drove up to Connecticut, I'd been part of a unit that had removed what was left of a five-year-old boy from an abandoned warehouse in little plastic bags. I mean, here you all were, talking about how the lowlifes were ruining Marion, and I'd just left a place where a child had been tortured and sodomized and butchered and cut up into little pieces . . . and my God, Jess; some of those pieces had been cooked and eaten.

I know this letter will never be mailed.

When you left, once I'd gotten over hating you so much, I talked about it a little. Mostly I talked to Billy, sometimes to a couple of older guys here at the precinct. Once I even spoke to the chaplain down at headquarters. I was really broken up and I guess I was looking for somebody who

*could make me believe it was all going to work out okay. I
wanted to hear that you'd come back after a while.*

*Well, nobody told me that, Jess, not even Billy, who says
anything I want him to say. What I heard was that it was the
job . . . that the things that make us good cops make us bad
husbands. They told me marriage was a casualty of the job.
For every police marriage that made it, there were a dozen
that went down the toilet. I don't know where they get their
statistics, but from what I can see they're not far wrong.
The only cop I know who seems to have a good marriage is
Pete Yorio and I don't know how he does it. Maybe it's just
luck. Who the hell knows?*

Who the hell knows . . . Vince stared at the letter. Of all
the times he'd tried to write, this was the first time he was
saying what was on his mind . . . what he'd wanted to tell
her all those years. He knew that sharing your innermost
thoughts was supposed to make you feel better, but all he
felt was embarrassed; embarrassed by his weakness, his
inability to come to grips with things the way they were.

"Got a cigarette, man?" It was one of a group of eight or
nine black teenagers occupying the holding pen.

Vince crossed the room and passed a pack through the
bars. "What'd they get you bums for?"

"Reefer, man. It's a bogus rap," one of them answered.

Vince smiled. "Sure. You tell that to the judge when you
see him Monday morning."

"Monday morning!" They all let up a howl. "This is
Friday, man. What they gonna do with us all weekend?"

He shrugged. "Keep you here, I guess."

"Keep us here? There ain't even a bed in this place!"

"Judge doesn't work on weekends," Vince said. "He's
gotta be out scraping the barnacles offa his boat."

"Oh man! Scrape his fuckin' boat while we rot in this
shithole . . . you jivin' us, man?"

"I don't jive." Vince retrieved his almost-empty pack of

cigarettes, lit the guy nearest the bars, and returned to his desk. He was about to resume writing when Tommy Ippollito walked into the squad room.

"What's happening?" Vince asked.

"Same old shit."

"Anything new on that double homicide?"

Tommy bristled. "Whaddaya doing, working for Boyle?"

"Hey, just asking, bro."

Tommy sat heavily across the desk from him. "Sorry. That asshole is double-shifting everybody until we get an honest collar."

"Got anything so far?"

"Yeah, we got a lot, but that prick wants everything yesterday. We know who did it. Everybody in the neighborhood fingered the little bastards. They're holed up somewhere around here. It's just a matter of smoking them out."

"Got a plan?" Vince asked.

"Shit, Boyle's ready to flatten the whole neighborhood with howitzers. Me, I'm more realistic. The way I figure it, they were all high on PCP or something when they did it . . . probably all of them are addicted to something or other. We just move their suppliers off the street for a couple of days and sooner or later they'll come crawling out of their holes."

"Boyle willing to wait that long?"

"Listen to this one . . ." Tommy leaned across the desk. "Boyle gets it into his head that the kids'll respond to a plea from their mothers, so he finds one who can speak English and puts her on Channel Two, eleven o'clock news. So she sits there in front of the cameras, moaning and slobbering and begging her little Angel or Rubin or whatever the fuck his name is to turn himself in to the cops, and Boyle is standing next to her beaming like he just won the goddamn lottery or something.

"And when she's all finished, he says, 'That was good,

Mother. We can only hope your boy will see it and come to us for help,' and she looks at him and asks, 'This goin' to be on *Dance Fever?*' And Boyle looks at her and says, 'No. This was broadcast live on the eleven o'clock news.' She says, 'Too bad. My boy don't ever watch no news . . . only *Dance Fever*.' How's that grab you for crackerjack detective work?''

Vince smiled. "Very impressive."

"Hey, you're not laughing, you okay?"

"Yeah, I guess so. Nothing I won't get over anyway."

"Anything you want to talk about?"

"No, not really. I was just trying to write a letter to my wife and nothing's coming out right."

"Wife?" Tommy looked surprised. "I thought you were divorced."

"Separated. She's living up in Connecticut with her family."

Tommy became serious. "Hey Vince, I know you don't want to hear this, but believe me, you're a lot better off."

"What the hell are you talking about?"

"Hey man, women just fuck you up."

Vince stared at him. "I don't believe that. You spend half your time trying to get laid—"

"I don't mean that!" Tommy protested. "Getting laid is one thing, but a relationship is something altogether different, man."

"I'm talking about marriage, for chrissake."

"Same fucking thing, man . . .'' Tommy's voice turned conspiratorial. "Lemme tell you, Vince. The trouble with relationships is that women don't tell the goddamn truth. I don't mean they lie deliberately or anything like that. They just say things because they think they're the right thing to say, not because they believe them. For instance, they're always carrying on about how they want guys to be smart and sensitive, right? Like they want a guy who's not ashamed to cry. Well, you just try being smart and sensitive around most of the broads in this fucking city, man. First guy comes along with a tattoo and a seven-fifty Harley-Davidson and starts kicking them in the teeth, they drop you like you had syph or something. Believe me, Vince, I tried smart and sensitive. It don't get you shit.''

Vince was laughing. "Okay, next time I see her I'll knock out a couple of teeth. Maybe she'll come back.''

Tommy retreated to his desk indignantly. "Go ahead and laugh, man, but mark my words, you'd be a lot happier if you did like me: Fuck 'em and feed 'em and turn 'em loose . . . no involvement, no unpleasant aftertaste.''

"Wish it was that easy," Vince said.

"Man, it's as easy as you want to make it. You, you want to make it hard, like you're always walking around with a sign on your back that says 'kick me.' ''

Vince was starting to get annoyed. "Come off it, huh. Where do you get all this shit anyway?''

Tommy threw up his hands. "Sorry I stuck my two cents in where it wasn't wanted. I don't wanna fight with you, Vince. It's just that in all the time I know you, I never seen you go out just to have a good time. Not once. I mean, stop me if I'm wrong . . . you go home at night, get a cold brew outa the refrigerator, maybe heat up a TV dinner, and fall asleep in front of the set. Well?''

He felt the air go out of him. "What the hell do you want from me, Ippollito. Look . . . it's eleven o'clock. You got so much action in your life, what're you doing hanging around this place for? Go on, for chrissake. Get the fuck outa here!''

"Hey man, you don't have to say it twice. I'm fuckin' gone.'' Tommy scooped up the papers on his desk and headed for the door. "Just remember, man. You're doing it to yourself.''

Vince stared at the unfinished letter and put it in his top drawer. It was all too pat, much too close to the truth. Tommy had nailed him like he was a specimen in a bug collection. Maybe he was too rigid. Maybe he was really afraid of letting his hair down, or allowing somebody else to get too close. Maybe he was afraid of being hurt again, of having to compete, share. It was all so goddamn complicated.

Eleven oh-five. It was the wrong time to call; too late if Jan was home, too early if she was out on a date. Tommy would tell him he was just being chickenshit and for once Tommy would be right. Just do it. Cut the crap and do it. He lifted the telephone and dialed.

"Hello." She sounded more bored than tired.

"It's Crowley. Did I get you out of bed?"

"I'm in bed but I wasn't asleep. Just reading."

"Anything interesting?" He winced when he said it.

"Uh, did you have a specific reason for calling me, Vince, or did you dial this number by mistake?"

He groaned. "I'm sorry, Jan. I'm tired and hungry and I guess I'm not making much sense. I've wanted to call you and try to straighten things out but every time I started to dial I'd freeze up. I guess I'm not much good at apologies."

"Nobody is." Her voice was softer. "Are you at work now?"

"It's quitting time. I don't suppose you'd be in the mood for a bowl of spaghetti, would you?"

There was a pause. "I might be persuaded. Does a glass of red wine go with it?"

He grinned. "Colinini's best basement vintage. I'll be there in forty-five minutes."

18

COLININI'S WAS THE kind of place where someone with
unpredictable hours, unhealthy eating habits, and an uncrit-
ical eye for cleanliness and good service could get a
home-cooked meal and a glass of homemade guinea red
almost any time of the day or night. Nestled in the shadow
of the Manhattan Criminal Courts Building, it catered to a
mismatched band of confederates from federal judges to
street hoodlums, united in an orgiastic truce of garlic and
oregano.

The decor was baroque, from the twenty-foot-long mural
depicting the canals of Venice lining an entire wall of the
restaurant to the sweeping red velvet curtain that separated
the bar and hat-check concession from the main dining
room. In contrast, the tables were bare, embellished only
with salt and pepper cellars, aluminum napkin dispensers,
and fluted glass containers filled with minced and dried
peppers. Vince led Jan through the jumble of patrons to an
empty corner table and held her chair while she sat. "Try
the linguine with white clam sauce," he said as he pulled up
a chair across the table from her. "It's the best in the city."

She squinted across the room at the menu, scrawled in

white chalk on a blackboard. "Not much of a choice, is there?"

He laughed. "You're used to those uptown restaurants where they heat everything up in a microwave. This is the real thing. The only one in the kitchen is Mama Colinini and she doesn't cook it until you order it."

Jan looked impressed. "Well, do you think she could fix me a salad?"

"Call it antipasto." He waved to the waiter, who passed him like he was carrying AIDS. "You have to be a little patient around here," he explained. "All of which gives me the opportunity to tell you that I'm sorry about the way things went last time."

"Please, don't apologize," she said. "I don't know why I took it so personally. It was my fault, not yours."

"Well, I promise there'll be no questions about your boss this time."

"I don't mind. It's just that there's nothing I could tell you about Stewart that would possibly help you—"

"Hey, this is supposed to be a date!" he interrupted. "I'm off duty now and I'm hungry as hell."

"Okay, but before we get down to eating and whatever else you have in mind for this evening, I just want to tell you that Stewart is in no way involved with that Dexter-Stark woman—"

"Whoa!" he said. "That's not an issue here. This is a date, remember?"

"Well, I just didn't want you thinking I'd work for somebody who was involved in that sort of sleazy business."

He was about to ask her what sort of sleazy business she was talking about when the waiter deposited an unopened bottle of red wine in the middle of the table. "This is compliments of Mr. Prestipino."

Vince spotted Tony Clams in the corner of the room, excused himself, and walked to where he was sitting.

"Thanks for the wine, Vito. I thought maybe you'd be mad at me by now."

Vito shrugged. "Why? Because your guys pulled me in on that Wellington heist? Hey, forget it, paisan. They gotta jerk me around every couple of years just to feel like they're earning their money. It's no big deal."

"They didn't have anything on you anyway, right?"

Vito chuckled. "You know me Vincent. I was in an all-night poker game in Newark . . . got about twenty witnesses who were willing to swear I never left the table." His gaze shifted to the far end of the restaurant where a short, burly man in a white silk suit, maroon shirt, and pale blue paisley tie was approaching. "I gotta do some business now, my friend." He extended his hand. "Enjoy the wine and give my best to your lady."

Vince returned to the table. "Tony Clams sends his best."

"Tony who?"

"Tony Clams. The guy who sent the wine. He's a lieutenant in the Carlo Madalena family."

"You mean he's a gangster?"

"I suppose you could call him that."

"He's the one who sent the wine?"

"The very same . . ." Vince grabbed the waiter by the arm as he passed and dragged him back to the table. "We'd like someone to uncork this bottle, a couple of glasses to drink it with, and a little food, if that wouldn't be too much trouble."

The waiter removed a corkscrew from his apron pocket and dug it resentfully into the top of the bottle. "The soup's minestrone and we're out of lasagna." He stood with his pencil poised over his order pad.

"Linguine with white clam for me and a small antipasto for the lady." Vince poured the wine into two water glasses on the table and handed one to Jan. "To us."

"To getting out of this place alive," Jan said.

He laughed. "Don't worry about Tony Clams. Him and me go way back."

"You mean you're friends?"

"Sort of. We respect each other," he said.

Jan shook her head. "I don't understand how a policeman can be friends with a . . . killer."

"He's no killer," Vince said. "But I wouldn't be so sure about the guy sitting with him."

Jan glanced nervously across the room. "Who's he?"

"Name's Pete Wentzel . . . Petie Roast Beef to most people. He's looking like he doesn't know me but I pulled him in on a homicide a couple of years ago."

"And he's out on the street?"

Vince shrugged. "That's the way it is sometimes."

She rested her chin in her palms and smiled across the table at him. "With all the interesting friends you have, I don't know why you waste your time with someone as colorless as Stewart Zeitlin. He couldn't hurt a fly."

"I never said he could, only that he might know somebody who could take me where I'm going."

"If you're thinking about Julia Dexter-Stark, forget it," she said. "I don't know anything about why she was in that file but I know enough about Stewart to know that he's far too levelheaded to get himself involved with a bitch like her."

He grinned. "That's pretty strong language."

"Well, I wouldn't know what else to call her. The woman has the morals of a mongoose. You must know that."

"I don't really know too much about her. Only what I read in the papers."

"Then you must have read about that dreadful orgy at her house in the Hamptons last year, when that starlet accused the movie producer of rape."

He shook his head.

She stared at him in disbelief. "You've gotta be kidding.

Where have you been for the past year—living under a rock or something? It was the hottest story on the TV news for months."

"I don't watch too much TV," he admitted.

"Well, you must have heard something about it. I mean the police were certainly involved in the whole business."

Vince shrugged. "Must've been a different precinct. What happened anyway?"

"There was a party at her estate in East Hampton last summer that lasted about a week according to all the accounts; alcohol, drugs, group sex, a real bacchanal from the accounts I read. Anyway, some young blond aspiring actress was found crawling along the highway about a mile from the house by a passing motorist, stark naked and bleeding . . . swore she'd been raped by half the people at the party."

"Who was the movie producer you talked about?"

"Serge something . . . a Rumanian, I think. He was the only one who was actually accused because he was the only one they could positively identify on the film."

"They filmed it?"

"I'm telling you, these people are really sick, Vince. They're so jaded and dissolute, there's nothing they won't do for kicks. That's how I know Stewart could never be involved with them. When they run out of sick things to do to one another they import deviates from the dregs of society to perform for them . . . the way fashionable uptown liberals would entertain Black Panthers back in the sixties."

Vince felt his skin begin to tingle. "What kind of deviates are you talking about?"

She shrugged. "You know: female impersonaters, transvestites, any oddball sexual deviant they could find, I guess. For all I know they're working on winos and bag ladies today."

There it was. Without knowing it, Jan had provided the

link between downtown Broadway and uptown Sutton
Place; the slime-ridden world of Marguerita and Charlene
and the insulated luxury of Julia Dexter-Stark. That was the
way investigations went sometimes. People who knew
absolutely nothing began talking and before long they were
giving up bits and pieces of information that were meaningless until they were fitted into the overall scheme. It was
like building a pyramid. Everybody contributed a brick
until the one left at the top was the killer. He was a long way
from that but the bricks were beginning to fall into place.

Dinner came· and he picked at it absentmindedly. As
much as he tried to relax and concentrate on Jan and the
evening ahead, his mind returned to the investigation. He
remembered what Tommy had told him; that he'd never
seen him relax and just have a good time. Maybe Tommy
was right, but as the pieces began fitting together he could
sense his heartbeat quicken, feel the vibrations of expectan-
cy on the tiny hairs of his arms, the skin of his face. He
guessed it was good time enough for him . . . at least for
now. It was the thrill of the hunt; the heightening awareness
that his quarry was getting closer.

It was better than sex.

19

GULLS AND DRIED saw grass rippling like the swelling tide with each scented gust of wind . . . beaten trails between the sandy hillocks cascading down to the ocean's edge and sky like robins' eggs stretching from the rim of the water to beyond the crested dune . . . The summer of his ninth birthday; the cold, hard sand at the water's edge and wave-tossed pebbles glossy as pearls gathered in a metal pail and hidden in his secret place, calcified shells and pieces of driftwood, horseshoe crabs and bits of broken glass worn smooth by the pounding of the waves.

His secret place was a hollow gully beneath an abandoned pier at Rockaway Beach, beyond the last dune . . . out of sight of his family's rented cottage by the road. From there he could plan his journeys, shore up the pier's defenses against attack from pirates by sea. His treasures were lashed to the wooden structure, a precaution against the incessant tide, which raked his stronghold daily and swept the floor clean of footprints and unwanted debris.

Each morning he would stand on the cool, flat sand and know that his were the only footprints that had ever occupied that place. He would look out over the unbroken horizon and know that he was the first to watch the sun

140

stretch from the water and draw shadows on the beach. Each day in solitude and solemnity he would claim that piece of sand and ocean for himself.

Driving along the south shore of Long Island, Vince was reminded of those days when things were a lot simpler. Westhampton Beach, Quogue, Hampton Bays; the seaside villages passed in nostalgic sequence and drew him further and further out of himself, away from the confinement of the day's routine. He crossed Great Peconic Bay where the ocean met the sound in slashing currents and swirling eddies, exhilarated in the answering screech of gulls, the faint, resonant clang of buoys, the thick, oily aroma of bass and bluefish drifting up from the inlets and estuaries.

Now the road ran through stretches of endless dunes and sandy beaches, bellying out to clusters of stilted cottages rising out of the sand in weatherbeaten clapboard. Through waterfront villages with coves and marinas and taverns with names like "Captain John's" and "Deadman's Float." It was still New York but it was a million miles away in tone and temperament.

He parked in front of the Suffolk County Municipal Building, a three-story brick-and-cement structure that seemed oddly out of place, and entered through a series of glass-and-metal doors. Inside, the place was empty except for an elderly janitor struggling with an oversized floor-waxer at the far end of the hall. "I'm looking for District Attorney French," Vince said loudly as he approached him.

The man turned the machine off. "Whaddaya want?"

"DA Thomas French," Vince said.

"Upstairs, to the right," he answered irritably. "You coulda read it on the directory when you came in."

"Yeah, I'll do better next time." He mounted the steps, found the DA's office tucked away in a corner of the building behind "Records" and "Department of Adult Probation."

"Anybody home?" he yelled into the empty reception room.

There was a momentary fumbling behind the closed office door before it opened and a tall, sandy-haired man in his early thirties appeared in a sweatshirt and jeans. "Hi. You Crowley?"

Vince shook his hand. "Sorry to pull you away from whatever you were doing on your day off."

The DA smiled. "It's no big deal. Always glad to help out the metropolitan PD whenever I can." He indicated an empty chair and motioned for Vince to sit. "Just give me a rundown on why you want to see the tapes again. Things were a little hectic when I talked to you on the phone yesterday."

"This is a murder investigation. A transsexual prostitute was killed and mutilated and dumped in the Bronx River in my precinct about a month ago. I know it sounds nuts but no matter how I work it, the name Julia Dexter-Stark keeps cropping up."

French shrugged. "Nothing about that dame sounds nuts to me. We got her tied in with more shit than you can imagine. If she didn't own half the people around here we'd throw her out for impairing the morals of the town."

"Anything you can make stick?"

"Not a chance. This babe's got more connections than the New York State Thruway. You think there's something in these tapes that can tie her in with your homicide?"

"I don't know what to think. My information is that these people were into some pretty weird stuff. The victim in this case knew Julia Dexter-Stark and it's just possible he might have been at one of those orgies they filmed."

"It's a long shot but you're welcome to look," French said. "There's only one problem. The court ruled those tapes were seized illegally and had to be returned. What I'm going to show you are bootleg copies and as far as either of us is concerned they aren't worth shit as evidence. If you happen to see anything you can take to court, you never saw it here, okay?''

Vince nodded. "It won't be the first time I've been handcuffed by the courts. I guess we all have to live with that."

French wheeled a portable TV into position in front of his desk and popped a cassette into a video projector. "Smoke if you got 'em, my friend. The film quality's not all that good but we're dealing with amateurs here. What they lack in technical know-how they make up for in enthusiasm."

The scenario unfolded quickly, blurred at first, zooming in on a naked man and woman in their late twenties or early thirties engaged in the act of foreplay. Vince felt an initial flush of embarrassment, then a tug of reluctant curiosity as they writhed together in active lovemaking, seemingly oblivious to the hand-held camera recording their efforts. Another female joined the action, then another. A second male who seemed more interested in mugging for the camera than responding to the attentions of the other three.

Vince tried to concentrate on their faces but the cameraman refused to oblige. He zoomed inward, blurring and refocusing to capture individual acts of penetration, the equipment disembodied, pink and viscid without passion, like open-heart surgery. The mild stirring he had first felt subsided as the heaving mound of flesh began to resemble anatomical gridlock. It was a classic case of too much of a good thing.

"Maybe we can save some time here," Vince said as French removed the spent cassette and started to insert another. "I'm looking for a transsexual male, mid-twenties, about six feet tall. You recall seeing anybody like that on any of these tapes?"

"You gotta be kidding," French said. "There are thirty-six tapes here and I can't remember one where anybody's standing up. Most of them are just like the one you saw. People crawling all over one another trying to find something to suck or to screw. It's just about impossible to tell where one leaves off and another one begins. Descriptions like that aren't gonna help you much in this circus.''

''How about just transsexuals. You remember seeing any of them?''

French thought about it. ''What do they look like?''

''Like women with balls.''

''It's hard to know for sure who belongs to what, but there was one . . .'' He rummaged through the pile of videocassettes until he found what he was looking for, inserted the tape, and activated the projector. ''This was one of their more artistic efforts, as I recall. There's even something vaguely resembling a plot.''

The show began with a fully dressed female, perhaps nineteen or twenty, seated alone on a sofa, reading a paperback novel . . . a steamy one judging from her agitated state. The more she read, the more aroused she became, heaving and sighing with each new line of breathless prose, allowing her free hand to wander across her ample breasts, beneath her skirt . . . kneading, caressing, driving herself to increased heights of horniness . . .

The doorbell rang and she answered it irritably, only to find an attractive woman selling magazines on her doorstep. She invited the woman inside, led her back to the sofa where they forgot all about the magazines and fell immediately into an impassioned clinch. The action advanced predictably until the horny book reader tore the underpants from the horny magazine seller, revealing her to be a fully erect male. ''That your transsexual?'' French asked over the footage.

''It's a transsexual, but it's not *my* transsexual,'' Vince answered.

Undaunted by the disclosure, the book reader proceeded to get it on with her new partner when the doorbell rang again. The action shifted to the door where the frustrated lovers encountered a male asking for directions . . . ''Hold it right there!" Vince said. "Can you freeze-frame that for me?"

French halted the tape. "What part?"

"The guy at the door, where we get a closeup of his face."

French rewound the tape and played it slowly forward until he reached the spot. "Doesn't look like any transsexual to me," he said.

Vince superimposed the face on his memory of the suspect's composite sketch: hair, forehead, brows, eyes, cheeks, jaws, nose, mouth . . . the similarities were uncanny; too close to be simply a coincidence. "That's not my transsexual, but it just might be my murderer. Any idea who he is?"

French studied the face. "Uh-uh; he could be just about anybody."

"Not just anybody, brother. Can I get a print of that face?"

French nodded. "Lab'll be open tomorrow. I can have one to you by late tomorrow afternoon." He noted the footage on the console and wrote it down. "Want to see the rest of the tape? From what I remember, the three of them get it going pretty good."

Vince grinned. "Another time, unless you can show me one starring Dexter-Stark herself."

"Not a chance. That was the big trouble with those tapes to begin with. The only one we could get even a half-assed make on was the producer, Popowitz, and even that wasn't good enough to get an indictment. Even if the court had let us use them as evidence, they wouldn't have gotten us very far. It seems that most of the people on those reels just showed up, did their bits, and disappeared. Julia Dexter-Stark and her bunch were content to just watch and be amused."

"Nobody was ever convicted of anything?"

"Not even a single indictment. The press made a big,

fucking deal about the whole thing but the truth is that the grand jury practically laughed us out of court. We were never really close to nailing anybody; not that I wouldn't have liked to. It's just that these people have enough money and clout to wear us all down with appeals. If you're going after them, make sure you have plenty of ammunition.''

"What would you get them for, if you could?'' Vince asked.

"Kidnapping, rape, sodomy, possession of narcotics, conspiracy to corrupt the morals of the Western Hemisphere, you name it. There aren't a helluva lot of public morals statutes they haven't broken. Why?''

"Just wondering. Maybe this investigation will turn up something you can use.''

"An eyewitness wouldn't hurt.'' French smiled. "Somebody of high moral character and impeccable reputation.''

Vince raised an eyebrow. "The last person I met like that was my old lady. She disinherited me when I became a cop.''

20

ANGELO NEGRI INTERCEPTED Vince on his way into Julia Dexter-Stark's building and took him to a corner of the lobby out of camera range. "I can't let you go up there, Vince. I got my orders."

"This is a homicide investigation, pal. What're you trying to do, obstruct justice?"

Negri groaned. "Gimme a break, willya Vince? This cunt's got nothing you want."

"As of today, she's suspect number one. That means she's up to her ass in a lot more trouble than you need. Now, how's about moving aside and letting me get to work."

Negri grabbed him by the elbow. "Look Vince, this job is all I got, you know what I mean? These people think all they gotta do is ask Angelo and he'll take care of it; like I got some real power to protect them. Dexter-Stark says she don't want no more trouble from the cops and I say 'sure' and everybody's happy. You go up there now and that makes me look like an A-number-one schmuck. How about it Vince, for old times' sake?"

Vince shook his head. "Come on Angelo. You know I

can't just drop it, even if I wanted to. I don't want any trouble with you but I'll go downtown and get some paper if I have to. I need to talk to this babe and I need to do it today, okay?''

Negri's shoulders slumped. ''Whaddaya want to go busting my balls for Vince? There's gotta be someplace outside of this building where you can question her . . . her boyfriend's place, her house on the island . . . anywhere but here.''

''Lemme get this straight. You want me to interrupt the normal procedure of homicide investigation and follow this broad all over the city just so you can look like a hero?''

''For old times' sake, Vince.''

''You gotta be fucking crazy, Angelo.''

Negri checked his Rolex. ''Look, today is Tuesday. On Tuesday she's at the museum from three to five-thirty.''

''What museum's that?''

''The Crawford, a private art museum near Gramercy Park. She's a trustee and they meet every Tuesday afternoon.''

''You're not shitting me, Angelo?''

''On my mother's grave Vince.''

''And you guarantee I'll find her there.''

Negri winced. ''Hey, come on, man. I can't guarantee nothing but that's where she's supposed to be . . . as God is my judge.''

Vince thought about it. ''Okay, Angelo. I'll go with you just this one time but you better be straight with me. If she's not at that museum you're in deep shit.''

Negri clasped his hand. ''I owe you for this, Vince.''

''You know it, brother.''

The trip to Gramercy Park was marked with the usual midtown traffic snafus. The line of motorists stretched and compressed seemingly without reason, screeching their brakes, honking their horns, fouling the air with their exhaust fumes. At one point Vince found himself stalled in

the line of march next to a blue-and-yellow hand-painted
van. "Need a couple of Blaupunkt speakers for your car?"
a young black yelled at him from the passenger's seat. "We
just checked our shipping manifest and they gave us two too
many."

"Got all the speakers I need," Vince answered.

"How about some first-rate Colombian blow?"

"How about if you get the hell out of here!" Vince
flashed his shield and the van took off as fast as traffic
would allow.

Farther downtown, he double-parked on Twenty-eighth
street, found a retail florist in the middle of the wholesale
market, and had a dozen roses sent to Jan. The cost was way
out of line on a cop's salary but he was feeling guilty about
his lack of attention during their dinner at Colinini's. His
mind had been on the case and even his lovemaking later on
had been routine and uninspired. Jan hadn't complained but
he'd sensed her disappointment. *"Don't give up on me
yet . . ."* he'd written on the card. *"There's life in the old
boy yet. Please give me one more chance to prove it."*

The Crawford Museum was a four-story converted
brownstone on the outskirts of Gramercy Park, a tree-lined
oasis in the middle of the chaos of Manhattan. Vince
climbed a flight of hewn granite steps to the massive oak
doorway and was informed by the security guard that none
of the trustees had arrived but that they were expected
momentarily. Given the choice of waiting in the hallway
with its forbidding twelve-foot ceiling, barrel-vaulted
chambers, and musty climate of impersonality, or waiting
outside on the steps, he chose the steps. No point in getting
carried away with this culture stuff, he reasoned. From what
he'd seen so far of Julia Dexter-Stark and her bunch, it
hadn't done a whole helluva lot to build their characters.

They all seemed to arrive at once, spilling out on the
sidewalk from black and gray chauffeured limousines. They
converged on the building, chatting amiably as they

climbed the stone steps. Julia Dexter-Stark was dressed in a rust-colored, one piece shift dress tied loosely at the waist, open-toed high-heel pumps and an understated mink stole draped loosely around her shoulders—a far cry from the nightgown she'd been wearing the last time he'd seen her. He waited until she was almost to the door and stepped in front of her, smiling. "I wonder if I might have a few minutes of your time?"

She seemed startled. "I'm sorry . . . I have a meeting scheduled now . . ."

"This will only take a minute." He took her by the elbow and escorted her gently off to the side.

"What's the meaning of this?" she hissed, once they were out of earshot. "I could have your badge for this!"

"There are a couple of matters I'd like to clear up here," he said softly. "Some additional information that's come to light since I saw you last time."

She glowered at him. "I have nothing to say to you, Detective. I thought I made that clear."

Vince smiled. "Now listen carefully, Ms. Dexter-Stark, because I don't want to have to repeat this. As of now, your friends over there think you and I are having a friendly chat, and that's the way I'd like to leave it. You can answer a few simple questions here or I can put the cuffs on you and drag you uptown in front of everybody. That might go over with some of your buddies out in East Hampton but this bunch doesn't look like the sort of characters who'd appreciate it. Now which way do you want it?"

She managed a strained smile. "My lawyers will eat you for dinner, flatfoot."

"We'll see . . ." He reached inside his jacket pocket and rattled the cuffs. "What's it gonna be?"

"Make it quick," she snarled through the frozen smile. "This is beginning to get embarrassing."

"Wouldn't want to embarrass you, ma'am." He handed her the black-and-white print French had provided from the videotapes. "Have you ever seen this person before?"

She glanced at it quickly and handed it back. "No."

"Take a little time . . ." He handed the photo back to her. "Maybe it's somebody who attended one of your parties out on the island?"

"I told you, I've never seen him."

"Let me refresh your memory. This is the guy who was asking directions in one of those stag films you and your pals made out at the beach last year."

She paled. "I have absolutely no idea what you're talking about. I know nothing about any films . . . which, by the way, were taken illegally by those storm troopers who invaded my home. And I've never seen the person in that picture before."

Vince pressed the photo into her hand. "One more time, *Ms*. Dexter-Stark. If I don't get the answer I want to hear, you and me are going for a ride together."

He could see the air go out of her. "It's a poor picture . . ." she stammered. "I can't really be sure."

"Just tell me who it *could* be."

"I can't really say for sure . . ."

"Give it your best shot," he urged.

She squinted at the photo. "It's so blurry . . . it could really be anybody."

"Try real hard. Think about that film that never was . . ."

She returned the photo angrily. "Well, I'm sure it's nobody I know, but it looks vaguely like Ronald Castanga."

"Who's he?" Vince asked.

"A friend of mine."

There was an awkward pause. "I'm gonna need more than that," he said finally.

"I should have known the name would mean nothing to you," she sniffed. "Ronald Castanga is a painter . . . an artist of rare and unusual talent."

Vince nodded. ''And where might I find this talented artist?''

''His studio is in East Hampton, not far from my home.''

''And will I be able to reach him there?''

She stiffened. ''I'm sure I haven't the slightest idea where you might reach Ronald. He doesn't apprise me of his schedule.'' She glanced nervously at her waiting companions. ''Will that be all?''

''For now.'' Vince placed the photo in his jacket pocket.

''In that case, I'm going to tell my friends that you're interested in the Castanga exhibit inside. They know he's a protégé of mine, so our talking like this won't seem too unusual.''

''Castanga has an exhibit in this museum?''

''An entire floor; seventeen major neo-impressionistic works, although I'm sure that means absolutely nothing to you.''

''It might. Mind if I go inside and browse?''

She raised an eyebrow. ''I wasn't aware the Gestapo had acquired a taste for fine art. I'll tell the guard to admit you once we're all safely inside.'' She wheeled and joined the waiting group.

Vince waited until everyone had entered and climbed the remaining steps to the door, where he was let in by the security guard. Inside, he found a stack of printed flyers on a desk by the entrance. There were four exhibits: a display of American Indian weaving; original stone carvings from Borneo; a collection of hand-fashioned dolls from the sixteenth century; and the Castanga show. He scanned the one-paragraph introduction:

Born in Rochester, New York, in 1956, Ronald Castanga received his early training at the Arts Institute of Buffalo and later at L'Ecole Graphis, affiliated with Le Sorbonne in Paris. His earlier works emphasize his emerging passion with the human form, its capacities and range, stretching anatomical limitations almost to the point of grotesquerie. His later works explore a rich variation of the organismal experience, verging sometimes on the rebarbative as in his epic oil, *Torso*, but always demonstrating the daring and virtuosity that have placed him in the forefront of the neo-impressionistic movement.

It read like one of Art Boyle's Integrity Reports; one of those documents designed to camouflage sheer bewilderment with language nobody understood. It was a safe bet that Castanga's paintings would make no more sense than his biography. If they were any good at all, whoever was in charge of writing about him would simply say so. "Ronald Castanga paints better than anybody else," they might say. "His stuff will knock your eyes out!"

It was baffling to Vince that the only time people like Julia Dexter-Stark said what was really on their minds was when they were abusing the cops. Looking at a painting on a wall, they would tell you that they were having a rebarbative experience, whatever the hell that meant; and when they spotted a policeman doing his job they would call him a storm trooper. He supposed it was only important for them to be understood when they were screaming about their rights; that they only needed to make sense to one another when their asses were on the line.

The Castanga exhibit was on the bottom floor, one flight down a narrow set of wooden stairs, through a fluorescent-lit corridor that opened up onto a series of connecting rooms. The first contained Ronald Castanga's earliest works: drawings in pencil, charcoal, and pastel of nude female models in various poses. For the most part they were realistic, rendered with care and detail, the measured strokes moving gracefully to emphasize each voluptuous curve. Vince guessed they were classroom exercises from his early school days.

The next room was filled with similar drawings, along with some watercolor and oil paintings scattered randomly about. The subjects were the same but his depictions of the models had become less faithful, running to torturous exaggerations of individual features; limbs and trunks twisted and magnified, malformed and misshapen in freakish caricature. These were of a later vintage, Vince noted; dating from the early to mid-seventies. It may have appeared to some that the artist was exploring new dimensions of his subject. To Vince, it was apparent he was becoming sicker.

Room three: The paintings had become larger now; only three enormous oils, each covering almost an entire wall. It seemed at first as if Castanga had abandoned the human form completely, seemingly content to fill his canvases with meaningless daubs of fiery color. Then, as Vince became accustomed to the spectrum of tones and shapes, he realized he was looking at the ultimate perversion of the human form; a noxious, heaving spillage of mortal entrails erupting from the remnants of pale cadavers like lava from a volcano . . . the grace and beauty of life turned inside out.

He stood transfixed before an enormous canvas titled *Torso*. Before him was the grim portrayal of evil that smothered him in his deepest chasms of gloom; the reeking, gurgling, sucking vision of life in its final agony, wave upon wave of purple and magenta intestines bubbling forth from the bowels of yawning craters torn into still-animated flesh. Instinctively, he choked back a wave of revulsion. It was the same sensation he'd experienced less than a month ago, the precise moment they had turned the body of Miguel Ramos belly up on the embankment of the Bronx River and watched his guts spill out into the mud.

21

NYPD FORM DD-5
COMPLAINT FOLLOW-UP   APRIL 6, 1984

DET. V. CROWLEY   ·   COMPLAINT #9892

SUBJECT: HOMICIDE/EMASCULATION OF MIGUEL RAMOS,
AKA MARGUERITA

DETAILS:

ON 4/6/83 A CRITIQUE WAS HELD AT THE 37 PDU OFFICE.
PRESENT WERE LT. ARTHUR BOYLE, DET. WALTER CUZAK,
DET. THOMAS IPPOLLITO, AND THE UNDERSIGNED; ALL OF
37 PDU.

ALL OF THE FACTS KNOWN ABOUT THIS CASE WERE DIS-
CUSSED AND IT WAS AGREED BY EVERYONE CONCERNED
THAT ALL INVESTIGATIVE LEADS HAVE BEEN EXPLORED
WITHOUT LEADING TO ANY SOLID INFORMATION THAT WILL
AID IN THE APPREHENSION OF THE PERPETRATOR(S). IT WAS
DECIDED THAT ADDITIONAL TIME SPENT ON THIS INVESTIGA-
TION WOULD BE FRUITLESS AND POSE AN UNNECESSARY
DRAIN ON AVAILABLE MANPOWER AND FACILITIES.

IT IS REQUESTED THAT THIS CASE BE MARKED INACTIVE. IF
FUTURE INFORMATION IS FORTHCOMING IT WILL BE GIVEN
IMMEDIATE ATTENTION.

CASE INACTIVE PENDING FURTHER DEVELOPMENTS.

The sidewalk in front of the precinct was swarming with
Hasidics dressed in long, black caftans and broad-brimmed
beaver hats despite the warm weather; carrying hand-
lettered signs; chanting, wailing, moaning, swaying back
and forth in cadence like a ritual conga line. PUNISH THE
MURDERERS, the signs read. GIVE US BACK OUR
NEIGHBORHOOD . . . WAKEFIELD CITIZEN'S ASSOCIATION
DEMANDS JUSTICE . . . END ANTI-SEMITIC BRUTALITY NOW!

Vince elbowed his way through the throng of protesters,
past a cadre of uniformed patrolmen who were trying to
contain the crowd, into the stationhouse, where a small
delegation of Hasids was arguing loudly with the sergeant at
the desk. Upstairs, the mood was somber as he entered the
Homicide room.

"What's all this?" he asked Tommy.

Tommy shrugged. "They're pissed because we haven't
arrested anybody in the Futterman homicide . . . what
else?"

"How's Boyle taking it?"

"Not well. He left word that nobody's to leave until he's
had a chance to talk to us."

"Where's he now?" Vince asked.

"Holed up in his office with a very official-looking
civilian sort of guy."

"Any idea who he is?"

"Who the hell knows? I don't think he's a Hasid . . . too
clean. Maybe an ADA or an IAD shoo-fly. The way things
have been going, I guess headquarters might be getting a
little edgy."

"Everybody inside, on the double!" It was Boyle,

standing in his office doorway. The civilian stepped out of the office behind him, shook his hand limply, and departed down the stairs. Boyle waited until everyone had entered the office and slammed the door shut.

"Okay. I wanna review every active case we're working on and nobody's leaving until we're finished. Any questions?"

Everybody eyed everybody else apprehensively.

Boyle retreated to the water cooler and popped a pill in his mouth. "In case anybody's interested, that guy who just left is a lawyer . . . a very important lawyer as it turns out. It seems he has a client who's decided to sue the city of New York, the Police Department, the Thirty-seventh Precinct specifically, and *me* in particular! And do you know who this high-priced, well-connected lawyer's client happens to be?" He looked directly at Vince.

"Beats me, Lieutenant."

"Try Julia Dexter-Stark, hotshot; and while you're at it, you might just enjoy knowing your ass is being sued, too. She's gonna nail all of us for public harassment, unlawful search and seizure, mental anguish, scratching our nuts, and any other goddamn statute her lawyer can find on the books. Whaddaya got to say about that, Crowley?"

"She's blowing smoke, Lieutenant. I stopped her on the street and asked her a couple of questions—"

"I don't wanna know what you did!" Boyle bellowed. "I don't give a rat's ass what you did . . . yesterday, last week, last year . . . ever! I got sheenies marching in the street, shysters in my office, heat from headquarters . . . I just found out the mayor is on his way up here to have his picture taken with those bearded bastards. Every shithead in the city with an ax to grind is lining up to get a piece of Art Boyle's ass and not one of you worthless humps is doing anything about it . . ."

He was hyperventilating, sucking and expelling air like a grounded carp. Vince looked warily at Tommy, who had suddenly found something fascinating on his shirtsleeve to pick at. Walt Cuzak was staring fixedly at the ceiling, drumming his fingers on his lap, forming wordlike shapes with his lips that Vince assumed were either prayers or obscenities.

"Is there anything I can do, Lieutenant?" Vince asked after an awkward pause.

Boyle plopped in his chair, poured a shot of bourbon into a paper cup, and tossed it down. "When I need your help, I'll ask for it. Where the hell were you when all this shit was going down? All of you—it's your goddamn job to protect your lieutenant . . ." His breathing was labored, like air escaping from a child's balloon. "I can't be expected to do it all myself. You'd think that once in a while somebody around here would realize the kind of pressure I have to put up with."

The room fell uncomfortably silent. Art Boyle seemed shrunken behind his desk, suddenly aware he was slipping over the edge. "Now where were we?" he sputtered. "Oh yeah, that Dexter-Stark thing. You say she's just jerking us off, Crowley?"

"She's got nothing, Lieutenant. I don't care what her lawyer says."

Boyle straightened himself in the chair. "Well, that's all immaterial. What we have to consider here is the effect on the department . . ." He was calming down. "After all, you and me don't count for a helluva lot in the big picture. The important thing is to put a stop to anything that could reflect negatively on the department. You agree on that?"

There was a mumbled chorus of assent.

"Good. Now let's take this Ramos homicide for starters. I've seen a lot of paperwork and so far no results. Where do we stand on that one Crowley?"

"Things are starting to shape up, Lieutenant."

"What the hell is that supposed to mean?"

"Just that, Lieutenant. I'm pursuing all possible leads."

"Any suspects?"

Vince cleared his throat. "At this time, nothing we can take to court, but I've got strong feelings on this one—"

"Feelings?" Boyle stiffened and looked around the room. "Okay, everybody listen up. I'm gonna want some feedback on this. Go on, Crowley, let's hear what you got."

Vince began. "Well, the way it goes down is that this Dexter-Stark dame has a direct connection with the deceased. She knew him as a waiter, recommended him to an uptown gland doctor, and paid his bill. Personally, I think she was probably humping him between meals and visits.

"So, Dexter-Stark has a house in East Hampton which is busted by the local constabulary on the grounds that some young chippie is found crawling near the premises in a naked state and she claims that a large group of Dexter-Stark's pals have been diddling her without proper introduction. The cops rake the premises, confiscate a shitload of illegal substance, along with a stack of homemade video-cassettes of the guests boffing each other like it's going out of style.

"I contact the Suffolk County DA and he invites me out for a private showing of said cassettes and during the show I see a dead ringer for my composite photo there on the screen. I confront Dexter-Stark with a blow-up of this guy's face and she acts like I just caught her shoplifting. After a little gentle persuasion, she finally admits she knows him as one Ronald Castanga . . . an artist, and genuine sicko in my opinion—"

"You've questioned this guy?" Boyle interrupted.

"Not yet, Lieutenant—"

"Then what the hell gives you the right to call him a sicko? What're you, a shrink all of a sudden?"

"No sir . . ." Vince could feel the muscles in his jaw tightening. "But I've seen some of his paintings and, in my opinion, they're the work of a real fruitcake."

Boyle poured himself another shot and walked around to the front of his desk. "That's it?"

"I know it doesn't sound like much now, but believe me, Lieutenant, this one just feels right to me. A couple more weeks and I ought to be able to build a real solid case."

"Against who . . . Dexter-Stark?"

Vince shrugged. "Maybe . . . I dunno yet. That whole crowd is sick enough to have done it. Maybe they all did it together, like a ritual sacrifice or something—"

"You got any proof of this, Crowley?"

"Give me some time, I'll get the proof."

Boyle glared at him. "How much time do you think the department can waste on a piece of shit like Ramos?"

"It's a homicide, Lieutenant," Vince protested.

"It's a dead fag, goddammit!" Boyle bellowed. "A routine, no-name, pervert floater that's giving me heartburn . . . busting my chops." He stared around the room. "Anybody want to comment on Crowley's case?"

Silence.

"Then I'll comment on it if nobody minds. In my considered opinion, what you got here Crowley is shit in a paper bag. I got half the Yids in the city of New York storming the gates, the mayor on the way up here, looking for a little free publicity, an unsolved double homicide involving residents of the precinct who just happened to be decent people and not perverts. I got IAD shoo-flies breathing down my neck; half my command is out sick and the other half is mutinous and uncooperative. I got a job that tears my heart out every day and you come in here and tell me you're out there harassing solid citizens instead of doing your job the way you're supposed to do it!"

Vince was stunned at the outburst. "I told you, Lieutenant, I'm pursuing all possible leads."

"My ass!" Boyle bellowed. "You told me you've been watching stag films when you're supposed to be on the job.

You told me you got somebody who looks a little bit like a description of a suspect you got from a couple of drugged-out fag whores. Just what kind of shit are you trying to feed me, Crowley?''

"I can make a case here, Lieutenant," Vince said firmly.

"And just what makes you so goddamn sure?''

He took a deep breath. "I told you Castanga was an artist. Well, I saw some of his work and he *painted* the body. The son of a bitch actually painted Miguel Ramos with his belly sliced open and his guts hanging out.''

"You can prove this? You can actually produce this painting for evidence?'' Boyle asked incredulously.

Vince shifted uneasily in his chair. "Well, I could, I suppose, but the painting wouldn't be enough in itself. It's not exactly a realistic painting, Lieutenant . . . more of an abstract if you know what I mean . . . kind of representing what's going on rather than spelling it out—''

"Let me get this straight," Boyle interrupted. "Do we have a painting of the deceased's body with guts hanging out or don't we?''

"It's more a feeling of guts hanging out,'' Vince hedged. "You really gotta see it to know what I mean.''

"I don't wanna hear about feelings!'' Boyle screamed. "Just tell me this: When a jury sees that painting are they gonna say, 'That's a liver . . . that's a spleen'?''

"It's hard to say, Lieutenant. I guess if they're real sensitive they might say that.''

"Sensitive?'' Boyle was shaking. "You been hanging out with the faggots too goddamn long, Crowley. I think you're becoming one of them, for chrissake!'' He sat, poured another cupful of bourbon, and tried to compose himself. "I'm shorthanded, I'm under a helluva lot of pressure; I probably should be in a hospital right now instead of out here taking all this shit. What I want from you men . . . what I *expect* from you is support, and above all loyalty. I want the Thirty-seventh to be known as the cleanest, smoothest-run detective squad in the city, and we can have that if we all work together.

"Look at it my way. Every day I have to come in here and take potshots from anybody who thinks they got a bitch against the department. You guys fuck up and I'm the one who takes the flak. Don't get me wrong; I know it comes with the territory, but if I'm under so much pressure that I can't function at a hundred percent, it filters down through the ranks and everybody's work starts to get sloppy. I think that's what's been going on here and I intend to put a stop to it before it drags the whole squad down the toilet. Now are you men with me or are you against me?"

Again the stunned silence, everybody looking nervously at everybody else.

"Okay. I'm gonna take that as a sign of support. We can get this squad moving again if we work together . . . show a little brotherhood and loyalty. That's about all I have to say on the matter. If there are no more questions, let's wrap it up and get our asses back to work. How about it men; are we gonna do it or are we gonna do it?" He was leaning across the desk, brimming with enthusiasm, like a fullback about to hurdle into the end zone.

"What about the investigation, Lieutenant?" Vince asked.

"Investigation?"

"The Ramos homicide."

"Oh yeah. We're gonna shitcan that one . . . not enough solid evidence to spend any more time on it. Starting tomorrow, I want you on the Futterman case with Cuzak and Ippollito."

"But Lieutenant, this is a good case—"

"It's a closed case. You're on Futterman starting tomorrow. Is that clear?"

"I'm off tomorrow," Vince muttered.

Boyle glared at him. "We can change that, too." He began shuffling the papers on his desk. "I think that wraps it up, gentlemen. Now let's get out there and act like we know what the hell we're doing around here." He busied himself in the paperwork as everyone filed out of the office.

"Thanks for backing me up in there," Vince said once they were at their desks. "Remind me to stick up for you guys next time your asses are on the line."

"Hey, come on," Tommy protested. "What are we supposed to do, for chrissake? He had his mind made up before we went in there and nothing was gonna change it."

"It'd be a different story if those were transsexuals protesting out there instead of Hasids."

"Sure it would, but there's not a fucking thing you and me can do about it," Tommy said.

"Let it go, man," Cuzak chimed in. "It's not worth getting yourself all bent out of shape over. We're talking about a dead fag here . . . let's not lose sight of that. They get themselves killed all the time because they hang out with scum. That's the way they want it, man."

"It's not like you're gonna get a commendation for this one," Tommy said. "Nobody gives a shit that this queen got snuffed and nobody gives a shit whether the killer gets caught. It's a no-win situation, man. Drop it."

"I don't believe I'm hearing this," Vince said. "You're telling me that it only matters when the victim is a politician or a businessman or some other pillar of society . . . that it doesn't count when a penniless, powerless vagrant has the bad luck to get himself butchered . . . right?"

Tommy gestured dramatically. "Hold it! I think I hear violins. You hear violins, Walt?"

"Yeah, I think so," Cuzak concurred. "It's enough to break your fuckin' heart."

Vince tried not to smile. "You guys are shitheads, you know that? A-number-one shitheads from the word go." He walked out of the squad room with Tommy's maniacal cackle in the background. Downstairs, the mayor's black Cadillac limousine had arrived in front of the precinct and the mayor was conferring gravely with several spokesmen from the enraged crowd of demonstrators. The TV cameras were rolling.

22

THE MAPLE TREES bordering the parking lot of the hospital had begun to bloom in earnest. Beyond the hospital grounds Vince could see spring greenery spreading out to trim, quarter-acre plots of manicured lawn and clipped shrubbery; landowners seeding and pruning, digging, fertilizing, clearing away the debris of winter and preening for the coming warmth. Vince parked in the almost-empty lot, gulped the fragrant air of the suburbs, and felt a twinge of guilt. His own house and grounds were going to seed, neglected like so many other fragments of his life that had been kept in good repair only when he'd been able to share them with someone else.

Now the effort seemed meaningless, a calculated stab at normality that wasn't fooling anybody . . . least of all him. He attended to the absolutely essential tasks—leaky toilets, clogged pipes, electrical outages—but that was about it. Once a week, an elderly cleaning woman named Mrs. Kuznetzov made a brave attempt at straightening and cleaning, but she could hardly keep pace with his accumulated debris. Her diligence was no match for his indifference.

He mounted the front steps and entered the vestibule of

the hospital. Here, the dull green, grease-coated walls and patched furniture, the persistent odor of disinfectant, the torn linoleum and shattered venetian blinds eased his guilt somewhat. Even by his own sloppy standards, Queens Hospital was a dump.

Billy was in his room, propped up in his gray, tubular metal bed, an intravenous plastic tube protruding from his right wrist and stretching upward to a bag of clear liquid suspended from a metal pole. "What's all this?" Vince asked the nurse who accompanied him.

She rearranged the pillows behind Billy's neck. "It's nothing to worry about . . . just a glucose solution."

"Anything wrong with him?"

"We've been just fine, haven't we?" She clucked and continued to fuss. "Yesterday we even spent some time outdoors, getting some sunshine."

"Why the tubes?" he asked.

"Routine. It's really nothing to worry about," she reassured him. "He'll be back on solids in no time."

Vince looked around the room. "Where's Jocko?"

She shook her head. "I'm sorry, I'm new here."

"His roommate, Jocko."

She reddened. "I think he passed on last week . . . I'm sorry."

"I'm sure it wasn't your fault." He smiled.

"I think it was cirrhosis . . ."

"Yeah, that'd be Jocko."

Jocko was what hospital insiders had called a "wet brain," an alcoholic who had destroyed so many of his brain cells he was incapable of taking care of himself. Most of the time, when he wasn't hooked up to some artificial life-sustaining contraption, he simply sat on the edge of his bed and stared off into space. Vince had never heard him utter a word and he doubted anybody else at the hospital had, either. He supposed everyone knew Jocko was a short-timer when they put him in the room they did. He was the fourth roommate to kick the bucket on Billy and it really didn't seem to bother him. There was a certain antiseptic logic to that.

"You're the first visitor he's had since I came to work here," the nurse said.

"Yeah. Not too many people come anymore."

"If you'd phoned ahead, we would have freshened him up for you . . . put him out in the day room for your visit."

There had to be a better way of putting that, a way that made Billy seem less like a piece of overripe fruit and more like a human being. "He's fine the way he is. I'm used to him this way."

"Do you come here often?"

Vince shrugged. "As often as time allows. He was my partner, before all this . . ."

"Then you're a policeman," she said.

He nodded.

She continued fluffing the pillows. "If you don't mind my asking, how did this happen to him?"

The question surprised him. For some reason, he'd expected her to know. "Gunshot. He took a shotgun blast in the chest. We were on surveillance, staking out a warehouse in the South Bronx. Billy got out of the van to stretch his legs and that was it. He didn't stand a chance."

"How awful," she said. "What was the reason?"

He shrugged. "They thought he was somebody else, that's all."

She shook her head sorrowfully. "Were you hurt?"

"Not a scratch. Billy was on the operation table more than ten hours. He died twice and they brought him back both times."

"It's a miracle," she said.

"Miracle?" He looked at Billy. "Call it what you want. Me? I'd call it a tragic mistake. He's been like this for four years now."

She looked embarrassed. "Well, where there's life . . ."

"Nobody's gonna do anything more for Billy Whalen," Vince said. "His mind is shot. All that time he was dead on the operating table, his brain was deprived of oxygen. Brain cells don't come back . . . ever."

"I'm sorry," she said.

"Me, too."

The nurse beat a hasty retreat out of the room and Vince pulled a chair next to the bed. He was sorry he'd let her go that way, feeling embarrassed about what she'd said. It wasn't her fault Billy was the way he was. She was only trying to bring a little cheer into a dismal situation. He supposed that if Billy could understand anything, he'd rather be treated like a simpleminded infant than neglected altogether.

"How're you doing, partner?" he asked. "They treating you okay since the last time I was here? I would've come a lot sooner, but things have been really hectic at the precinct . . ." He blushed at the lie. "You know, asshole Boyle's been coming down real hard on everybody lately. He hides in his office, drinks himself shitfaced, and dreams up all kinds of crazy plots against him. I swear to God, Billy, I don't think the poor son of a bitch'll last another month.

"Everybody else is okay, though. They all said to say hello. I talked to the Mosquito and he told me to say hi. Remember Morty Silverman? He was asking about you a couple of weeks ago. Even Tony Clams said to send his regards. You shoulda seen the beautiful job he pulled on the Wellington Armored Car Company . . . slickest goddamn thing you'd ever want to see. I tell you Billy, you want professionalism, give me an old-timer every time. They pay attention to detail; know what I mean?

"I saw Jessy last month. She's in a hospital, too . . . a place called Silver Hills. It's not exactly like this joint, but I guess the less said about that the better. I gotta tell you that it shocked me, though, her having a problem with booze and pills like that. It was always you and me who were the big drinkers, not Jess. Remember the summers out in Rockaway? Jeez, Jessy and Marcia put us both to bed almost every night.''

He hadn't meant to mention Marcia, it had just slipped out. Vince had managed to put her out of his mind, to mask the anger and hurt he'd felt when he realized she'd turned her back on Billy. It was during a telephone conversation they'd had almost two years ago, when she'd called the precinct for some information on Billy's family disability benefits. He'd been deliberately cool, knowing she hadn't visited the hospital in a long time. He'd also heard through the grapevine that she'd started seeing other guys. Finally he'd confronted her about it.

"He's dead to me, Vince," she'd answered unemotionally. "I still love him. I'll always love the man he was and cherish what we had together, but I have to think that way. I'm still alive and I have to go on living. I can't wrap myself in a black shawl like some old Irish grandmother and spend the rest of my life lighting candles to his memory. I'm still a young woman, Vince.''

Maybe Marcia was remarried by now. Maybe she was living in another state or another country. He had no way of knowing. All he knew was that he was the only one who cared enough to keep coming . . . to keep the memory alive.

"Jessy's old man wants to give me money," he went on. "He offered me megabucks to let her divorce me without a fuss and to let him raise the girls like proper little nutmeggers. Can you imagine that, the nerve of that son of a bitch? He's already got the girls, he's got Jessy, but he just can't be happy until he owns me, too. Well, brother, you and me know that ain't gonna happen, not in this lifetime.''

He laughed. "What the hell would I do with all that money anyway, an Irish kid from Queens like me? I'd probably blow it all on broads or the horses or something stupid like that. It'd be like casting pearls before swine, eh Billy? Besides, who the hell knows? Maybe Jess and me will get back together after all. She didn't say yes but she didn't say no either. I don't have to tell you that's what I really want, Billy. We both know my life hasn't been shit since she left.

"It's just that I don't know how things could be different if she did come back. I mean, we really never talked about why it was she left in the first place. It was me, I know that, but I'm not sure what part of me it was. Maybe it was just being a cop, and I can't change that . . ." He paused. "Not now, anyway."

The afternoon sun had positioned itself outside of Billy's window, throwing spears of dusty light through the cracks of the venetian blind, definitive shadows on the walls and floor of the room. Vince walked to the window and drew the blind shut. Somehow the sunlight was an intrusion, a spotlight that warped the privacy of his confessional.

He returned to the bed and took Billy's hand. It was cool and waxen, riddled with tiny discolorations from intravenous injections, limp, seemingly without weight. "She never really understood about me being a cop Billy, you know that? Maybe it was because I never told her. It's hard to tell a woman that it's all tied up with being a man. Women think that's all a lot of macho crap . . . the John Wayne thing. But I'll tell you something Billy: I don't think there's a whole lot of things I could have done with my life that would make me prouder about myself. I don't think any woman could understand that. Women need love. They can't imagine what it's like to need respect.

"And now we got woman cops . . ." He shrugged. "You and me know what that's all about. It's a fucking joke, that's what it's about. What we oughta do is tell the bad guys 'Look, we gotta have women on our side, so you guys should have women criminals just to make it fair.' "

He laughed. "I'll have to tell the Spring Man about that one. From now on, the Mafia's got to have fifteen percent women criminals or we call off the game . . ."

He felt a slight movement in Billy's hand. For the first time in more than four years Billy was smiling at him. "Oh my God! Billy, can you hear me?" The hand remained limp but the smile was fixed. Vince ran out into the hallway and found the nurse. "He's moving. I swear to God! I made a joke and he laughed at me."

She returned to the room, took a look at Billy, and checked his pulse. "Stay here. I'll be back in a minute."

Vince stood by the open doorway, afraid to breathe too hard, fearing too much movement might break the spell. She was back in a few seconds, accompanied by a doctor who looked like he hadn't had a good night's sleep in a couple of years. He brushed past Vince without comment, placed a stethoscope to Billy's neck, and shook his head. "Nothing doing here. This guy's dead as a doornail."

Vince just stood there. "How? What caused it?"

The doctor removed the stethoscope and placed it in his jacket pocket. "I don't know. Are you a member of the family?"

"No, I was his partner."

"Then I'll have to ask you to leave." He pulled the sheet up over Billy's face.

Vince was riveted to the doorway. "Just a few minutes. I want to say good-bye."

"I have to seal off this room—"

"When I'm finished!" Vince glared at him.

The doctor rubbed his eyes. "Sure . . . why not? Just don't touch anything and stop by the front desk on your way out." He motioned for the nurse to follow him and left the room.

Vince moved to the side of the bed and pulled the sheet away from Billy's face. The grin was still there, impish and animated as if he were contemplating some uproarious practical joke. Even his eyes seemed more alert than before, and Vince could swear his chest was moving evenly. It was an illusion, he knew. He'd seen too many dead bodies to delude himself that he was seeing any more than a shadow of remembrance. It was like that before the funeral directors got ahold of them and wreathed them in heavy-lidded silence, before the cosmeticians took away their last traces of humanity.

Then they became hard and pasty and rigid in their attitudes. Their faces were the same face; their hands set thoughtfully with rosary beads and missals; empty chests that seemed too wide and starched. How many dead men had he seen over the years? How many funerals had he attended? There was his grandmother Kate, and Sister Mary Dominick of Our Lady of Lourdes . . . his father.

They had knelt and recited the Sorrowful Mysteries: the Agony in the Garden, the Crowning with Thorns. He had watched his mother grow old before his eyes, right there in front of the gleaming brass-and-mahogany casket. Her face seemed to fall apart in hollows and gaps that strained to create a shadow of her youth. He hadn't wanted to see it, but it was too obvious to ignore. She lost her youth that day and with it her last vestiges of illusions. Her time for dreaming had come and gone.

And now it was time for him to mourn for Billy, and the tears he'd choked back that day at his father's funeral began to find their way down the ridges of his face. He cried for Billy and the songs that would never be sung, the stories that would never be told. He cried for his father, for Jessy, for himself, for the times that never were and never would be. He cried as if each painful spasm unlocked a desperate knowledge he had hidden all his life. He cried with dignity.

Then it was time to stop.

23

THE FOLLOWING DAYS were a blur, Vince putting in the time without thinking, without feeling. There was routine to keep him busy, the details of a new case he could pretend to be interested in, paperwork. He went through the motions mechanically, assuming that keeping active was the best way to dull the ache. He accepted the consolation of old friends and younger cops who hadn't known Billy but understood what losing a partner meant. He prepared himself for Billy's funeral.

Hero cops get a big send-off in New York, and Billy got the best the city had to offer. It made no difference that the had been doing nothing more heroic than taking a leak alongside a surveillance van when he was shot; no difference that he had spent the last four years as a vegetable waiting to die at the city's expense. He was shot in the line of duty and that entitled him to all the pomp and pageantry a slain officer deserves.

Billy would have enjoyed it, Vince thought as he stood in a fine drizzle in front of Saint Patrick's Cathedral. As much as he hated police brass and city politicians pandering to the mobs and preening for the cameras, he would have gotten a lot of cynical satisfaction at all the fuss and inconvenience he'd put them to: file upon file of crisply uniformed policemen marching somberly to the mournful cadence of muffled drums; the legions of New York's finest honoring their fallen comrade. Ranks of assembled dignitaries standing in the rain; the plaintive wail of bagpipes from the Emerald Society's fife and drum corps playing "Ballad for a Fallen Warrior"; the slow, inexorable advance of the funeral cortege as it bore Billy's body to its final tribute.

A sleek black hearse pulled alongside the curb and deposited the flag-draped coffin into the waiting hands of Vince and the other pallbearers. They accepted the salutes of the ranking police brass lining the steps to the cathedral, the respectful nods and bared heads of the collected dignitaries: assemblymen, congressmen, the mayor, the archbishop. They stood discomforted in the drizzle, honoring a dead cop they had never known in life; a symbol of their own vulnerability they did not dare ignore.

The pallbearers deposited the coffin on a wheeled platform inside the vestibule and accompanied it to the front of the cathedral where they took their seats alongside the honored guests. The archbishop, accompanied by an army of lesser church luminaries, passed the coffin, entered the sacristy, and began the service: "Eternal rest give unto him, O Lord; and let perpetual light shine upon him . . ."

Vince sat stiffly, barely aware of the ritual surrounding him; the robed priests and acolytes, the pungent aroma of incense, the mechanical responses of the congregation, the dull resonance of the cathedral bell . . . "Be merciful, O Lord, we beseech Thee, unto the soul of Thy servant William, for whom we offer Thee this sacrifice of praise . . ." It washed over him like the shadows of a dream, a vague unwanted intrusion on his solitude and his grief. "Eternal rest give unto him, O Lord. May his soul and the souls of the faithful departed through the mercy of God rest in peace . . ."

Billy was buried in Woodlawn Cemetery, not far from

the Thirty-seventh, where he had served his final days. There was a gathering of notables, not as large as the one at the cathedral but impressive nonetheless. The archbishop was gone but in his place the department chaplain performed a dignified graveside service and delivered a mercifully short eulogy:

"Friends and relatives. We gather here today to pay homage and to say good-bye to William Whalen; our husband, our friend and confidant, our brother officer; stricken down by an assassin's bullet in the line of duty. It is not our business here, to ponder and proclaim the injustice of his death, nor is it our purpose to glorify his life. In the final analysis, the taking of life is God's province, and so we must proclaim our finite submission to His almighty will. And if glory is to be imparted to the life of William Whalen, let it be the reflected glory of a life lived in the service of his God and his fellow man, for only God can glorify. We can but remember."

Then the mist was shattered by the lament of a single bugler blowing taps and presentation of the furled and folded flag to his widow. One by one, the guests filed past to offer her their condolences, then went to their waiting cars and left the cemetery. Vince waited until almost everybody had left and walked to where she was sitting. "Hello, Marcia." He took her hand.

"Hi. How've you been, Vince?"

"Okay I guess. How are you doing?"

"I'll be all right. Did Jessy come?"

"Uh-uh. We're separated. She's up in Marion with the girls. To tell the truth, it just never occurred to me to call and tell her about it."

"I'm sorry," she said. "I hope you can work it out."

He paused. "How's your life going?"

"It's fine now, Vince. Thanks for asking."

"If there's anything I can do . . ."

She eyed him sadly. "I'm sorry about Billy, Vince."

"I should be saying that to you."

"No . . ." She squeezed his hand. "You're the one who's grieved the most. I hope it'll be better for you now."

"Yeah. Maybe it'll be better for both of us."

"Take care of yourself, Vince."

"You, too."

He made his way through the wet grass to the car where Tommy was waiting. "Move over, brother. I feel like driving."

"We going back to the precinct?" Tommy asked.

"Well, we could go out and get drunk."

Tommy shrugged. "I wouldn't give you a real hard time about that. I never knew the man but I'll hoist a few to his memory."

Vince drove through the cemetery gates and turned onto 223rd Street. "It wouldn't be fair to Billy, the way I feel," he said. "I couldn't put a proper load on as tired as I am, and Billy deserves my best effort. You do what you want after you've let me off at the station. I'm gonna check out and get myself some sleep."

Walt Cuzak was holding down the fort when he arrived. "How'd everything go?" he asked.

"As good as these things go, I guess. Anything happening here?"

Cuzak leafed through his papers. "You had a call . . . Shem Weisen from the ME's office. Says to call him back." He handed Vince the note.

Vince dialed the number on the sheet and was put on hold. He called back after eight minutes of silence and got the coroner on the second try. "You guys ought to do something about communications around that place," he said.

"Hey. This is the bureaucracy," Wiesen said defensively. "Besides, most of the characters in this joint have stopped communicating on a permanent basis."

Vince ignored the joke. "It's been a tough day, brother.

What'd you call about?''

"You know your castrated DOA transsexual?''

"Yeah. What about him?''

"Well, I got another one just like him down here. They fished him out of the East River at six-thirty this morning.''

"Same MO?'' Vince asked.

"Same everything, with a few added flourishes. I think you ought to take a look.''

"Thanks, buddy. I'll be there in twenty minutes.'' He hung up the phone and headed for the door. "If Boyle gets back, tell him we better reopen the Ramos case. Tell him we got a regular crime wave on our hands.''

He rode the siren all the way to Jacobi Hospital, running red lights and snarling traffic in his wake. It occurred to him on the way that murder wasn't the sort of thing that would make most people forget their troubles, but in his case it seemed just the tonic he needed. Two killings with the same MO didn't exactly make a crime wave but it could be enough to force Boyle to rethink the case. He double-parked in an "Ambulance Only'' area and bounded up the hospital steps.

"So you think it's the same guy?'' he asked Shem Wiesen as they descended the stairs to the morgue.

"Gotta be. The case wasn't publicized enough for it to be a copycat. We'll know for sure after he's autopsied, but I can pretty much guarantee you the cause of death is the same: asphyxia and shock brought on by torture. This bird's gonna keep it up until he gets it right.'' He led Vince down a narrow corridor lined with stainless steel vaults until he found the one he was looking for. "You know, that's the funny thing about psychopaths. They can never leave well enough alone . . .'' He slid the heavy metal drawer open and removed the sheet from the victim's face. "This guy's gonna keep it up until he makes enough mistakes to trap himself. It never fails . . .''

Vince stared at the body in the drawer. The face was

puffy, partly from the beginnings of bloat and partly from a purplish, mottled bruise that ran from beneath her matted blond hair, down the entire left side of her face. There were numerous scratches and contusions, even a few missing teeth, but the identity was unmistakable. It was Jeanne, Charlene's girl friend. "I can get you a positive ID on this one," Vince said.

"Friend of yours?"

"Friend of a friend," Vince answered. "What were the additional flourishes you mentioned on the phone?"

"Cigarette burns, for one; and it seems there was coitus just before or just after death. I found fresh semen in the anal cavity and in some of the wounds."

"You mean they had sex?"

"Well, the killer did. I doubt the victim was alive to enjoy it. It looks like our psychopath is also a necrophile."

"Spare me the technical stuff," Vince said. "Can I go to my boss and tell him this is the same murderer?"

Wiesen shrugged. "Tell him anything you want." He pushed the drawer shut and locked it. "By me, it's the same guy. Some other pathologist might see it different, but as far as I know, I'll be doing the autopsy and my word'll stand."

"And your word is that it's the same guy."

"Fuckin' A."

24

"I'M SO SCARED, man . . . you don't know how scared I am." Charlene sat across the table from Vince in a coffee shop not far from the Medical Examiner's office. "I'm gonna be next, man!"

Vince nodded. "I'd be scared, too, if I were you."

"What's gonna happen to me? This guy knows who I am. He knows I was Jeanne's friend. What am I supposed to do when he comes after me? Tell me that?"

Vince stirred his coffee slowly. "We're doing what we can, Charlene, you know that."

"So go on out and catch the motherfucker. That's your job, ain't it?"

"I wish it was that easy."

"What's your problem, man? I gave you a description. He ain't gone no place since then. All you got to do is send some cops out looking for him. Shit, if it was some uptown society bitch that got snuffed you'd send out a fuckin' SWAT team."

"Maybe, but that's not the point. The point is that this guy's out there and he's gonna kill again soon unless we stop him. I know it's not fair, but you're looking at all the manpower the department's willing to assign to this case. If

I don't get him, nobody's gonna get him. And he'll get you; you can count on that.''

"Oh, man!" Charlene moaned. "What're you trying to do, make me more scared than I already am? I don't hardly leave my room anymore. It's like a nightmare.''

"Well, it won't get any better unless we do something about it.''

Charlene stared at the ceiling. "So whaddaya want from me, man? I don't know nothing about this crazy man who's doing all these killings. I just want to be left alone to live my life. Is that too much to ask?''

"The problem is that you're already in it,'' Vince said, "whether you like it or not. This psychopath has already killed your two closest friends and it doesn't take an Einstein to figure out that you're probably next on his shopping list . . .'' He paused to let the thought sink in. "Now, we can sit around and wait for him to show up, or we can go out and get him. It's really up to you.''

Charlene gaped at him. "You want *me* to go out there after him? You gotta be out of your fuckin' mind, man!''

"I'm not asking you to go out after him,'' Vince reassured her. "All I want is for you to hit the clubs at night, same as you always do. Keep your eyes open, and if you see the son of a bitch give me a call. I'll take care of the rest.'' He handed her one of his cards.

"No way, man!'' she howled. "I ain't setting myself up for no psychopathic killer. Whattaya take me for, some kind of fool?''

Vince reached across the table and handed her a twenty-dollar bill. "I'm not setting you up, Charlene. I wouldn't even bring it up if I thought there was any real risk. You're safe as long as you don't go off somewhere with this guy. If you see him, you pick up a telephone, call the number on that card, and sit tight. He's not gonna do anything if you're surrounded by other people.''

Charlene looked at the twenty. "What if I don't see nothing?"

"That's okay, too. You just keep in close touch, and as long as I think you're straight with me, I'll see that you're taken care of."

She shook her head. "Man, you know what you're asking?"

"I'm asking you to help me catch the guy who murdered your two closest friends."

"I'm so fuckin' scared, man . . ."

"It'll be all right, Charlene. Just remember to call if you see anything suspicious."

She folded the twenty around Vince's card and opened her purse. "I'm really taking a chance, Crowley."

He spotted the glint of a small-caliber nickel-plated revolver tucked inside the pocketbook. "I hope you have a license for that thing."

She stared at him in amazement. "You gotta be kidding. Who's gonna license somebody like me? This was Marguerita's. I found it in the hotel after you left."

"You could get yourself in a lot of trouble carrying that around."

She laughed. "What do you think I'm in now? I'm probably gonna get killed no matter what I do." She stuffed the card and money into her purse and snapped it shut.

Vince paid the check and accompanied her outside.

"Over here, honey . . ." A street-hardened, platinum-blond transsexual waved to Charlene from across the street.

"Who's that?" Vince asked.

"Lucia, my girl friend."

He felt a tug of resentment. "You sure as hell didn't waste any time, did you? How long has Jeanne been dead—two, three days?"

She stared at him icily. "You got no right to talk to me like that, Crowley. What do you know about it anyway?"

He was embarrassed. Where the hell had that reaction come from? "Sorry . . . guess I'm just a little on edge."

"Yeah. Me, too." Charlene crossed the street and embraced the newcomer. From where he stood, Vince could distinguish the imprint of a tattoo on the blonde's right hand, and the indistinct traces of a knife scar running the length of her cheek, partially obscured by layers of chalky makeup. For some irrational reason he felt sad. He'd hoped Charlene would do better.

Boyle was waiting for him back at the squad room. "What's this shit about another fag getting iced?" he asked.

"Just that, Lieutenant. Another transsexual was murdered over in the Forty-fourth. Same MO, probably the same killer."

"Well, that's their problem," Boyle snorted. "We got enough problems around here without opening that can of worms again."

"Yessir. What do you want me to tell Detective Schwartz when he calls?"

"Who?"

"Detective Schwartz from the Forty-fourth. The coroner's office noticed the similarities to the Ramos homicide and notified them over at four-four. I was told to expect a call from this Detective Schwartz. What do I say?"

Boyle eyed him quizzically. "Tell him what you've got, of course."

"Well, sir, it's just that I was pretty close to breaking that case, and if I give him all my information they're gonna get the collar. I don't know how that'll look down at Division . . . after we reported the case was hopeless and all . . ."

Boyle looked like he was going to hyperventilate again. "You jerking me off, Crowley?"

"No sir. I just wouldn't want somebody else to get the credit for our work, that's all."

"Do you really have a case here or are you pulling my chain?"

"I think I have a good case, Lieutenant. I'd be glad to review it with you, if you think it'd do any good; but like you say, we're dealing with a lowlife faggot here . . . not the kind of homicide that'll keep the solid citizenry awake nights."

Boyle drew himself up indignantly. "That's not your decision to make, Detective. We don't pursue investigations around here on the basis of race, creed, *or* sexual preference. Every murder victim is entitled to police protection . . . regardless. You got that?"

Vince bit his lip. "Yes sir. I guess I lost my head for a minute there. Shall I proceed with the investigation on that basis?"

"You're to proceed with the investigation forthwith."

"And what about the four-four, sir?"

"What about them?"

"Shall I coordinate my investigation with Detective Schwartz?"

His eyes went blank. "Coordinate with the four-four, yes; but make sure we get credit for the collar."

They were interrupted by a clamor on the stairs outside the squad room. "What the fuck's going on out there!" Boyle screamed into the hallway.

Walt Cuzak appeared first, followed by a string of uniformed officers, plainclothesmen, and civilians. Behind him, Vince could hear a rising chorus of outraged Hasids spilling from the street into the precinct: "*Butchers! Anti-Semites!*"

"It's two of the kids wanted in the Futterman homicide," Cuzak said breathlessly as he reached the top of the stairs. "Their lawyer just surrendered them to the desk sergeant."

The assemblage filed into the homicide room, leaving the roar of screaming Hasids behind the closed door. There were two youths, about seventeen years of age, manacled and frail-looking in the middle of the crowd. There was nothing menacing about them; nothing to suggest they might be capable of bludgeoning two helpless old people to death. They seemed like average kids to Vince, the kind he saw every day and waved to in the parks and playgrounds of the Bronx. "They make a statement?" he asked Cuzak.

"Not yet. Somebody's on the way over from the DA's office now. They'll probably confess if we can keep them alive long enough. It's real ugly out there."

"Who are they?"

"The tall one's Enrico Vargas. The little one's his cousin . . . Jose or Jesus, something like that. They've only been in this country a couple of months."

Vince watched as Boyle supervised their lockup in the holding pen. They seemed bored, annoyed at all the commotion around them. Their lawyers shouted last-minute instructions to them in Spanish and they nodded disinterestedly, apparently unconcerned or unaware of the magnitude of the charges against them. Vince had seen it all before—the mindless, unfeeling savvy of the street kids who filtered through the holding pen on their way to bigger and better things. Jail held no terror for them; neither did the prospect of premature, violent death. It was as if they'd lost a vital part of what it takes to be a human being somewhere in the twisted alleyways of their childhood.

"They don't look too worried," he said to Cuzak.

"You should've seen them downstairs when the TV cameras were rolling. They were real bigshots then. They'll be on the six o'clock news where all their campañeros can see them. They'll be neighborhood heroes before the day is out."

"They juvies?" Vince asked.

Cuzak shrugged. "What the hell difference does it make?" He motioned toward the two youths, lounging casually against the cell bars. "Whatever goes down for

them, it'll have been worth it. Even if they fry, neighborhood kids will be spray-painting their names on the play-
ground walls for a while. That's a form of immortality,
brother.''

"You're beginning to sound like a social worker," Vince
said.

"Nah . . . just a realist. If I had my way, I'd just hand
them over to those beards downstairs, let 'em practice a
little of their eye-for-an-eye justice.''

"They'd still be heroes."

"Yeah, but it'd hurt a lot more.''

NYPD FORM DD-5
COMPLAINT FOLLOW-UP   APRIL 11, 1984

DET V. CROWLEY   COMPLAINT #9892

SUBJECT: HOMICIDE/EMASCULATION OF MIGUEL RAMOS,
AKA MARGUERITA

DETAILS:

1. ON 4/11/84, IN THE COMPANY OF DET. IPPOLLITO, I
   VISITED THE HOME/STUDIO OF RONALD CASTANGA,
   LOCATED AT DUNE ROAD, EAST HAMPTON, N.Y. TELE-
   PHONE # (516) 555-1120, AND INTERVIEWED SAME.

2. INTERVIEWEE STATED TO UNDERSIGNED THAT HE HAD
   ATTENDED SEVERAL PARTIES AT THE HOME OF JULIA
   DEXTER-STARK IN 1982 AND 1983, AT WHICH PARTIES
   TRANSSEXUALS PERFORMED SEX ACTS.

3. INTERVIEWEE FURTHER STATED THAT AT NO TIME DID

HE PARTICIPATE IN THE AFOREMENTIONED ACTS AND
THAT HE DID NOT KNOW THE DECEASED.

4. INTERVIEWEE DENIED THAT HE WAS HOMOSEXUAL BUT
ADMITTED TO BEING BISEXUAL AND FURTHER ADMIT-
TED TO FREQUENTING BARS AND DISCOTHEQUES THAT
CATER TO HOMOSEXUAL TRADE.

5. INTERVIEWEE ADMITTED THE POSSIBILITY THAT HE MAY
HAVE MET THE DECEASED AT SOME TIME IN ONE OF
THESE ESTABLISHMENTS BUT DENIED MEMORY OF
SAME.

6. INTERVIEWEE WAS GENERALLY COOPERATIVE.

CASE ACTIVE. INVESTIGATION CONTINUES.

The drive to East Hampton was quiet; Tommy scribbling
earnestly in his notebook and Vince rehearsing his strategy
for the interrogation of Ronald Castanga. There were
several approaches that might work, depending on
Castanga's emotional stability, his psychological makeup,
and, of course, his guilt or innocence. That factor would be
established in the first ten or fifteen minutes of questioning.
Criminals gave themselves away in their mannerisms: in the
faint tremble of their voices, the darting, unnatural quick-
ness of their eye movements, the imperceptible beads of
sweat that appeared on their foreheads and upper lips—
symptoms that would mean nothing in a court of law but to
a trained interrogator they were as good as a confession.

"Carry the radio with you when we go in there," he said
to Tommy. "And leave it on, loud."

"What the hell for?" Tommy looked up from his
notebook.

"I dunno. It makes civilians nervous. Like they're not
sure whether they're being recorded or not."

"Come on. Any asshole knows the difference between a tape recorder and a radio," Tommy said.

"Maybe . . . maybe not. Call it a hunch. This guy's an artist and that makes him kinda flaky to begin with. The radio looks real official and all that squawking'll probably rattle his cage a little bit. Who knows?"

Tommy shrugged. "It's your investigation. You handle it the way you want. Me, I'd just walk in there, Mirandize the son of a bitch, tell him that we had him nailed colder than a nun's cunt, and wait for him to react."

"Yeah, I thought about that," Vince conceded. "The only problem is these people have a habit of calling their lawyers as soon as they see a shield. If we're not careful we could lose him."

"So what're you gonna do, cuddle up to him?"

"Maybe. For a little while anyway; at least until I can get a reading. I'm curious about what kind of a guy he is."

Tommy nodded. "Yeah. You wonder what kind of scumball would carve up a faggot and fuck him after he was dead."

"I'm more interested in what kind of guy would paint that awful shit I saw in the museum." Vince grinned. "Getting paid for that crap's got to be a crime of some sort."

• "Hey, that's good . . ." Tommy began writing in the notebook. "I'll try to fit it into my best-seller."

"I thought you were writing about whales, for chrissakes," Vince said.

Tommy looked wounded. "I never said *I* was writing about whales. I said Herman Melville wrote about a whale: Moby Dick. If you weren't such an ignoramus you'd know that."

Vince let it go. "So what's this one about?"

"Science fiction; about a future society that breeds a form of idiotic humans for organ transplants and interstellar garbage men."

Vince rolled it over in his mind. "So what's that got to do with what I said about Castanga's art?"

"Oh Jeezus!" Tommy slid back into the seat. "Melville never had to put up with this kind of shit. I don't know how I'll ever write an intelligent book as long as I keep hanging out with illiterates."

"Probably not," Vince agreed. "Not a bad idea though, interstellar garbage men. It's something we could do with the bad guys when the prisons get full-up."

Tommy eyed him critically. "You fucking me around, Vince?"

Vince laughed. "No. I think it's great you're writing a book, I really do. It's something everybody says they oughta do and they never do it. You're doing it and I respect you for it. Billy used to write, you know that?"

Tommy reddened. "Well, it's just something to kill time—"

"Maybe I'll even write a book after I retire," Vince went on. "God knows I've seen enough in the twenty years I've been on this job."

"Cop books are a dime a dozen." Tommy shrugged. "What kind of stuff did Billy write?"

"Poetry, mostly. Some short stories. I didn't understand most of it, to tell the truth, but he had a special way with words."

Tommy let a few moments of reverential silence elapse. "Too bad about him going that way."

"No, it was better. What's too bad is that he had to hang around all that time and lose his dignity. People just forgot what he'd been. It would've been a helluva lot better if he'd gone down the day he was shot."

Tommy began writing and paused. "Okay if I write about that or are you saving it for your book?"

Vince laughed. "Be my guest." He pulled the car onto a sandy shoulder and stopped in front of a weatherbeaten clapboard house forty or fifty yards from the waterfront.

"Number one thirty-two. This must be it. Don't forget the radio." He locked the car, removed his wallet and shield from his jacket pocket, and accompanied Tommy to the front door.

The young man who answered his knock looked even more like Vince's composite sketch of the killer than the image he'd seen in the videotapes. Medium built, light complected, with brown hair, hazel eyes, and no visible scars or contusions; he appeared more like a clerk or librarian than a psychopathic killer. Even his opening manner was disarming:

"Hi. I'm Ron Castanga. I hope you didn't have any trouble finding the place. We had a bad blow out here last month and they haven't gotten around to replacing the street signs that got knocked down."

Vince flashed his shield. "Ronald Castanga. I'm Dectective Crowley from NYPD Homicide. This is Detective Ippollito. We'd like to ask you some questions concerning the murder of Miguel Ramos, also known as Marguerita. Mind if we come in?"

Castanga stepped aside and ushered them inside the house; a cavernous, hollow shell that had been gutted to accommodate hundreds of canvases, hanging from the paint-encrusted walls behind huge plastic drop cloths draped from the ceiling like colorful, abstract tapestries; piled haphazardly in bunches along the splattered floor. The place reeked of oil and turpentine, almost overpowering the faint, sweet aroma of reefer that wafted down from the thin, yellow cloud floating just below the ceiling.

Castanga smiled. "Like I told you on the phone, I have no recollection of ever having met anybody by that name but I'll be glad to assist you in any way I can."

"I'm glad to hear that . . ." Vince sat on one of three upright wooden chairs Castanga had provided for the occasion and nodded to Tommy, who turned up the volume on the radio. "The truth is that every way we turn in this investigation, your name and your face keep cropping up . . ." He reached into his pocket, retrieved the police mug shot of Miguel Ramos, and handed it to Castanga. "I'm sure there's a logical explanation for it and that's where you're going to have to help me out. This is a picture of the murder victim. Please look at it carefully and tell me if you've ever seen him before."

Castanga studied the picture. "I'm sorry, the face just isn't familiar . . ."

"Okay." Vince handed him the more recent mug shot. "How about this one?"

He squinted his eyes. "Is this the same person?"

"About a year later."

A flicker of a smile crossed his face. "I'm afraid not, Detective."

Vince took the photos and opened his notebook. "Mr. Castanga, I have sworn statements by several individuals who attended parties at the home of Ms. Julia Dexter-Stark, indicating that both you and Mr. Ramos were involved in making home videotapes at those parties. I have further information that you have been known to frequent the Blue Parrot nightclub and Cruise Control discotheque, and that you were seen in the company of the deceased at both of those establishments prior to his death. Would you care to confirm or deny that information?"

Castanga remained impassive. "Am I being charged with anything, Detective?"

Vince cleared his throat. "Well, that will depend on your answers."

"Because if I am being charged, I'll want my attorney present during any questioning."

Vince shot a glance at Tommy. "I don't think that'll be necessary . . . unless, of course, you have something to hide."

Castanga grinned. "That's very good. You're very adroit at keeping the suspect on the defensive."

"I never said you were a suspect," Vince corrected him.

Castanga sat forward in his chair. "Then let's call a spade a spade, Detective Crowley. I have nothing to hide and I certainly don't mind answering your questions if you think I can provide you with any information that might lead to the capture of a murderer. God knows I have no sympathy for murderers, but I also have no sympathy for people who patronize me or insult my intelligence. You're here to pump me for information and I am willing to be pumped, so long as I'm not treated like a complete imbecile. Now, shall we do this thing fairly or shall I dial my attorney?"

Vince nodded. "Okay, Ronald. What would you consider fair?"

"For starters, you can turn off that stupid radio. I'm not in the least intimidated by it. It just makes it harder for me to hear your questions."

Vince looked at Tommy, who had begun to redden. "Fair enough. Anything else?"

"I don't know the individual in those photographs. That's not to say that I never met that person or that I don't know others who may be acquainted with him. I'm more than willing to waive my constitutional safeguards and answer any reasonable questions you have in order to help you in your investigation; and, as thorough interrogators, I'm certain you'll be able to extract information from me that I am not even aware I possess. All I ask is that you don't attempt to frighten or coerce me. I do not frighten easily and I have an uncanny ability of seeing through shallow, fraudulent tricks. Grant me that courtesy and I'll sit here and answer your questions all day long."

Vince took a deep breath. "Okay, Ronald, I'm gonna take you at your word. The truth is that I don't have a real strong case here—a lot of circumstantial evidence; a lot of hypothetical theories . . ." He glanced at Tommy, who looked like he was about to choke. "What I need from you is some straight talk about your relationship with the deceased. I *know* there was a relationship. I'm not just trying to scare you with that.''

Castanga sat back and lit a cigarette. "If there was, I'm certainly not aware of it.''

"What about the party at Julia Dexter-Stark's place?''

He smiled. "Dear Julia. Whatever did she tell you about that awfully boring evening?''

"The police didn't think it was so boring,'' Vince said. "They arrested half the guests before the night was over.''

"Including yours truly.'' Castanga smiled. "It was really quite a drag.''

"What about that stag film you starred in?''

"Oh God, which one? There were films at all of Julia's parties. It was practically part of the curriculum. Everybody got up and sang or danced or did something dreadfully unfunny for the camera and Serge Popowitz would prance around giving orders like he was John Huston or somebody and we'd all get stoned and silly and collapse into a heap on the floor. That's all there was to it.''

"I'm talking about the tape where you show up asking directions from a blonde who's going down on a transsexual. You remember that one, don't you? We got about five minutes of you in living color.''

Castanga didn't bat an eye. "God, how could I ever forget that disaster?''

"Then you were in the film.''

He seemed surprised. "You have it on tape, don't you?''

"And you took part in the sexual acts—''

"Certainly not,'' Castanga protested. "The whole thing was a farce, a black comedy if you like. I suppose my role in it was stupid but it was just a lark. There was nothing sinister or menacing in any of it.''

"How about sexual?'' Vince asked.

"Certainly there was sex. That was the whole point, but I never took part in any of it. My part was passive

. . . transitory, as Serge called it.''

"And the others, the transsexuals who took part in the tapes. Did you know any of them?''

"I suppose I met them, but I didn't really know them.''

"Didn't you recruit some of them from the Blue Parrot and Cruise Control?''

He smiled thinly. "Did I admit to having been in those places?''

"You have been there, haven't you?'' Vince asked.

"I suppose so. There are very few places in New York I haven't been. If you'd simply asked I would have told you that. There was no need for you to try to trick me into telling you.''

"Those places cater to transsexuals,'' Vince said.

"So what was an all-American boy like me doing in places like that, right?'' he asked.

"The question occurred to me.''

"I've been there for kicks; I've been there for sex; I've been there just to mute the awful boredom. Does that answer your question?''

"Are you a homosexual?''

"No,'' Castanga answered emphatically.

"So why hang out in the fag joints?''

He paused momentarily. "I've explored my sexuality, Detective Crowley. Plumbed the heights and depths of my eroticism as it were, experimented with all sorts of feelings and experiences. I don't think that makes me queer.''

"Maybe not,'' Vince conceded. "But my killer was seen in both of those places just prior to the crime and I don't have either the time or the inclination to figure out whether he was plumbing the depths of his eroticism or just looking for a victim. I gotta go on what I've got Ronald, and what I've got doesn't look real good for you.''

Castanga smiled. "Touché, Detective Crowley. A truly formidable riposte. I'll try not to underestimate you in the future.''

"I'd appreciate that, Ronald," Vince said. "This is a murder investigation and I find it's best to get right to the point."

"And the point is that you consider me a suspect, right?"

"Everybody's a suspect in a homicide investigation, Ronald. You haven't given me any reason to exclude you."

"Oh God, don't exclude me, whatever you do." Castanga groaned theatrically. "Rejection is the dread of all true artists."

Vince closed his notebook. "I'm sorry you feel this is a joke, Ronald. It'd make things a lot easier for everyone if you took it seriously. We're talking about murder here. I don't find anything funny in that."

"Of course not." Castanga hung his head sheepishly. "Forgive me, Detective Crowley. I realize my waggish behavior is sometimes woefully inappropriate. From this point on, I'll do anything I can to help you out."

Vince took a miniature 35-mm camera from his jacket pocket. "I don't suppose you'd care to pose for another picture? Just for a lark, of course."

Castanga smiled. "You know I don't have to do this."

"I know."

He assumed an exaggerated pose. "Then take your best shot, Detective. I never could resist the greasepaint and the crowd."

26

BACK AT THE precinct he received another bonanza: two transsexual lovers who were willing to admit they had seen Castanga with Marguerita on the night of the murder. Tommy had been doing his job, checking every facet of Castanga's life: his telephone records, mailman, fuel delivery service, anyone who might shed light on his movements at the time of the crime. He'd circulated Castanga's photograph in all the bars and hangouts, finally hitting pay dirt with the bizarre pair at the Blue Parrot.

Vince read aloud from their written deposition: "Evelyn and Francesca . . . born Edward Louis and Robert Francis Hayes. Is this address legit or do we find an empty lot when we go looking for them?" he asked Tommy.

"For today it's legit; a welfare hotel in Chelsea. Better get them quick if we're gonna use them, though. You know how these scumbags move around. Next week they're liable to be in San Francisco."

"We could put them in protective custody," Vince thought aloud. "Tell 'em the slasher's got them penciled in for next week . . ."

"No way," Tommy said. "They're pissing in their pants now. They'll clam up if we drag them up here for any

196

reason, believe me. The only way I could get them to sign that statement was to promise them immunity from testifying.''

Vince laughed. "*You* promised them immunity? I'll bet the DA's office would love to hear that."

Tommy shrugged. "Hey come on, man. You gotta do what you gotta do; know what I mean?"

"Well, we're gonna have to get them up here to pick him out of a lineup sooner or later."

"Let's worry about that when the time comes."

Vince scanned the deposition. "It doesn't say anything here about them seeing Castanga and Marguerita leave together."

"They were dancing," Tommy said. "Cheek to cheek, and too much in love to notice that sort of thing."

"Gimme a break," Vince moaned.

"I know it's not a lot," Tommy said. "But it places Castanga with the victim sometime after three A.M. on the morning of the murder. One more thing . . . both of these cookies agree that Ramos was shitfaced drunk when they saw him. They said he could hardly stay on the barstool."

Vince slipped the deposition into the file jacket. "The Blue Parrot . . . that's pretty far uptown for Marguerita, at least for that time of night. My bet is they left there and went someplace in the immediate area. It was too late to head back downtown and Marguerita was probably too stoned to make the trip anyway."

"The shape he was in, Castanga could've taken him out in an alley and carved him up," Tommy said.

Vince shook his head. "I don't think so. It wouldn't be like Castanga to do something that haphazard. This is a very organized guy, a guy who ties his shoes by the numbers. I think he had a place all set up nearby. Now if you were a killer and you needed a place to butcher somebody in the East Bronx at three in the morning, where would you go?"

Tommy rolled his eyes. "Jeez, there's only about a

thousand places in this cesspool . . . ''

"Let me put it another way. Suppose you needed a very private place in the East Bronx where you could bring a chippie at three A.M., do anything you felt like doing, and not have to worry about anyone asking embarrassing questions?''

"Hump Heaven!" Tommy said triumphantly.

"Sounds good to me. Grab your jacket and let's get going." He led Tommy down the stairs two at a time and into the waiting squad car.

Hump Heaven was the Golden Gate Motel, a ramshackle assortment of decaying wooden cabins at the edge of Ferry Point Park, in the shadow of the Whitestone Bridge. The motel was operated by Pasquale "Sally Boy" Uggerio, a known front for the Thomas Felice crime family of Malba, Queens, directly across the bridge. The Felice family used the motel as a kind of foreign embassy on the territory of the Carlo Madalena family in the Bronx . . . a place where they could meet in relative seclusion and iron out their differences.

It was also an illicit lovers' paradise, a place where anything and everything was tolerated and no questions asked, where anybody with strange sexual appetites could bring manacles or machinery or any kind of contraption that suited their fantasies, groan and moan and holler to their heart's content without being disturbed. It was a perfect place for violence; a perfect place for Ronald Castanga to do his stuff.

Sally Boy Uggerio was watching a small black-and-white TV behind the cashier's desk when Vince and Tommy arrived. He was not overwhelmingly happy to see them.

"What the fuck do you want, Crowley?" he growled.

Vince threw a forearm to Sally Boy's throat and sent him crashing against the rear wall of the office. He stepped behind the counter, directed a full frontal kick to Sally's groin, and stomped heavily on the knuckles of his exposed right hand. "A little respect when you're talking to the police, huh Sally? How many times I gotta tell you?"

"You're breaking my hand!" Sally wailed. "Lemme up for chrissakes!"

Vince stepped back and allowed Sally to pull himself to a sitting position against the wall. "Now let's start all over again," he said evenly. "Hello Sally. How's the motel business?"

Sally grabbed his crotch and moaned. "What'd you have to go and do that for Crowley? I ain't done nothing to you."

Tommy reached down and removed a .38 snub-nosed revolver from Sally's inside jacket pocket. "You have the right to remain silent. You have the right to be represented by an attorney . . ."

"What the fuck's going on here?" Sally screamed. "What am I being busted for?"

Vince grabbed him by the lapels and dragged him to a standing position. "It's like this, Sally baby. We got you on all kinds of shit. We got you for complicity to commit murder. We got you for harboring known criminals; for pandering; for operating a premises for the purpose of prostitution. We got you for littering the fucking street . . ."

Sally's shoulders slumped. "Okay, Crowley. Whaddaya want?"

Vince looked at Tommy. "What do we want from this scum-bucket, partner?"

"Maybe a little information, partner."

"Maybe a little *straight* information," Vince corrected him. "We're not in any mood for bullshit."

Sally closed his eyes and groaned. "Just let me sit down, okay?"

Vince waited while he slumped heavily into a patched vinyl chair, then handed him Castanga's photo. "When was the last time you saw this guy."

Sally stared at the snapshot. "I dunno . . . he looks like

a lot of guys who come in here.''

"You gotta do better than that, Sally . . .''

"I swear to God!'' Sally wailed.

"He would have been with this . . .'' Vince handed him the mug shot of Marguerita. "Last month, around the twelfth.''

Sally looked at the picture and nodded. "This one I remember. She was so fuckin' bombed, the guy practically carried her to the room.''

"And was this the guy who was with her?'' He gave Sally Castanga's picture again.

"It's hard to tell. There's nothing special about this dude. There was nothing special about that dude either. It could've been him.''

"What do you mean 'could've been'?'' Vince demanded.

Sally shrugged. "You want me to say it was him? Okay, it was him. You happy now?''

"Now let me see the register,'' Vince said.

"You gotta be kidding, Crowley. You don't think he signed his right name, do you? Nobody in this joint signs their right name, for chrissake!''

Vince leafed through the dirt-smeared, yellowing pages of the motel's register until he reached the right date. "Smith . . . Smith . . . Smith . . . Jones . . . Poppins. Who the hell is Poppins?'' he asked.

Sally shrugged. "How should I know? Some fag comes in and tells me he's Mary Poppins. Who am I to argue?''

Vince tried not to smile. "Do you remember what room you gave them?''

"Probably fourteen or fifteen. I remember the guy wanted a clean room. Those two are the cleanest I got.''

"Which one, fourteen or fifteen?''

"Fifteen,'' Sally said emphatically.

"How can you be so sure?''

"Whaddaya busting my chops for?'' Sally wailed. "You

want a room, I give you a room. I'm trying to be cooperative here. I don't want no more trouble with you guys!''

Vince tore the page from the register and put it in his pocket. "Okay Sally, let's have a look at room fifteen.''

Sally shrugged. "Suit yourself, but you ain't gonna find nothing there. There've been a hundred guys in there since then. The place's been cleaned a half a dozen times.''

Vince was glad Sally hadn't shown him one of the motel's bad rooms. Number fifteen smelled like wet bed linen and compacted garbage. They combed the premises, scraping samples of grime from the floor and walls. "I told you you wouldn't find nothing,'' Sally said from the open doorway.

Vince glared at him. "I'm sending a forensics team in here tomorrow. Don't rent this room to anybody until they're out of here.''

Outside of the smell and the obvious filth, there was nothing apparent to link the place with Marguerita's murder. There was a broken shower head, bent downward, protruding impotently from the grease-smeared tile wall like an old man's penis. A dirt-encrusted tub. A shattered window stuffed with oily rags. A basketball-sized hole in the wall that somebody had roughly filled with globs of plaster and neglected to paint. "This is your cleanest room?'' Vince asked.

"Whaddaya want from me?'' Sally shrugged.

They left the room and headed back to the office. "Okay, you guys. You got what you wanted. Now how about leaving me in peace?'' Sally pleaded.

"Not quite,'' Vince corrected him. "I still need the license plate of the car the guy was driving.''

"What do I look like, the motor vehicles bureau?''

Vince eyed Sally coldly. "Now you're getting cute with me again. You and me both know you snap a Polaroid of every plate that comes in and leaves this pesthole.''

"Where'd you hear a thing like that?"

"I know the scam. You shoot the plates, send a copy of
the photo to the john, and threaten to expose his extracurri-
cular activities unless he pays up. Right?"

"No, no—" Sally shook his head vehemently.

Vince turned to Tommy. "Okay, partner, put the cuffs
on this scumbag."

Sally raised a hand. "Awright already. Just wait here. I'll
be back in a couple of minutes."

Vince followed him into a room behind the office. There,
the neatly paneled walls, plush carpet, and oval mahogany
conference table stood in marked contrast to the sleaziness
of the rest of the place. Sally walked resentfully to a row of
gray metal file cabinets at the far end of the room and began
sifting through one of the drawers. "You know I'm a dead
man if any of this gets out."

Vince placed a fraternal hand on his shoulder. "Would I
let that happen to a friend of mine? Hey, don't worry about
a thing, Sally baby. I want you right where you are. Who
knows what kind of slime they might replace you with if
they punched your ticket? You and me, we got a kind of
understanding . . . know what I mean?" He took the photograph Sally handed him and put it in his pocket without
looking at it. "See how I trust you, paisan? Shit, it takes
years for two people to develop that kind of relationship."

27

THE PLATE CHECKED out; a gray 1983 Mercedes four-door sedan registered to Ronald Castanga at the East Hampton address, but a thorough check of the car by a forensics team failed to turn up any new evidence. Same with Hump Heaven; no blood stains, no fingerprints, no real evidence of any kind that a crime had ever been committed on the premises.

Vince sat in the darkened projection room at the DA's office with Tommy Ippollito and viewed the television pictures that had been taken by the Crime Scene Unit on the morning of Marguerita's murder. The hand-held videocamera danced down the muddy embankment and zoomed in on the limp, floating body of Miguel Ramos, facedown in the water. It backed away, trained a shaky lens on the Emergency Service police unit as they carried it toward shore, and recoiled momentarily as the body was turned and Marguerita's entrails spilled out onto the ground. It was all too familiar, fixed in his mind like a recurrent dream that always ended in exactly the same way.

"Anything about the embankment strike you as unusual?" he asked Tommy.

Tommy shook his head. "A lotta mud, that's about it."

"That's right; a lot of mud and no footprints."

Tommy shrugged. "He coulda wiped them away after he was finished. It was raining pretty hard that night. They might've just washed away."

"It's possible," Vince conceded. "But what about drag marks? Ramos was pretty heavy, and Castanga's no Mr. America. He would've had to drag the body down the embankment. There's just no way he could have carried it. So how come there were no drag marks? How come there wasn't even a trace of blood anywhere around there?"

Tommy thought about it. "He might've dropped the body off the bridge."

"No . . . there were no broken bones, not a single sign of forced impact. The body was put there by somebody who was able to get it down forty feet of steep, muddy soil without leaving a trace. Pretty good work if you ask me."

The videotape ran out and Tommy shut off the machine. "There's another screwy aspect to this thing. As soon as ESU turned the body on its back, all the guts poured out like somebody had turned on a faucet. I mean *all* the guts. I don't remember the ME saying that anything was missing. That means our killer had to maneuver all that rough territory, carrying a body that was split open like a side of beef, and not lose a single giblet along the way. Now *that's* really good work."

They looked at each other. "The body had to be wrapped," Vince said.

"I think so," Tommy agreed.

"Taken into the water in some kind of bag that was tight enough to hold everything in; placed facedown in the water and then unwrapped . . ."

"That still doesn't explain why there were no drag marks," Tommy said.

"It would if the bag was lowered from the top of the bridge by a rope or a chain. That might also explain why we couldn't find any bloodstains at Hump Heaven or in Castanga's car."

"He woulda had to be awfully careful," Tommy observed.

"He is," Vince said. "Let's get somebody out there on the double to check that bridge. If we're lucky, we might find some rope fibers or metal scrapings lodged in the cement."

"You got it." Tommy left to call headquarters and Vince reran the videotape, hoping to see something that would confirm his new theory. There was only one unsteady shot of the top of the bridge and that was too brief and out of focus to be of any use. He ran the tape through and replaced it in the file just as Tommy returned.

"Guess who called you?" Tommy asked excitedly.

"Beats me."

"Try Ronald Castanga." He grinned. "He left a number where you can call him back." He handed Vince a folded sheet of paper.

Vince shook his head. "What the hell do you think this is all about?"

"Maybe he wants to confess."

"Fat chance." He lifted the phone and dialed the number on the sheet. "Hello, Ronald? This is Detective Crowley. I understand you tried to reach me at my office."

"Hey, Crowley. Good to hear your dulcet tones again." Castanga was as breezy as ever. "Tell me, do you like to fly?"

The question took Vince by surprise. "In an airplane?" he asked.

"Well, that's the only way I'd try it," Castanga said.

He paused. "I guess I'm not overly fond of it. It gets you from one place to another, that's the best I can say for it."

"Too bad," Castanga said. "I was going to ask you if you wanted to go flying with me this afternoon."

Vince raised his eyebrow at Tommy, who was listening in on the extension. "You a pilot?" he asked.

"A damn good one," Castanga answered.

Vince couldn't believe what he was hearing. "And you want me to go for a ride with you?"

"Sure, unless you'd feel funny about it."

"No, no, I'd love to go flying with you. Anyplace in particular you wanted to go?"

"No . . . just up over the city. I'm on my way to the airport in about fifteen minutes. Can you meet me there?"

"Which airport?"

"Flushing, in College Point, Queens; just over the Whitestone Bridge."

"I know where it is," Vince said, trying to disguise the excitement in his voice. "I can be there in about a half hour. That okay?"

"I'll be waiting at hangar Eighteen A. See you then." Castanga hung up.

"You're not really going?" Tommy asked when Vince put down the receiver.

"You bet your ass I'm going. When was the last time a suspect in a murder investigation called you and asked you to spend a couple of uninterrupted hours with him?"

"Never," Tommy conceded. "But even if one did, there's no way you'd get me up in a private plane with him. What if Castanga decides to end it all and take a header into Jamaica Bay with you sitting next to him? This guy's a fruitcake, you know. That may be just what's on his mind."

"I'll take my chances. Just tell headquarters where I am and phone Flushing Airport in a little while for a copy of his flight plan. If you don't hear from me by close of day, you can come after both of us."

He dropped Tommy off at the precinct and headed for the airport. Funny, the way things worked out, he thought, driving over the bridge to College Point. Just about everybody he'd encountered had busted his balls. They'd gone out of their way to avoid answering his questions, impede his progress, and be generally uncooperative. They had screamed about their rights, assailed him as a pig and a storm trooper; come at him with icy sarcasm, outright hostility, and threats of reprisals; they had placed secretaries, security guards, and high-priced lawyers in his path; and even succeeded in bringing the wrath of Asshole Boyle down around his shoulders in an effort to obstruct his investigation. And here this guy was, falling all over himself, trying to provide clues that might just lead to his own capture and conviction. Who the hell could explain a thing like that? It was a weird and wonderful world.

Castanga was waiting outside of hangar 18A, beside a single-engine Cessna that was fueled, running, and ready to go. "Ever been in one of these babies before?" he shouted over the noise of the engine.

"No!" Vince shouted back. "That's what I wanted to talk to you about. Maybe you and me could just have a nice talk here in the hangar . . . you know, away from all the noise and gas fumes and all."

Castanga smiled. "Don't worry, I'm a very good pilot. I have over a thousand hours without a single mishap."

"It's not that . . ." Vince hedged. "I, ah, don't know whether this is really the way to go about it—"

"You're not afraid of me, are you?" Castanga asked.

Vince drew himself up. "You better not start to believe that, Ronald."

"Then guts it out."

He steeled himself and walked to the plane. Castanga helped him inside from the right wing, then entered himself from the other side. He secured the doors, ran what seemed like an interminably long instrument check, and tested the seat belts. "It's really quite safe." He tried to reassure Vince, who was gripping the sides of his seat. "You have a lot better chance up here than you do in city traffic."

"That's what I hear . . ." Vince tried to sound relaxed. "I guess I'm just used to city traffic. I kinda know what to expect from it."

"There's nothing different up here," Castanga said as he pulled the plane off the tarmac apron onto the cement runway and began to taxi. "Just don't panic if it gets a little bumpy up there. Wind currents are just like potholes. They're uncomfortable but they don't cause any real problems if you're careful." He paused at the end of the runway, waited for clearance from the tower; then, in a sudden surge, before Vince knew what was happening, they were airborne.

Vince felt his stomach catapult into his chest as the ground began to fall away. For a moment, the realization that he could have avoided all of this, that this had been his choice, penetrated his mind like a bullet wound. He wanted to scream, to grab the controls from Castanga's grip and force the airplane back to the ground; feel the reassuring earth beneath his feet once more and know that he was no longer a frail missile hurtling through hostile space. He wanted to throw up.

"Don't close your eyes," Castanga said. "That'll just make it worse. Try to concentrate on a fixed point in the aircraft until the nausea goes away."

Vince gulped. "How'd you know I was sick?"

"Everyone is their first time."

Somehow, knowing that helped. In a few minutes he was feeling well enough to hazard a tentative look out the window at the ground below. "How high are we?" he asked.

"Five thousand feet."

"Is this as high as we're gonna go?"

Castanga laughed. "Try to relax. It's a beautiful day for flying."

Vince could identify a few landmarks from the tiny world below: Point Lookout, Jones Beach, Montauk. They were heading east, away from the setting sun. "Where are we going?" he asked.

Castanga shrugged. "I thought we'd just cruise around, unless there's something in particular you'd like to see."

"You're the pilot," Vince said.

Castanga smiled. "I hardly ever know where I'm going when I fly. I file a flight plan because it's required, and then I just go wherever my instincts take me."

"Isn't that dangerous?" Vince asked.

"Not really. It's different up here than it is down there. None of the confusion; none of the muck and corruption of the city. It's pure and uncluttered up here, almost spiritual."

Vince surveyed the almost cloudless horizon. "I guess you have a point, but I still like the feeling of solid ground beneath my feet. I guess it's my conditioning or something."

"Don't you ever get fed up with the filth and depravity you see down there?" Castanga asked. "You're a policeman; I'm sure you see more than your share of it. Doesn't it ever get to you? Don't you just want to scream sometimes?"

"Maybe," Vince conceded. "But that's part of my job. I try not to dwell on that sort of stuff. The world's not such a bad place once you get to know it."

Castanga frowned. "Really, Crowley . . . I expected more from you than that saccharine, simpleminded pap. Doesn't the gore and perversion you see every day make you want to puke sometimes?"

"That's kind of a strange question, coming from somebody who's as fascinated by gore as you seem to be," Vince said.

"You're speaking about my work—"

"Those paintings of yours; they're all about guts and intestines, aren't they?"

"I suppose you could say that, in a very conventional sense. But as allegory, they go far beyond that."

"I'm afraid you just lost me."

Castanga grinned. "It's all a matter of how you look at them. It's highly unlikely that anyone buying one of my works will see it in the same way I painted it. Art is a very subjective thing. Don't you think?"

"I wouldn't know about that; but if you'll excuse my saying so, I wouldn't want one of your painting hanging over my fireplace. It'd give me the heebie-jeebies."

Castanga seemed surprised. "Really? After what you have to live with every day?"

"I may have to live with it but I don't have to like it," Vince said.

Castanga mulled it over for a moment. "I think you're the exception then. Granted, my work isn't to everybody's taste, but I really believe most people have an overwhelming preoccupation with the macabre. They may be revolted by it but there's a certain fascination in their revulsion. All you have to do is look at history to see that. Look at the films that are making money . . . chain-saw murders, decapitations. We've even established museums dedicated to the ghoulish and macabre. Every half-assed traveling carnival has a wax display of blood-curdling murders that all those square, gray little people out there just flock in to see. We've institutionalized horror, Crowley; packaged it so the public can go and pretend to be horrified by it all. They can live out their bizarre fantasies without actually having to do anything about them. Maybe that's why so many people find my work irresistible."

"Then there are the ones who actually go out and do something about those sick urges," Vince said. "They're the ones who I get to deal with."

Castanga nodded. "True. I imagine this case you're involved in now is a case in point. I wouldn't be at all surprised if you believed that the killer had somehow crossed that invisible line between fantasy and psychotic behavior.''

"I try not to complicate it too much," Vince said.

Castanga began to laugh. "You are determined to remain unregenerately pedestrian, Crowley. Aren't you ever tempted to go beyond that plodding, unimaginative world of yours and explore the abstracts of your calling? God, doesn't it become terminally dull for you after a while?''

"I try to keep things moving," Vince said.

"Good lord! Police work *is* supposed to be a science, isn't it? Hasn't it ever occurred to you that there may be aspects of this investigation that go beyond pounding the pavement? There's forensic science, pathology. I even recollect that you have your own little museum of homicidal horrors at the Manhattan morgue . . . the sixth floor, I believe.''

"How would you know about that?''

"I've been there," Castanga said. "Call it research, if you want. I spend quite a bit of time down at the morgue. I guess you could call it a creative tool.''

"Not too many people would see it that way," Vince said.

"Not too many people are getting fifty grand a canvas.''

The point was well taken. They flew for a while without talking, Vince feeling more at ease and Castanga seeming to become more mellow, as if his escape from the ground had somehow freed him from worry. "Aren't you curious why I asked you to go flying?'' he asked finally.

"I figured you'd get around to telling me.''

"The truth is, I like you. I know that may be a little hard for you to understand, what with you trying to pump me for information. But the fact is, I understand it's all part of your job and I wouldn't respect you if you weren't doing it the best way you knew how.''

Vince raised an eyebrow. "You like me?''

"Sure. There's something genuine about you that I don't

usually see in the circles I travel in.''

"You'll excuse me if I tell you that I think that's a crock of shit, Ronald," Vince said evenly. "I mean, here you are, a celebrity . . . probably a millionaire. You hang around with artists and writers and movie producers and a bunch of people whose biggest problem in life is finding something weird enough to snap the boredom in their lives. And you expect me to believe that you can't wait to strike up a friendship with a New York City cop? Come on, Ronald. Give me credit for having half a brain anyway."

Castanga shook his head sadly. "I'm sorry you feel that way Crowley, I really am. I never thought of this as being a matter of class. I assumed you and I could overcome that kind of pettiness and establish an interesting relationship."

"That's not the way I work," Vince said. "I go where the investigation leads me. It really doesn't make any difference whether you like me or I like you or we hate each other's guts. Facts are facts, evidence is evidence. That's the only way I know how to do it."

Castanga scowled. "What a pity. I had you figured for a more dimensional person than you're turning out to be. I presumed that an effective homicide detective would need to transcend that kind of linear reasoning. Certainly killers are multidimensional individuals. It would only seem reasonable that their pursuers be at least resilient enough to comprehend them . . . their inconsistent behavior patterns."

"You seem to know a lot about the way killers think," Vince said.

"Aha—back to basics." Castanga laughed. "You never tire of it, do you? Frankly, it amazes me that you can keep from exploding, stifling those growling abstractions that surface from time to time. Being prosaic *all* of the time must be an exhausting enterprise."

Vince shrugged. "I don't have a big problem with it. I sleep okay at night."

In a terrifying instant, the bottom fell out as the airplane began losing altitude, plummeting downward, propelling Vince upright in his seat, straining at the leather harnesses that held him.

"Jesus! What's going on?"

"Sorry. Must've brushed the control by mistake . . ." Castanga was grinning smugly as he straightened out the plane.

Vince sat silently, letting his stomach settle. "I think we oughta go back now, Ronald."

"Now you've gone and allowed yourself to be intimidated," Castanga said. "Does that mean the interrogation is over?"

"For now."

"But we'll get together again, won't we? I'd hate to think this little dance of ours was over, especially when it offers such infinite possibilities."

"You'll be hearing from me," Vince said.

"You're not afraid I'll seduce you . . . emancipate you from your comfortable cop's perceptions?"

"I'll take my chances." Vince watched Castanga out of the corner of his eye. "Just get us back on the ground where I have some room to operate. I'm a better dancer down there, know what I mean?"

Castanga smiled. "Where you and I will be on equal footing, right?"

"Wrong," Vince said evenly. "The street's my turf."

28

THE CALL CAME in over the car radio as he drove back to the precinct: a double homicide on the 2300 block of East Tremont Avenue. Vince hit the siren and pushed traffic out of the way until he'd reached the scene, double-parked behind a blue-and-white and clipped his identifying shield to the outside of his jacket.

"What went down?" he asked a uniformed officer who was diverting traffic from the area.

"Two killings . . . man and a woman, both shot. Bodies are upstairs on the third floor."

He entered the house, a faded yellow, four-story Victorian frame structure, made his way up two dingy flights of stairs past a file of dumbstruck friends and relatives of the victims, and encountered Boyle and Cuzak on the third-floor landing.

"It's that pimp Ball-Bearings and some white bimbo," Cuzak said. "Somebody just opened up on them when they were in the sack and blew them to pieces."

Vince walked past them into the bedroom where CSU was clearing the premises for prints and evidence. The victims were as they had been found: Ball-Bearings spread-eagled on his back and the woman sprawled across the foot of the bed, the upper portion of her body resting partly on the blood-splattered wooden floor. They were both bleeding profusely from multiple gunshot wounds that punctuated almost every exposed area of their naked bodies.

"How do you make it?" he asked a CSU detective standing near the door.

"Revenge killing . . . maybe a drug deal that went sour."

"Any leads?"

He shook his head. "Nah. Nobody knows nothing. The killer climbs two flights of stairs, empties about four clips of forty-five ammunition into them, and walks out without disturbing a soul. It's fuckin' amazing how they can do that."

"Could there have been more than one shooter?" Vince asked.

"Hard to say. I can tell you this, though: Whoever did this was pretty goddamn mad about something. It looks like they just kept shooting, reloading, turning the bodies over and pumping more rounds into them after they were dead. There are bloody prints all over the place." He pointed to the blood-stained sheets and walls. "Whoever did this didn't care much whether they left any clues."

Vince walked to the side of the bed and looked at the bodies. Part of the female's lower jaw had been torn away by gunfire, and there was a gaping hole where her left eye had been. "Any ID on the woman?" he asked.

"Driver's license is made out to a Delores Prestipino," the CSU detective answered.

"That figures."

"You know her?" Boyle asked from the doorway.

"No, but I know who she is." He walked out into the hallway and took Walt Cuzak aside. "Does this look like a professional job to you?"

"No way. No self-respecting pro would leave a sloppy mess like this. This's fucking disgusting."

"That's the way I see it," Vince said. "You know the dame is Tony Clams's wife."

"No shit?"

"She's been fucking this black turd for a couple of months now. Frankly, I'm surprised Vito waited so long before he went after them."

"You think he blew them away himself?"

"Sure, he had no choice."

Cuzak shook his head. "I don't get it. Tony Clams could've imported a gun to do the job. There was no reason for him to even get his hands dirty. Why would he want to set himself up this way?"

"He's a Sardinian," Vince said.

"What's that supposed to mean?"

"Too much to explain now . . ." Vince headed for the stairs. "Just call in an APB on Tony Clams and send a backup unit after me. I'll be at Colinini's Restaurant on Baxter Street in the Village."

Call it intuition. Vito was at his usual table when Vince arrived, seated behind a huge portion of clams oreganata that had barely been touched. He smiled a tired smile. "Sit down, Vincenzo. I been expecting you."

Vince sat across from him. "We found Delores and Ball Bearings, Vito. It's a real bad scene."

Vito poked at the clams absentmindedly. "You want some of these, Vince? I got no appetite tonight."

"Did you hear what I said Vito? We found their bodies."

Vito just nodded. "Tell me, Vincenzo; how long we known each other . . . fifteen, twenty years?"

"Yeah, something like that."

"You know, I always liked you, Vince . . . even when you were a pissy-assed rookie busting my runners in Brownsville I thought you were a good boy."

There was an awkward silence. "Why'd you do it, Vito?" Vince asked finally.

He shrugged. "You know why, Vince."

"I mean why did *you* do it? You could've had the job done for you. Christ, you musta left a hundred prints in that room."

Vito looked tired, his eyes puffy and bloodshot, the corners of his mouth drooping, his skin the color of old plaster. When he spoke the words seemed far away, as if he'd spoken them into a tape recorder years ago and was just now activating the machine. "Did you ever stop to think why it was you became a cop?" he asked.

"Sometimes. Why?"

"I mean, is it because you like long hours and short pay? Did you stick around all these years because you get a kick outa putting your life on the line every day? What's the real reason, my friend?"

Vince shrugged. "What're you getting at, Vito?"

"Just this. You and me are a lot more alike than you think. We can walk down any street in the neighborhood and guys step aside for us. They may not like us but they give us plenty of room, know what I mean?"

"Maybe."

"Look, I may not like that badge you carry but I respect it . . . and I respect you because you don't dishonor it. I'll blow you off the street if you get in the way of my business, but I won't ever shame you . . . or the badge. That's not the way men act."

"You know I'm gonna have to take you in, Vito."

Vito lifted a clam shell with his fingers and poured the contents into his mouth. He chewed the clam lustily and wiped his chin with a checkered napkin. "I know what I am, Vincent. I'm a fat man—a fat, funny man who didn't have no business being with a beautiful woman . . ." His voice was trembling. "But you know, to me she was a diamond. Every minute I was with her I couldn't believe my good luck. Vince, I swear to you, I'd walk in a joint with her and people would stop talking. I'm not shitting you. They'd just sit there and gawk at her like she was a movie star or something. Not bad for a fat man, eh, paisan?''

There was a commotion at the door and Vince turned to see two uniformed patrolmen walking toward the rear of the restaurant. He excused himself and met them halfway into the dining room.

''Need any help?'' one of them asked.

''No. Just wait outside for a couple of minutes. There won't be any trouble here.''

He returned to the table. ''You carrying a piece, Vito?''

''Nah.'' He held up his hands. ''Check if you like.''

''It's okay. Do you want to finish your dinner or come with me now?''

Vito shrugged. ''You gonna put the cuffs on me, Vince?''

''I don't think that's necessary. We'll just be a couple of old friends leaving together. How's that?''

He nodded. ''It's better this way, Vincenzo. If I gotta go down, I'm glad it's you who's gonna get the credit.''

Vince smiled. ''Don't give me that shit, Tony Clams. We both know your lawyer'll have you sprung in an hour. There's no way a guy as well connected as you are is going down for this one. Next year this time you'll be eating linguine with your goombahs back in Sardinia.''

Vito looked off into space. ''You know, she coulda had anything, Vince . . . anything I had was hers. If she needed younger guys we coulda worked something out. She didn't have to go and shame me that way . . .''

''It's time to go now, Vito.'' He handed his hat across the table.

''You know, a man ain't got much he can take with him; a little pride, a little respect. You take that away from a man and he's got nothing left, you know what I mean? The other ain't worth shit—money, cars, houses. What counts is the way guys look at you when you walk into a room; what they say about you after you walk out. That's the stuff that stays.

A man works all his life for that . . ." His voice trailed off.

"You ready now, Vito?"

"I gotta take a leak, Vince. Okay if I go to the can for a minute before we leave? I'm a little nervous. Don't worry, I ain't gonna run. No way a fat man like me could get through that little window in there anyway. You can even come in with me if you want to."

"It's okay, Vito. I'll be waiting here when you get back."

He watched as Vito shuffled slowly to the men's room, older now than Vince remembered him, and shrunken, his once massive bulk seeming lost in the blue silk suit hanging limply around him in untidy folds and drapes. Vince knew his reassurances to Vito had been a sham and he knew Vito understood that, too. Vito had violated a cardinal rule by committing the crime himself, by sticking his body in the firing line when it would have been a simple matter for him to get the job done by somebody else. Obviously revenge was more important than his personal safety. Obviously, this was the way Tony Clams wanted it to turn out.

Around him, the bustle of patrons at Colinini's continued to feast, oblivious to the small drama that was unfolding. The air was thick with the wafting aromas of garlic, wine, and cigarette smoke; muffled conversations and the cacophonous tinkle of silverware and glasses. There was a homely familiarity to it all, Vince thought, a fundamental sort of symmetry in the surroundings that made his job seem less oppressive. It was shattered in an instant by the penetrating crack of a single gunshot echoing from the men's room.

29

VITO'S FUNERAL WAS only a little less impressive than Billy's had been. The assembled dignitaries wore expensive silk suits and black homburgs rather than uniforms; hugged and kissed one another profusely on the stone slab steps of Saint Anthony's Church; conferred in hushed, reverential tones as they departed the ceremony and climbed into sleek, black limousines for the trip to the cemetery; followed by a convoy of flat-bed vehicles overflowing with floral sprays of every color and configuration.

Thomas "Ducks" Frattiani, Paulo "The Owl" Lacarrubba, Gaiatano "Chops" Bruno . . . Vince registered the names in his head as he sat across from the church in an unmarked car. There was a delegation from the Treppino family in Newark; one from the Felice family in Queens; visitors from as far away as Buffalo and Cincinnati; Carmine "The Pest" Renzullo and Augie "Little Leo" Brogno representing the Mauro family in Hoboken. All in all, it was a gathering that Tony Clams would have appreciated; a final demonstration of respect for a fallen comrade who had gone out bloodied but unbowed.

There were other uninvited vehicles in attendance: blue-and-whites to control the snarl of traffic, unmarked police vans filled with surveillance equipment that monitored the comings and goings of the guests, motor scooters recording the license plates of every car in the area; even a few FBI observers who watched the proceedings with the same keen interest that seasoned Kremlinologists would show the Moscow May Day Parade. Even his enemies rendered Tony Clams's remains the respect he craved in life. Even his most bitter rivals came to bring luster to his tarnished pride.

Vince watched the ornate mahogany coffin borne from the church by the pallbearers, followed by Vito's immediate family and a file of clergy led by Monsignor Luigi Bottonne, the so-called Mafia Priest. He knew he would miss Vito and felt no guilt over that. Vito had been an adversary worthy of respect, a man of integrity who played by the rules even when the rules served him poorly. His code was a centuries-old tradition of honor and courtliness that had become sadly out of date in a selfish world. He had been an almost gentle dinosaur in an age of piranha.

He stayed until the cortege moved slowly out of sight and turned the car toward the precinct. It was a good day to be buried, he thought, one of those leisurely spring mornings when the earth seemed to heave with bounty. The smell of life everywhere, penetrating the dull gray buildings and closeted alleyways, bringing texture to the flat, unyielding fabric of the streets, brilliance to the leaden overcast of sky. The earth would rest softly on Tony Clams, he thought. It would be kind.

There was a note on his desk when he got back to headquarters: *Call Dennis Sloan . . . 555-3300*. It was a New York number, probably his brokerage firm in downtown Manhattan. Vince felt a tugging resistance, a kind of inner dread that told him Sloan's message would be trouble; and trouble was the last thing he needed that morning. Reluctantly, he lifted the phone and dialed.

"Vincent, I was hoping we could get together for lunch." Sloan's voice was calm, unctuous.

"I'm a little tied up here. Is it something we could talk about on the phone?"

"I'm afraid not," Sloan said. "It would only be for an hour or so. I'd appreciate your taking the time."

"Okay . . . you have any place special in mind?"

"How about the Securities Club? The food's not so hot but they make a decent drink."

"What time?" Vince asked.

"It's just after eleven now. Do you think you can make it down here by noon?"

Vince checked his watch. "Sure. I'll meet you there."

"Good. I'll make a reservation." Sloan hung up the phone.

The Securities Club. It was probably one of the places Vince hated most in the world, running a close second or third behind Bloomingdale's and all of Fairfield County, Connecticut. It wasn't the food, which was certainly better than the frozen dinners that were his usual staple; or even the atmosphere, which boasted a bar that was cleaner and better stocked than the saloons he generally hung out in. He supposed it was what the Securities Club stood for, the cult of bonded, old-boy clannishness that made him feel like a turd in an orchid garden. It was the old class thing again, and it was him.

Tommy burst into the squad room, out of breath. "Guess what? We were right. There were tiny hemp fibers imbedded in the cement at the top of the bridge and they match fibers found in the trunk of Castanga's car."

Vince made a jubilant fist and punched the air. "We got him now, partner. Did Forensics find any fibers like that when they swept Hump Heaven?"

Tommy shrugged. "I dunno. I didn't think to ask. They would've checked that out, wouldn't they have?"

"Not necessarily. They were looking for blood and signs of violence when they were out there. They might've just dumped everything else into bags and forgotten about it. Check it out for me, willya?"

"You going someplace?" Tommy asked.

"Yeah, for a couple of hours. Call Quinlan over at the prosecutor's office and try to get an appointment for later this afternoon. I want him to see what we've got."

"You think he'll give us the go-ahead for an arrest?"

"No way. Not on a circumstantial case like this, but I want him to be involved. The way things are breaking it could happen any time now, and I want us all to be ready when it does. And get an okay from Boyle to place a loose trail on Charlene. I got a feeling Castanga's getting ready to make another move."

"Why not place her in protective custody?"

"Because I want her out in the open where he can see her. Just do what I say, bro. I'll be back around three." He grabbed his jacket and bounded down the stairs.

Sloan was waiting for him at the Securities Club bar, nursing a martini straight up. "Good to see you, Vincent." He offered his hand. "I was afraid you might not come."

Vince sat down next to him. "Why?"

"Well, after that unpleasantness last time . . ."

Vince shrugged. "What's done is done. What did you want to talk about?"

"Jessica, mostly . . ." Sloan stirred his drink with his forefinger. "She's drinking again."

"I thought she was doing great in that place."

Sloan shook his head. "The doctors said she was resistant to treatment, that she was filled with denial, whatever that is. At any rate she checked herself out of Silver Hills against medical advice last Tuesday and went on a bender. I got a call from the Meriden police yesterday. They were holding her in the drunk tank of the local jail. Apparently she became boisterous and caused some damage in one of their taverns."

"Where is she now?" Vince asked.

"Home, of course. I went to Meriden and personally bailed her out. She's under sedation right now."

Vince tried to visualize Jessy causing a disturbance in a saloon. "It just doesn't sound like her."

"I doubt you'd recognize a lot about her now," Sloan said. "She's just not the same person she was a few years ago. I think this whole business between you two had a more profound effect on her than any of us had suspected."

"You think she's drinking over the separation?" Vince asked.

Sloan nodded. "That, and a lot of other things. It hasn't been easy for her, you know."

"I don't think it's been easy for any of us."

"I don't mean just the separation. I think that's part of it but I believe the real trouble started a long time ago."

Vince eyed him suspiciously. "I'm not sure I get your drift."

"I think you do, Vincent." Sloan peered at him over the rim of his eyeglasses. "Surely you'll have to accept a measure of responsibility for everything that's happened. You can't just walk away from a situation that's largely your fault."

Vince felt himself becoming angry. "Let me get this straight. Are you trying to tell me it's my fault Jessy has a drinking problem?"

"No, it's not that simple. The people at the hospital told me that. But I do believe that most of the stress Jessica has had to live with these past years is a result of the life you forced on her—"

"Forced on her! I never forced anything on Jessy. We loved each other. We both had to make sacrifices."

Sloan paused. "Perhaps, but hers were greater."

"Who the hell are you to make that kind of judgment?" Vince asked.

"I'm her father and I've known her all of her life. I know

how she was raised and I know how much she's had to give up.''

Vince shook his head. "This is crazy, you know that? I'm sitting here listening to you tell me it's my fault Jessy got herself loaded and arrested up in Meriden. That's bullshit!''

"I'm not saying anything of the sort," Sloan corrected him. "If you'd been listening, you would have understood that I feel a large part of Jessica's problem comes from the pressures she's had to deal with since her marriage to you. That, for whatever reason, she was never able to make the adjustment from being a pampered debutante to being the wife of a cop. Don't get me wrong, Vincent; I'm not here to defend Jessica or to criticize you. I know my daughter, and I know that at her worst she can be selfish, irrational, and cruel; but she is my daughter, and if I don't look out for her, who will?''

"I did the best I knew how," Vince said lamely.

"I'm afraid it wasn't enough," Sloan said. "As much as the two of you may have loved one another, I don't think you stood a chance of erasing that social chasm that existed between you. Call it culture shock if you want—''

"That a medical opinion?" Vince asked.

"That's a father's opinion and I'm entitled to it, just as you are entitled to yours. Our bickering like this won't help Jessica, and that is my primary concern. I was hoping we might pull together.''

"In what way? I've already told you I'm not willing to sign away my rights or give away my daughters. What more can I say? If Jessy wants a divorce, I won't fight it. That's her choice to make.''

"I'm not asking for any of that," Sloan said. "It's become quite clear that Jessica wants to remain married to you. I belive she's prepared—even eager—to effect a reconciliation, provided certain changes take place.''

Vince felt his heartbeat quicken. "What changes?''

"We both know that you're eligible for retirement in a few months. What Jessica and I would like, would be for you to do it—retire; leave the police force once and for all."

"That's it?"

"It's the main thing," Sloan said. "Of course the two of you couldn't possibly live on your retirement benefits."

"I could get another job."

"Exactly. And I believe I can help you in that area."

"In what way?"

Sloan took a long drink of his martini. "I can offer you a job with my firm. I can provide employment that will allow both of you to live comfortably for the rest of your lives."

"What kind of job do you have in mind?" Vince asked.

"That would be pretty much up to you. Despite what you may think, I've always believed you had a good mind . . . if a somewhat undisciplined one. There are a number of positions that I'm sure you could easily handle."

Vince paused. "And if I refuse?"

Sloan turned icy. "If you choose to be selfish . . . if you refuse to live up to your responsibilities as a husband and father, I can only say that any sort of reconciliation would be out of the question."

"Is that Jessy's decision, or just yours?"

"We've spoken about it," Sloan said.

"And she agrees?"

"I wouldn't be here if she didn't."

Vince leaned across the bar. "Mind if I have a drink?"

Sloan signaled the bartender. "What's it going to be?"

"Irish whiskey . . . Jamieson's if they have it; and a draft beer chaser."

Sloan waited until Vince had downed the whiskey. "I don't expect an answer from you today, but I want you to consider my offer. You and Jessica have a very comfortable life ahead of you if you make the right decision."

"A comfortable life . . ." Vince said, almost to himself.

"Think about it."

Vince looked around the bar, out into the dining room beyond. The place was packed with businessmen drinking, eating, just relaxing, in three-piece suits and manicured contentment. For all the crowd, the place was strangely quiet . . . tailored and mirthless and tight-assed as a drum.

Everybody seemed comfortable.

30

DESPITE LUNCH WITH Sloan, it was turning out to be a red-letter day. A telephone call to Tommy confirmed that identical rope fibers had been found in the previous sweep of Hump Heaven, clinging to the bent shower fixture in the bathroom. Knowing that, it was simply a matter of putting the pieces together to reconstruct a plausible setting for the crime. Marguerita had been heavily drugged, bound with rope, and dragged to the bathroom, where her body had been hung from the shower fixture in the tub and systematically butchered like a side of beef in a slaughterhouse.

Still, there was the absence of any sign of struggle, the lack of witnesses, and the fact that Forensics had been unable to uncover traces of blood. That was the uncanny part. Bathtubs were historically a favorite location for murders, especially messy ones, because the killers believed they could wash the evidence of the crime down the drain with careful scrubbing. The facts proved otherwise. There were always minute traces of blood ground into the tiles and caulking of the tub that no amount of washing would remove. Almost invisible to the naked eye, these traces were usually enough to give trained pathologists a clear picture of the victim, age to shoe size.

That element was missing in this case and Vince knew it was a vital link in his investigation. He leaned against the glass-enclosed telephone booth in the lobby of the Securities Club and tried to form a mental image of the crime scene: Marguerita's limp form dangling from the metal shower fixture, knees bent behind her; the coarse fibers of the rope tightening around her neck, causing her to slowly strangle. It must have been an unbelievable scene of carnage, he thought. There was no way the killer could have prevented the blood from erupting out of Marguerita's massive wounds and splattering everything in the vicinity.

That might indicate the victim was strangled in the motel and butchered somewhere else. It would explain the lack of blood traces, but it wouldn't square with the facts. Shem Wiesen told him that asphyxiation was the cause of Marguerita's death and that the castration and mutilation happened *prior* to that. The murder and butchering had to have occurred in the tub; there was no other way it could have happened.

He found his car where he had left it, a parking ticket fluttering beneath his windshield wiper. Angrily he removed it and surveyed the area until he spotted a squat, black meter maid ticketing another unfortunate victim about a block away. "Didn't you see the 'DETECTIVE ON CALL' sign on my visor!" he shouted as he approached her.

She turned slowly and fixed him with a baleful stare. "You a police officer?"

He felt himself stiffen. Every impulse in his body told him to produce his shield and make this fat bitch regret the day she had ever fucked with Detective Vince Crowley.

"You a cop or you just wastin' my time, honky?" she demanded.

There was a one-in-a-thousand chance she was an Integrity Officer, one of the slimeballs from IAD that prowled the streets like barracuda, looking for dishonest cops. She looked stupid and slow but that could be a trick. Maybe others were watching; maybe she was wearing a wire. He felt his hand unclench from his wallet and fall limply to his side. "Forget it." He walked back to the car.

That was stupid, he thought as he pulled onto the FDR Drive and headed north. Asshole Boyle had everybody in the precinct so uptight they were seeing IAD shoo-flies behind every garbage can. The meter maid was just another of the hundreds of surly minority morons the city had hired to do a job even the dumbest cop could perform infinitely better. There was a moment when he considered going back to confront her but he decided against it. There would be somebody back at headquarters who could take care of the ticket.

The image of the bloodbath that must have occurred at the motel stayed with him as he drove through lower Manhattan. It was as if the absence of blood at the scene was a part of the bizarre game the murderer had been playing, another mind twister to test the competence of the police who were investigating him. He was smart enough to pull it off in a way that was obvious but clever enough to be easily overlooked; like the comic-strip drawings he remembered from childhood; the ones that asked, "Can you find ten things wrong with this picture?"

There were a lot of things wrong with the picture he constructed of Marguerita's murder, inconsistencies that troubled his trained investigator's mind. There was too much precision . . . an almost antiseptic quality that seemed to contradict the brutal nature of the crime, like the measured brushstrokes he'd seen in Castanga's paintings.

He visualized them, imprinting each gruesome canvas on his recollection of the murder scene. There were similarities but there were also differences; nothing really incriminating unless a morbid preoccupation with people's insides was a crime. Not enough to go on there, not yet. Castanga had lectured him about history . . . about how people down through the ages had been fascinated with grisly murders, how they'd even established museums to memorialize the more sensational crimes. He'd even been to the New York City Morgue. Research, he'd called it; a creative tool. He'd talked about the museum upstairs, the chronicle of gruesome crimes throughout the city's history . . .

The morgue museum . . . something clicked. A picture flashed into his mind like a lightning bolt and disappeared; too faint an image for him to form an impression. He tried to reconstruct it, like an aging lover reaching back into his memory for a scrap of sexual arousal, forcing out the extraneous impulses of his brain until the image reappeared and forced him bolt upright in his seat. Instinctively, he pressed the accelerator to the floor and sped toward the nearest exit.

The morgue museum was in the Medical Examiner's office at 520 First Avenue in downtown Manhattan. Vince passed the security guard in the lobby and took the elevator to the sixth floor where the grisly collection was housed in a square room of approximately thirty feet, divided into six rows of individual exhibits. He began at the rear of the room and worked his way slowly down aisle one. There was a collection of human skulls, bashed and broken in a variety of ways; along with clay and plaster replicas of the heads as they had appeared in death, their wounds faithfully reproduced in sculpture and paint. Vince studied them and found no connection.

Farther on, he encountered a display of severed human parts: fingers, hands, ears, pieces of innards; all carefully preserved in sealed jars of alcohol, the dates and manner of their removal, as well as the names of their previous owners, dutifully written on index cards pinned above them. Vince stopped at several jars containing, among other things, genitals: a severed breast, an entire vagina, a half dozen penises of varying lengths and hues. He closed his eyes and pictured Marguerita's body, the gaping wound where her genitals were supposed to be. None of the parts had ever been found . . . not even stuffed inside the body, as Shem Wiesen had suggested sometimes happened in cases like this. Was it possible they had been removed and left lying in plain sight, like a parlor game where the guests try to find a collection of articles hidden in open view? Where the hell do you hide a penis . . . a severed breast?

There was still no connection. If genitals were a part of the clue, they were too obscure to be what he was looking for now. He moved on to aisle two and a series of complete human skeletons and bodies manufactured of plastic, metal, and cloth; representations of famous suicides in the city's history. There were several hangings that Vince took particular care to scrutinize: a middle-aged female suspended from the ceiling, her head twisted grotesquely to one side in a final, wrenching death spasm; a male child, no more than ten or eleven, crumpled at the end of a knotted cord tied to a bed frame; a plaster mannequin opened at the neck to reveal the organic damage resulting from asphyxiation; a disembodied skull and upper spinal cord showing the results of a broken neck. He formed a mental image of Marguerita's body dangling from the shower fixture and superimposed it on each of the exhibits. Nothing fit.

Aisle three was devoted to weaponry, the instruments of murder accompanied by graphic depictions in two and three dimension of their use in famous crimes: pistols, rifles, automatic and semiautomatic machine guns, knives, hatchets, garden tools, garrotes, blunt instruments, curtain rods, bows and arrows, blow-guns, razors—even a garter belt and nylon stocking. It seemed that almost anything mankind had developed for his betterment and convenience had been used to rub somebody out at one time or another.

Nothing yet; not there or in the next aisle, an assemblage of photographs depicting bodies torn apart by explosives: pipe bombs, letter bombs, incendiaries, bombs placed in automobiles, buildings, public conveyances. As gruesome as the destruction was, it had a kind of random, impersonal feel to it; less savage than the one-on-one violence of some of the other exhibits, less sickening than the clinical disembowelment of Marguerita.

The exhibit continued with a display of vehicular homicides and deaths that were closely associated with automobiles. Vince found it curious that a great many people had taken the time over the years to catalog this strange collection. It was hard for him to visualize somebody placing the stuff of violence in alphabetical, chronological, and categorical order. Violence was violence, murder was murder; and while it could be an absorbing study, it seemed to Vince too energetic to be committed to dusty museum shelves. It was his business, and seeing it in displays and photographs simply left him cold. It was the sort of thing where you just had to be there.

Suddenly it was in front of him: a nine-by-twelve black-and-white photograph set in a cheap wooden frame, the upper right-hand portion bleached to a pale amber from the effects of moisture seeping through the cracked glass cover. The faded index card above the picture listed the particulars: MARY FRANCES MAHONEY, MURDERED JULY 23, 1957, ASPHYXIATED BY HANGING AND EVISCERATED BY KILLER OR KILLERS UNKNOWN.

Vince stared at the photo and felt his skin tingling. The body, or what was left of it, was suspended by the neck from a wall shower fixture, exactly as Marguerita had been. It was tightly wrapped in what appeared to be a kind of plastic cloth covering the entire body except for the head and a portion of the middle torso which had been carved open, allowing Mary Frances Mahoney's intestines to spill out onto another plastic cloth shrouding the tub below. The effect was similar to a giant baked potato wrapped in foil and sliced open to reveal its overflowing bounty.

The plastic drop cloths spread around the scene were placed in such a way that it was impossible for blood and excreted gore to stain the tile or woodwork. The killer had been thorough and fastidious, planning every detail careful-ly to minimize the mess, right down to the deliberate, meandering incision in the victim's lower abdomen . . . surgically inflicted, same as Marguerita's had been.

Things were beginning to make sense—the murder, the mutilation, the disposal of the body. He'd been unable to locate blood at the crime scene because it had all been disposed of with the drop cloths, along with Marguerita's butchered body, trussed up like a Smithfield ham in a clean outer cloth and transported to the park where it could be easily lowered from the top of the bridge into the water.

The drop cloths! Castanga's East Hampton studio had been filled with plastic drop cloths, spattered and smeared with every color imaginable. It would be entirely in character for Castanga to have hung the bloodied cloths around the place, knowing the police would be walking all over them, unable to distinguish between blood and paint stains, not knowing the evidence they needed was trampled beneath their feet. He must've gotten a big kick out of that.

Vince stood before the photograph for a few more seconds, fixing the details in his mind before leaving. He took the elevator back to the lobby floor, approached the guard at the desk, and flashed his identification. "Where do I get authorization to remove a picture from the museum upstairs?"

"What for?" the guard asked.

"Evidence in a homicide investigation."

He shrugged. "I dunno. Nobody ever asked that question before."

"Well, why don't you call your supervisor and find out?"

"Why not?" The guard reached for the telephone on his desk.

Vince found a pay phone at the other end of the lobby and dialed Tommy at the precinct. "I think we got Castanga nailed. We got him screwed, blued, and tattooed."

"How's that?"

"Too much to explain now. Did you get an appointment with Quinlan?"

"Sixteen hundred hours today, partner. You want me to be there?"

"You bet your ass, bro. This is too good to keep to myself."

"Meet you there."

"Hold it." Vince stopped him before he hung up. "Who's handling parking tickets up there these days?"

31

FIRST ASSISTANT BRONX County DA Tom Quinlan was lean, rock jawed, and tough, a faint wisp of salt and pepper shading at his temples the only hint that he was forty-seven years old and no longer the New York City Welterweight Golden Gloves boxing champion he had been in 1957. When he laughed, which was often, his flat Irish face seemed to fold in on itself in creases like an aging concertina, with a full set of even, white teeth that flashed from jawbone to jawbone. When he was serious, which was not all that often, the tiny creases in his forehead and around his mouth deepened, the glint in his blue eyes misted over with concern. Today he was serious.

"I've gotta tell you that what you're giving me is all circumstantial," he said, fingering Miguel Ramos's manila file jacket on his desk. "It just isn't enough."

"I know it's circumstantial, but it's good circumstantial," Vince protested. "I've seen you issue warrants on a helluva lot less than this."

"Not for some down-and-out drag queen," Quinlan said.

"Forget drag queen . . . forget everything except there's a murderer out there running loose and he's gonna do it again. I got him leaving the bar with the victim a couple of hours before she's killed. I got him at the motel with her. I got matching rope fibers from Castanga's car, the motel, and the bridge where the body was dumped. I got photographic evidence that the suspect himself leads me to, that shows me exactly how he committed the crime, and I guarantee you if you get me a warrant to search his studio I'll find the drop cloths he used to wrap the victim's body . . . covered with the victim's blood.

"Sure, today he's just slicing up transsexuals, but I know this guy, and he doesn't seem like the kind who stays excited about any one thing for a long time. Tomorrow he might decide it'd be more fun to murder cops or DAs or their families . . . who the hell knows?"

Quinlan smiled for the first time. "Jeezus, Crowley. You got more shit than a Christmas goose, you know that? You know what you're asking me to do? I can't go around issuing licenses for cops to break in on citizens without good cause. Get me an eyewitness, for chrissake. You say this Castanga is playing games with you; trick him into a confession. Short of that, there's nothing here I can take into court."

Vince moaned. "If you'd get me a fucking warrant, I could give you all the evidence you want. Look . . ." He leafed through the manila jacket and produced a coroner's form, showing the exact position of the incision in Marguerita's abdomen, drawn in red felt-tip marker on a black-and-white line representation of a male human body. He placed the form alongside the picture he'd taken from the museum. "Tell me those wounds aren't identical."

Quinlan shrugged. "So they're identical. So what?"

"So you give me the authorization to go in there and nail the son of a bitch."

"I wish it was that easy." Quinlan got up from his desk and walked to his office window overlooking the Grand Concourse. "Come on Vince, you've been around long enough to know how these things work. This guy

Castanga's big time . . . a lotta money, a lotta connections. I let you trample all over his civil rights and he's got a barrage of high-priced lawyers hanging my ass out to dry.''

"I'm not talking about trampling over anything. All I want is a couple of minutes inside with a forensics team to determine whether those plastic cloths are covered with Marguerita's blood, that's all.''

Quinlan leaned back against the windowsill. ''Why not just ask him for the drop cloths? Maybe he'll let you have them.''

"You gotta be kidding.''

"Why not? You said yourself he likes to do the unpredictable.''

"That's not unpredictable, that's stupid,'' Vince said. ''I tell you Tom, I'm so goddamn certain we'll find blood on those cloths I can taste it. Believe me brother, this one's gonna be good for both of us.''

"Proof,'' Quinlan wailed. ''Where's the proof?''

Vince looked across the room at Tommy, who shrugged helplessly. ''Look . . . I'm not the kind of guy who calls in old markers, but I need this one, Tom. Now you remember the Sabbitini case a couple of years ago? Remember it was my testimony that let you convict that scumbucket?''

Quinlan nodded. ''Sure, you did your civic duty as a good cop and a good citizen. You told the truth.''

Vince just stared at him.

"Come on, Crowley, you know that bastard was guilty as hell.''

"Evidence was pretty circumstantial as I recall.''

"You're not telling me you lied up there, are you?''

Vince remained impassive. ''If I remember right, you got a nice promotion out of that one.''

Quinlan walked to his desk, lifted the manila file folder, and leafed absently through the pages. Finally, he looked at Vince and grinned. ''You know, your ass sucks grass, Crowley. *You* know you're humping me around, *I* know you're humping me around, Tommy over there knows a good hump job when he sees one . . . shit, I'm not even being kissed, so how come I don't mind it?''

"So you'll get me a warrant?''

"It must be old age," Quinlan said. "Hardening of the arteries to the brain or something. I'm throwing my whole goddamn career right down the toilet.''

"You kidding?'' Vince ran a playful hand through Quinlan's hair. "They'll make you the fucking mayor for this one.''

"I'll end up back in night court," Quinlan moaned.

"Love ya.'' Vince grabbed Tommy by the arm and exited the DA's office.

Obtaining the search warrant and rounding up a forensics team took almost two hours. That, plus another hour of driving through heavy rush-hour traffic, got them to Castanga's East Hampton studio shortly after seven. It was still light enough to see the house clearly, silhouetted against the trailing sun of daylight saving time, which had begun the day before. Vince pulled the car onto the sandy shoulder of the road and stepped out, followed by the team from the forensics van, a CSU car, and two plainclothes officers in a separate vehicle. They crossed the thirty yards of barren space that lay between the house and the road and knocked loudly at the door.

"Doesn't seem to be anybody home," Tommy said after a wait of several minutes.

Vince tried the door and found it locked. "Check around back and see if there's an open door," he directed the plainclothes officers. "Stay there if it's locked. If he's inside I don't want him running.''

The house was securely locked all around. Vince looked at Tommy, shrugged, and smashed his left elbow through one of the bottom glass panes in the front door. He reached through the jagged opening, released the latch, and pushed the door inward. "Whaddaya know, it was open all along.''

Inside, the pervading smell of turpentine and paint only seemed to magnify the emptiness. Everything was as it had been: tubes, bottles, and cans of paint strewn casually about; brushes, piled canvases . . . the spattered drop cloths. Vince pointed to a closed door at the rear of the house and Tommy approached it silently. He drew his revolver, stood to one side, and carefully turned the door handle. "Nothing here," he said after a careful inspection.

Vince walked the periphery of the room, peering behind stacked canvases and metal cabinets until he was satisfied the place was empty. "Okay. Let's get the forensics guys in here to have a look at that plastic."

The team worked quickly and efficiently, combing the house for weapons, traces of rope, and signs of violence. A detective from Latent dusted exposed surfaces for prints while a CSU officer photographed the premises with a 35-millimeter camera. The drop cloths were numbered alphabetically and as samples were scraped from them or portions cut away, they were systematically recorded on a grid by one of the forensics detectives. Anything that looked like it might be dried blood was collected, placed in sealed plastic bags, and cataloged.

"How's it look?" Vince asked Detective Bill Reid, head of the unit.

He shrugged. "Could be blood. I'll know for sure when we get it back to the lab."

"What's your gut feeling?" Vince pressed.

"If I had to make a decision right this minute? I'd say we got a helluva lot of blood here . . . I'm ninety-nine percent sure of that."

Tommy emerged from the adjoining bedroom with a small cardboard box. "Take a look at this. Maybe one of these is the murder weapon."

The box contained a variety of knives, mostly flat tipped, all scraped clean and looking relatively new. "What do you make of it?'' Vince asked Bill Reid.

He examined them one by one. "They look like palette knives to me, the kind artists use to smear paint on their canvases; probably not sharp enough to do the kind of damage we're looking for." He handed the box to another member of the team. "We'll take 'em along anyway. You never know what'll turn up in analysis."

There was an ashtray filled with cigarette butts that was emptied intact into a separate plastic bag for a saliva comparison with the butt found at the scene of the crime. None of the butts was a Merit, Vince noted, but that wasn't particularly relevant. It was his experience that people these days were changing their cigarette brands as often as they changed their socks. It was a subtle form of relieving the guilt they felt for smoking in the first place, he thought. If they weren't locked into any one particular brand, they weren't really hooked. He lit an unfiltered Camel and inhaled deeply. It was the only brand he'd smoked since high school.

"What happens now?" Tommy asked, as the forensics team packed their gear and began to leave. "Assuming all this stuff checks out."

"We bring Castanga in for questioning."

Tommy looked around the empty room. "Suppose he's split for good?"

"Not likely. My guess is that he doesn't think he's pushed us far enough yet. He's still having fun with this thing."

"Do we wait here for him to come back?"

"No. I want him to have some time alone . . . to know we've been here and try to figure out how much we found."

Tommy grinned. "Too bad we can't leave one of those cards the Electrolux salesmen put in the mailbox: 'Sorry I missed you this time around but I'll drop by next time I'm in the neighborhood.' "

"He'll know we've been here," Vince said.

"We gonna put the place under surveillance?" Tommy asked.

Vince walked to the open door and observed the surrounding landscape, flat and treeless, broken only by an occasional dune rising out of the horizon. "You tell me where I'm gonna hide a surveillance vehicle out there."

Tommy shrugged. "How about a chopper?"

"You've been watching too many Clint Eastwood movies."

Tommy threw his hands in the air. "Okay . . . just don't blame me if this guy takes off on you."

"He won't," Vince said emphatically. "He'll realize what we've got and he'll try to cut his losses. My guess is, he'll probably throw his attorney at us next."

"I hope you're right." Tommy gathered up his gear and followed Vince out to the car. "Hey, I been meaning to ask you," he said, once they were underway. "That case you mentioned to Tom Quinlan; the one where your testimony sent the guy up . . ."

"The Sabbitini case."

"Yeah, Sabbitini. You didn't really lie on the stand, did you?"

Vince shot a cynical glance across the front seat of the car. "Sabbitini was scum. He wiped out an entire family—grandmother, wife, an eleven-year-old boy, and a baby girl sixteen months old—over a drug deal that went bad. The son of a bitch deserved a lot more than he got."

"Yeah, but did you lie on the stand?" Tommy persisted.

There was a long pause. "Cops don't lie," he said finally.

POLICE DEPARTMENT
CITY OF NEW YORK

FROM: COMMANDING OFFICER 37TH PRECINCT DETECTIVE
      UNIT
TO: POLICE JURISDICTION CONCERNED
SUBJ: REQUEST FOR FIELD INFORMATION

1. ATTACHED IS A PHOTOGRAPH OF A SUSPECT IN A
   HOMICIDE BEING INVESTIGATED BY THIS COMMAND.

2. IT IS REQUESTED THAT ANY FIELD INFORMATION POS-
   SESSED BY YOU RE: THE POSSIBLE LOCATION OF THIS
   INDIVIDUAL BE FORWARDED TO THIS COMMAND.

   DO NOT APPREHEND OR APPROACH THIS INDIVIDUAL!!!

3. DESCRIPTION: MALE, WHITE, 5 FT. 9 IN., 28 YRS.,
   MEDIUM BUILD, DARK BROWN HAIR, BROWN/GREEN
   EYES, NO APPARENT SCARS OR PHYSICAL DEFORMITIES.

SUBJECT MAY DRIVE A LATE-MODEL MERCEDES (BLACK OR DARK BLUE) WITH LICENSE PLATE J3666S.

4. SUBJECT IS SOUGHT FOR QUESTIONING IN THE HOMICIDE OF A TRANSSEXUAL MALE WHO WAS CASTRATED AND DUMPED INTO THE BRONX RIVER.

5. MATTER IS CARRIED UNDER 61 #9892, CASE #1735, DET. V. CROWLEY AND T. IPPOLLITO ASSIGNED.

6. KINDLY TELEPHONE ANY PERTINENT INFORMATION TO THE 37TH PDU AT 212-555-1011, 12, OR 14.

LT. ARTHUR M. BOYLE, COMMANDER

Vince scanned the sheet and Castanga's accompanying photo and slipped them under his bronze PBA shield paperweight, on top of a pile of neglected paperwork he'd allowed to accumulate for several years. It had been almost a week since they had swept the East Hampton studio and so far Castanga had failed to reappear. Questioning his friends and checking his favorite haunts had turned up nothing. The bulletin was standard procedure, but Vince didn't expect it to produce any results. He was convinced that Castanga was holed up somewhere in the area and that he would surface when it suited his purposes, not before. In the meantime there was nothing to do but wait.

It was close to quitting time on the four-to-twelve shift; a slow night with little to do but brush up on reports, drink coffee, watch TV, and shoot the shit. Pete Yorio was back after an eight-week terminal leave, cynical as ever, busting everybody's chops like he never went away. He'd decided to stay on the force rather than retire after twenty years of service, and that buoyed Vince's spirits. Pete was one of the few old-timers left at the Thirty-seventh, one of the guys who'd been there with him at the beginning. They shared a lot of history. If he'd quit, they would have thrown him a beer brawl; but as it was, nobody had said a word about his decision to stay. He'd just shown up one day ready to work. Nobody made a big deal out of that.

He was sitting at his desk at the far north end of the squad room giving Tommy the needle, winking broadly at Vince when Tommy took the bait. "Hey, when are you gonna get a haircut?" he yelled across the room. "You rookies are all the same . . . look like a buncha faggots instead of police officers."

Tommy pretended to be watching television.

"And all that shit you guys wear—gold chains and earrings. Earrings . . . Jesus! Hey Vince, what would they have done to us if they caught us wearing earrings at the old seven-three?"

Vince grinned.

"They woulda hung our asses from the duty roster, that's what they woulda done. Man, today anything goes: hippies, homos, midget cops, minority cops, women cops . . . you can give me the old days any time."

"Hey man, you can have 'em," Tommy shot back. "You want the old days, you go down to any one of those mick saloons in Castle Hill and you'll find all the old-timers sitting at the bar with spongy noses and fried livers crying in their beers about how terrific everything used to be. Go on, shithead. That's where veterans like you belong."

Yorio grinned. "Hey, dago, I don't need a bunch of old drunks to tell me the way it was. Vince here remembers, don't you Vince? Remember Brownsville? Remember Big Mama Lou?"

"Jeez!" Vince put his head in his hands.

"You shoulda seen my partner Vince here." Yorio laughed. "One of the truly great exploits in the history of the police department."

"Mama Lou . . ." Vince shook his head. "I'd almost forgotten about her."

"How could you forget Big Mama Lou? It was your one chance to be a hero and you blew it. You probably woulda been an inspector today if it wasn't for Mama Lou."

"What happened?" Tommy asked.

Yorio leaned back in his chair and crossed his legs. "Well, Vince and me were on foot post in the old seven-three back in sixty-four. Now there's this big black bimbo named Mama Lou running whores out of a house on our beat . . . checks in at about three-fifty, three seventy-five pounds, wouldn't you say, Vince?"

"More like four hundred."

"Four hundred pounds," Yorio went on. "Ass as big as a beer wagon and mean as a snake . . . I tell you, this was one mean bitch. There wasn't nobody in that neighborhood about to mess around with old Mama Lou and that includes yours truly and PO Vince Crowley. Well, she's got this boyfriend named Candlestick who can't weigh in at more than a hundred twenty-five pounds soaking wet . . ." He removed a wrinkled handkerchief from his hip pocket and wiped his eyes, which were beginning to tear.

"Now they run a good house," he went on. "Candlestick out on the street drumming up trade and Big Mama Lou inside taking care of the girls . . . busting heads if anybody tries any rough stuff. Everybody's happy. The house is making money, the girls are making money, the johns are fucking their brains out. It's an ideal situation until Mama Lou hears from the grapevine that little Candlestick is sampling the merchandise and whacks him upside his black head one night. Well, Candlestick, he just loses it, pulls a knife on Mama Lou and cuts her in the arm. She grabs him, throws him on the ground like a dirty wash, and sits down on his face . . . I mean smack on the poor bastard's nose."

Now Vince and Tommy were both laughing. Yorio was on his feet, embellishing the story with grunts and grimaces; prancing around the squad room in a fit of laughter. "So the girls run out on the sidewalk and start hollering *'Murder! . . . She's killing him!'* Me and Vince hear all the commotion and haul our asses in there where she's still sitting on Candlestick's face. By the time we get there, she's already been sitting on him maybe fifteen, twenty minutes, and she ain't moving for nobody. All the whores are hooting and hollering and me and Vince are pulling and tugging and cursing like a son of a bitch and Big Mama Lou's just sitting there with her arms folded like a goddam buddha or something . . ." He wiped his eyes again.

"Anyway, I don't know how we did it, but we finally got her offa him and by that time he's already purple and smelling like a ten-day-old fluke. *'Do something!'* the whores are screaming. *'Give him mouth-to-mouth . . .'* Well, I look at Vince and he looks at me and we both take a whiff . . . I mean, it was *bad* brother, old Mama Lou ain't seen the inside of a bathtub since V-E Day. And we both crack up . . . we fucking fall on the floor laughing. It's crazy; everybody's screaming their lungs off, Big Mama Lou's sitting on the floor and she can't get up if she wants to, old Candlestick is stiff as a board, and we can't stop laughing. It was really embarrassing, man."

There was a pause. "So what happened to Candlestick?" Tommy asked.

"He died."

"That's fucking sick," Tommy said.

"I guess so." Yorio went back to his desk and busied himself with paperwork.

"Is he shitting me?" Tommy asked Vince.

"Pete's an upstanding police officer. He wouldn't lie."

"It happened just the way I told it," Yorio said. "On my old man's grave."

"That's twisted, man." Tommy returned to the TV.

Vince took his empty mug to the coffee machine and filled it for about the tenth time that evening. He stopped in front of the television set and watched the anchorman from Channel Seven news recounting the day's miseries: a family of five killed in a fire in Newark; a twelve-year-old murdered for his radio in Bedford-Stuyvesant; an IRT subway derailment that sent thirty people to the hospital . . . There was a visual of an automobile being lifted from a body of murky water by a crane. Vince noticed the CSU detectives on the scene, their orange jumpsuits emblazoned with the words CRIME SCENE written across their backs. "Get a load of these hot dogs," he said. "They pull out the glad rags when they know they're gonna be on camera."

"Hey, shut up!" Tommy interrupted him. "Listen to this."

Vince turned his attention to the audio voice-over: ". . . and Staten Island police are proceeding on the theory that they may have uncovered an organized-crime graveyard . . ." The visual shifted to a canvas-wrapped body being removed from the trunk of the car. "The one body police have been able to identify so far is that of Noah Weinberg, former manager of the Wellington Armored Car Company, which was robbed of nearly six million dollars last month . . ."

"Hey, remember him?" Tommy said.

"Yeah." Vince returned to his desk and began chewing unenthusiastically on a slice of cold pizza. "A real sneaky-looking guy as I recall."

"Had piggy little eyes," Tommy said.

The telephone rang and Vince lifted the receiver. "Crowley!"

"Hello, Crowley. How're you doing?"

Vince sat bolt upright. "Is that you, Ronald?"

"Sure is. I thought I'd call and congratulate you on

figuring out about the drop cloths . . . pretty nifty piece of detective work there. I guess I underestimated you on that one.''

"Can you hold on a minute, Ronald? I got a call on the other line. Let me get rid of them and I'll be right back to you. Just stay where you are." He punched the HOLD button and yelled across the room to Tommy, "It's Castanga! Start a tape next door and get this recorded. And tell switchboard to run a trace, pronto!"

He waited a few seconds and released the button. "I'm back, Ronald. Where are you calling from?"

"You don't seriously expect me to answer that, do you? I may be plucky but I'm not stupid."

"You're in a lot of trouble, Ronald," Vince said. "Everything checked out. Those plastic sheets were covered with Marguerita's blood. We got the rope you used to tie her up with—"

"You keep calling that abomination 'her.' '' Castanga interrupted him. "Miguel Ramos was a male."

"Okay, Ronald . . ." Vince tried to sound soothing. "I think I understand how you feel."

Castanga laughed bitterly. "Don't patronize me, Crowley! You haven't the vaguest idea how I feel. Your plodding cop's instincts could never rise that high."

"So why not come in and we'll talk about it?"

"You're really something, you know that?" Castanga snarled. "You never run out of tired cop stratagems, do you? When are you going to realize you're dealing with a different sort of individual here?"

Vince kept his voice even. "Look, Ronald. There's nothing here that you and me can't work out between us. Tell me what you want and we'll meet someplace and talk about it. I'm sure you have things you want to say and I'm willing to listen. I'm a reasonable guy, Ronald. How about it?"

There was silence on the other end. "Anything I might say would elude you," Castanga said finally. "You couldn't possibly grasp the creative implications of what I'm doing."

"Try me," Vince said.

"You can't see . . . nobody could understand the power . . . the soaring feeling of artistic accomplishment I can achieve in one explosive moment of ultimate creation. It's the only true creation on earth, you know . . . It erupts into being at the precise moment it dies. I can't describe the joy it gives."

Vince shrugged helplessly at Yorio, who was listening in on his extension. "I think I understand some of what you're saying, Ronald. It's kinda like sex, isn't it?"

"Christ no!" Castanga exploded. "That's what I mean. Your emotional grasp is so limited you equate every positive feeling with sex. God, Crowley; talking to you is like talking to a head of lettuce."

"I hear you . . ."

Castanga moaned. "You're incredible, Crowley. I know you're just trying to keep me on the line long enough to trace this call. I'll save you the trouble. I'm at the PATH bus terminal, for all the good it'll do you. I'll be long gone by the time you get here."

"Now, listen to me, Ronald."

"Why? You have nothing to say that would interest me in the least, Crowley. I hope you'll have expanded your intellectual horizons by the next time we talk. This is becoming an awful bore." The phone went dead.

"You get any of that?" he yelled to Tommy in the next room.

"Every deranged word."

"How about the trace?"

"I don't think we had him on long enough."

Vince grabbed his jacket. "Let's get down to the PATH

terminal anyway. Maybe we can scare up somebody who saw him leave.''

''You think he was really calling from there?''

''Why not? It makes the game more exciting for him.''

Tommy shook his head. ''Give me a good old-fashioned ice-pick murder any day. All this intellectual sparring is giving me a headache.''

33

May 5

Dear Jessy,

   I had lunch with your father last week and he told me about your trouble. I'm sorry, I really am. I'm sorry I wasn't there for you, not just in Meriden but all along the line when you needed help. I don't know whether I could have changed anything but I wish I'd made a better effort. I wish there was something I could have done a long time ago that could wipe out the last couple of years altogether. I wish you and I had stayed the way we once were.

   I've thought about this as much as I've ever thought about anything in my life, Jess, and I can't honestly tell you I've figured anything out. I guess I always loved you as much for the things I couldn't understand about you as I did for the things that made sense. There was always a part of you that remained a mystery to me and in a way that made it exciting. Maybe that's the part of you that got away from me. Maybe that's the part you lost yourself.

   The fact is, it kills me to think of you in a drunk tank. I form a picture of it in my mind and I almost go berserk. It kills me to think of you being hurt or humiliated in any way and if I thought I could make you better by taking the blame for your problem I'd do it. I swear I would. But I've searched inside of me and I know I tried to be the best husband I could . . . the best man I knew how to be. I don't know any other way of putting that.

Your father seems to think that none of this would have happened if you hadn't married a cop . . . that it all can be set straight if I leave the force and start a different life . . . that somehow or other your drinking and your recovery are all in my hands. Jessy, I don't think I ever had that kind of power and I'm sure I never will.

I'm a cop and I know I've spent a good part of my life apologizing for that . . . as if being a cop was settling somehow, being less than I was capable of being. A lot of us do that. Well, I've got to tell you Jessy; I've thought about doing something else, about being somebody else, and it just makes my blood run cold. I've seen lawyers and insurance salesmen and stockbrokers and I know I couldn't make you happy by being one of them. I'd be too miserable myself to care much about you or anybody else.

I can't honestly tell you what it is about being on the force that works for me. I only know that when I'm here, when I'm doing the things I've learned how to do, I feel strong. I feel like a man. When I'm away from it I can feel that strength slipping away from me. It's that simple. I'm doing what I want to do with my life and I'm sorry you were never able to accept that. I'll have twenty years in a few months, and the way things look today, I'll probably sign on for another tour. I can't look very far beyond that.

Take care of yourself, Jessy, and watch over my girls for me.

Get well my darling,

Vince

He addressed the envelope and placed it in his inside jacket pocket. Across the room, Walt Cuzak was leafing gloomily through a magazine he'd pirated from Boyle's wastebasket. "You want some coffee?" Vince asked, heading for the machine.

"Nah." Cuzak shook his head vigorously. "That shit'll kill you."

Vince poured himself a mugful and returned to his desk. "What's that you're reading?"

"*Prevention* Magazine," Cuzak answered. "It tells you how you can keep from getting sick in the first place."

"Doesn't seem to do much for Boyle."

"Boyle's an asshole. This stuff'll really work if you do it right. It's all what you eat, man. Most of the shit we put in our bodies would kill an orangutan."

Vince took a swig of the bitter coffee and checked his watch: 9:37. Almost an hour and a half to go. So much of it was just sitting around waiting for something to happen. If the guys who wrote the novels and TV shows knew what it was really like they'd have a tough time making police work look so glamorous.

"Hi there, stranger." It was Jan, standing in the doorway with a box of Kentucky Fried Chicken tucked under her arm. "I thought you might be hungry."

Vince was surprised, and very glad to see her. "What're you doing in this neighborhood?" He walked to the door and kissed her lightly on the lips.

"You know; if the mountain won't come to Muhammad . . ." She handed him the chicken.

"I'm glad to see you, I really am." He led her to the desk and pulled up a chair for her. "I would have called but we're into this homicide—"

"Forget it," she interrupted. "I called last week and they told me about your partner Billy. I'm very sorry."

"Me too," he said. "Jan Webster, meet Walt Cuzak."

He pointed to the other end of the room. "Walt's our resident health nut. Want some of the colonel's best, Walt?"

"No way, brother." Cuzak walked to the desk and shook Jan's hand. "You wouldn't happen to have any carob peanuts in that box, would you?"

Jan laughed. "I'm afraid not, but join us anyway, please."

"You saved my life," Vince said, opening the box. "I haven't eaten since breakfast."

Cuzak shuddered as Vince bit into a crusty brown drumstick. "You're gonna die, brother . . ." He turned to Jan. "No offense intended."

She smiled. "None taken. What's wrong with Kentucky Fried?"

"It tastes good," Vince broke in. "Walt thinks food's gotta taste like cardboard to be healthy."

"Hey man, that's not true," Cuzak protested. "Did you ever taste Dutch apple yogurt? It's delicious."

Vince made a face and wiped his chin with a paper napkin.

"Give me Colonel Sanders anytime. I'll die with a smile on my face."

"It does smell awful good," Cuzak was wavering.

"Go on. One piece won't kill you," Jan said.

He eyed the open box and bit his lip. "Maybe just a wing." He rooted around in the chicken until he found the smallest piece and bit into it tentatively.

"See? You didn't die," Vince said.

Cuzak finished the wing and had another, then a fat, juicy breast and a drumstick. By the time he was finished, the box was empty and he'd risen out of his bad mood. "How'd you two get together?" he asked.

"Vince was investigating a homicide," Jan said. "He came to question my boss."

Cuzak shook his head thoughtfully. "It happened just like that, huh? Jeez, I wish it was that easy for me."

"You're looking in the wrong places," Vince said.

"Nah, the health club's a good place. A lot better than the bars."

Vince winked at Jan. "You gotta be kidding. The women in that place would rather go home and look at themselves in a mirror than look at someone else."

Cuzak ran a finger across the bottom of the box and licked the residue of fried batter. "Maybe you're right. The last gal I took out to dinner from there started doing stretch exercises in the middle of the restaurant. It was embarrassing as hell."

Vince took Jan by the elbow. "Come on, I'll show you around the place." He led her into the robbery room, then downstairs through the lobby, into the turnout room, lockers, and administrative department.

"That's it." He shrugged at the end of the tour. "Not exactly 'Hill Street Blues,' is it?"

"It's great." Jan looked at her wristwatch. "I really can't stay, but I wanted to thank you for the roses. I was touched."

Vince felt himself blushing. "I had to do something . . ."

She laughed. "Never apologize for sending a girl flowers. We appreciate little things like that."

"I meant what I said on the card."

"I know you did." She squeezed his hand and accompanied him outside to where her car was parked. "Call me?" she asked.

"Sure." He kissed her softly on the lips. "Tomorrow or the day after."

He watched her car disappear over the crest of the hill and turned toward the station. It was nice, he thought, to be involved again; even if the involvement was weighted down

with uncertainties. That was his fault, he knew, and it was
up to him to change. It was time for him to begin expanding
his horizons . . . to give the rest of the world a chance and
start building his life again.

Jessy's letter weighed heavily in his pocket.

34

FIVE FORTY-SEVEN A.M.; boredom was the enemy. Two hours, thirteen minutes till quitting time and no way to make the time pass any faster. Night tours were enjoyable out on the street, probably Vince's favorite duty, but landing the borough watch from midnight to eight A.M. on a slow night was as close to dying as he wanted to come. The silence was oppressive, interrupted by spells of penetrating awareness that bounced familiar objects in and out of his consciousness like Ping-Pong balls: the faded cinderblock walls, the lockup, the file of squat, metal desks overflowing with reams of unattended paperwork, threads of an old movie flipping lazily across the face of a television screen that had lost its vertical hold, layers of yellowing bulletins obscuring one another on the walls, a clock with hands that wouldn't move . . .

Walt Cuzak was nodding at his desk, leaving Vince alone with his thoughts: Jan, and the warmth he'd felt earlier that evening. Jessy, and the mute realization that it was really coming to an end. The night shift provided too much time for reflection and too much reflection was the kiss of death for cops. There were too many unresolved conflicts

. . . too many skeletons and hobgoblins pressing in on their memories, searing their souls. The chaos of the job was their only relief, the one potent weapon they possessed that could muffle the reality. It didn't exactly offer peace of mind but it kept most of them from morbid distraction.

The metallic squawk of the telephone was a welcome relief.

"Hello, Crowley, I've been thinking about you." Castanga's voice was distant, unemotional.

"Ronald?"

A hoarse laugh. "Who else would be thinking about you at this time of night?"

Vince signaled for Walt to start a trace. "I dunno, Ronald. You seem to have all the answers. Why don't you tell me?"

"Oh, come on, Crowley," Castanga cooed. "Don't tell me you're tiring of our little tête-à-têtes. And I thought you and I were beginning to establish a real rapport."

"Look Ronald . . . if it's all the same to you, I'd appreciate it if you cut the shit. I've got things to do and I can't spend all my time playing word games on the phone with you. If you've got something new to tell me, just say it and let me get back to work, okay?"

There was a moment of silence. "You really are marvelous, you know that Crowley?" Castanga said finally. "Trying to draw me out by pretending you don't really care. A delightful ploy; one that would probably work on most of the slugs you have to deal with. But we both know you care very much, don't we Crowley? We know that getting your hands on me is the most important thing in your mundane, trivial existence. I excite you; admit it, Crowley. Can't you feel your heart pounding faster when you talk to me?"

"Honestly, Ronald? Uh-uh. You're just not my type."

Castanga laughed. "I think that's why I like you so much, Crowley. No matter how stellar the opportunity, you can be counted on to miss the point entirely.''

"And just what is the point?'' Vince asked.

"The point is you and me, Crowley . . . the reality of us. This monumental joust of life and death that's going on between us. Don't tell me it doesn't exhilarate you as much as it exhilarates me. I don't think I've underestimated you on that point.''

"Is that all this is to you, Ronald . . . some kind of game?''

"Yes, it's a game—a supreme challenge. The chance for both of us to be everything we can be. Good God, Crowley, open your eyes for once in your life. I'm giving you the chance to share the moment of absolute creation. Don't blow it!''

Vince felt his stomach churning. "I'm not sure what it is you're trying to tell me, Ronald—''

"To be honest!'' Castanga exploded. "Just stop being a cop long enough to admit the excitement you feel. Admit it, goddamnit! Admit your heart pounds when you simply think about what I've done . . . what I'm about to do.''

"Want to run that one by me again?'' Vince said.

"You heard me, Detective. You didn't think I was about to rest on my laurels, did you? I'd be denying my own creativity if I did that . . . squandering the gift. Oh no, my friend, the best is yet to come. Everything that's happened up to this point has been prelude . . . setting the stage for my final, greatest exhibition.''

Walt Cuzak slipped a note under his nose saying that they'd successfully traced the call to a downtown pay phone. Vince signaled wordlessly for him to send units to the address while he held Castanga on the line. "So you're having another exhibition of your paintings?'' he asked.

Castanga chuckled. "You could say that.''

"At the Crawford Museum again?''

"Not this time. I'm afraid even those enlightened souls would shrink in the face of my masterpiece. No, this time

I've taken unusual pains to match my subject to its surroundings . . ."

Vince shuddered. "Are you telling me that you're planning another killing, Ronald?"

"I've told you I'm having an exhibition and you're invited." Castanga giggled. "You should be flattered, Crowley."

His mind was racing. "Where Ronald? Tell me where to go and I'll be there—"

"Oh, come now. Let's not take all the adventure out of the game. You're going to have to rely on your own resources for *something*. I have confidence you'll be able to figure it out."

"Are you giving me some kind of clue?" Vince asked.

"I've already talked too long. Be a good cop and follow those lumbering instincts you're so proud of. See you at the exhibit Crowley. Ta-ta for now." He hung up.

That was it. If there was a lead in anything Castanga said, Vince had missed it, and there was no time for quiet reflection. If clues were to come they would have to reveal themselves as things progressed. He grabbed his jacket, stopped at the front desk only long enough to check out a radio, and headed outside to the car.

He was on the Bruckner Expressway in minutes, speeding down the FDR Drive with his siren wailing, leaving scattered, angry motorists snarling in his wake. It was only a little past six A.M. but the city was already alive, its arteries choked with trucks and vans delivering produce and dry goods to downtown merchants, double- and triple-parked in the narrow side streets to offload their cargo in heavy traffic.

An illegally parked panel truck ground traffic to a halt between Madison and Fifth. Vince tried to back up, saw the way was blocked by gathering vehicles, and squeezed through a narrow opening at the curb; the sickening screech of collapsing metal telling him the opening was tighter than he'd thought. Startled pedestrians bolted into doorways and alleys as he rolled across the sidewalk, punching the siren in angry bursts like a volley of warning shots.

He arrived at the address at 6:16, a cheerless, gray office building with a bank of telephones lining the lobby. Units from the immediate area were on the scene as he double-parked in front of the entrance, cordoning off the site, questioning building employees and curious bystanders who had begun to gather. Nobody had seen anything and that was no surprise. Castanga was gone, as Vince had suspected he would be. The only question was where.

Several of the responding patrolmen lounged near a blue-and-white at the curb, the vehicle's short-wave radio barking staccato calls into the still morning air. Vince reached into his jacket pocket and realized he'd left the precinct without his cigarettes. "Can I bum a butt?" he asked as he approached them.

"Who's this guy we're looking for, anyway?" one of them asked as he handed Vince a filtered Chesterfield.

"Name's Castanga; wanted for a string of transsexual homicides." Vince clipped the filter and lit the cigarette.

"What kind of homicides?"

"Transsexual. You know . . . men who have operations to turn themselves into women."

"You gotta be kidding." The patrolman grinned at his partners. "We oughta be giving the sumbitch a medal instead of hunting him down. He's doing the city a favor, getting rid of shit like that."

Vince felt his anger rising and held it in check. Ninety-nine out of a hundred cops in the city would react the same way if it wasn't their case to solve. There was nothing personal in it for them; no reason for them to identify with the victims. They hadn't invested a big part of themselves in the hunt.

The radio crackled under the conversation: *Call the area*

five . . . Sector Charlie . . . One-eight-six to nine-eleven Avenue A . . . Apartment three-C . . . See the woman on possible B&E . . . The patrolmen rested against the vehicle, oblivious to the radio's blare, the uninspired drone of the female dispatcher's voice no more than background accompaniment to the day's routine. The skill of isolating important calls from irrelevant ones was a learned one. Rookie cops listened for them; veterans picked them up instinctively.

Units respond to ten-thirteen at the Elsinor Hotel . . . Twenty West Twenty-fifth Street . . . Possible female DOA . . . Keep 'em coming . . . The call came at him like a mortar blast. He tensed and waited for the repeat, making sure there was no mistake, then bolted for his car and screeched out into traffic.

A bedraggled crowd of onlookers had gathered outside of the hotel by the time he got there, harsh, flat silhouettes of rheumy-eyed vagrants and luridly costumed drag queens frozen in the hard reflective glare of flashing lights from patrol cars that had already arrived on the scene. He pushed his way through the mob and bounded up the front steps into the lobby, where a group of uniformed officers and plainclothes detectives had gathered at the open elevator door, surrounded by a motley assemblage of the hotel's residents, a woeful assortment of pimps, hookers, welfare castoffs, and transvestites pressing through the thin cordon of policemen, straining to get a better view.

He identified himself to the first patrolman he approached. "What's going on here?"

"Body's down there." The patrolman pointed to the exposed elevator shaft.

Vince peered through the open elevator door and saw a uniformed policeman at the bottom of the shaft, bending over a motionless female form. "Is she alive?" he yelled down.

The officer looked up and shook his head. "No way!"

Vince strained to get a better view in the murky darkness of the shaft. "Is she a blonde?" he asked.

"Nah . . . redhead."

"Tattoo on her right hand?" Vince yelled again.

There was a short pause. "Uh-huh . . . a butterfly I think."

It was Lucia. For a brief, puzzling moment he felt relief that it wasn't Charlene. He turned to a plainclothes detective who was questioning two drag queens by the side of the elevator. "How the hell did she end up down there?"

"That elevator never works," one of the queens lamented in a high-pitched fit of pique. "The elevator door opens and there's nothing there . . ."

He faced the crowd. "Did anybody see what happened here?"

A fussy, black transvestite pushed through the crowd. "I didn't see it but I heard it. I live right next door and I could hear them in the hall."

"Hear them doing what?"

"There was a guy knocking her around."

"Knocking who around?"

"The one down there . . . I think."

"Was there anybody else? Was Charlene with them?"

"I only heard that one . . . she was screaming."

"Why didn't you do anything?" Vince asked.

He shrugged. "Everybody's always screaming around here. It's usually no big deal."

Vince turned to the detective in charge. "Has anybody been upstairs?"

He nodded. "Apparently she came down from the sixth floor. We ran a sweep and all the apartments were empty. If there was anybody up there they split when the fun started."

He elbowed his way through the crowd to the front desk

and ordered the night clerk out of his plastic barricade. "What do you know about this?" he demanded.

The clerk shrugged. "I told the cops everything I know."

"About what?"

He stood dumbly. "You know, man . . ."

"No, I don't know, scumbag. You tell me."

"Hey, I don't want no trouble," he wailed.

"Didn't you see anything . . . hear anything?"

"I don't know nothin', man."

"You don't know what's at the bottom of that shaft?"

The clerk shifted uneasily. "Yeah . . . I know."

"So how'd she get there?"

He shrugged.

"I'll tell you how she got there, scumbag. She fell down a faulty elevator shaft. Why wasn't that elevator working?"

The clerk seemed stunned. "What the fuck are you coming down on me for? I ain't done nothing. That elevator never works, man."

"Why?"

He wheeled and headed for the cage. "I'm calling my lawyer, man. You can't pull this shit on me. I'm straight with everybody—the cops, the building inspectors—everybody got theirs. What kinda asshole shakedown is this anyway?"

Vince backed him against the cage and spoke in a measured whisper. "Tomorrow . . . after everyone is gone and you're here all alone, I'm coming back here and I'm gonna blow you away like the turd you are . . . understand?"

He began to sweat. "Whatta you want from me, man?"

"The girl, Charlene. What happened to her?"

"I dunno. They both went upstairs at the same time."

"What time was that?"

"Two, three o'clock. I'm not sure."

"Were they alone?"

"Yeah, but guys came in after that . . . Johns, you know."

"Was this one of them?" Vince handed him Castanga's photo.

"Mighta been." He shrugged helplessly.

Vince returned to the crowd at the elevator shaft and passed the photo among them. Nobody responded. "Okay if I have a look upstairs?" he asked the detective in charge.

"Be my guest." He motioned to a uniformed patrolman nearby. "Accompany the detective to the sixth floor and give him any assistance he needs."

They climbed the concrete stairs and entered Charlene's unlocked apartment. Everything seemed in place. No sign of struggle anywhere. "Was anything taken from this apartment?" he asked.

"I don't think so. CSU and Forensics haven't been here yet."

Vince walked slowly around the small apartment, systematically searching for anything that seemed out of place. The waterbed, the wicker table, the beanbag chairs, the artificial blaze in the fireplace . . . everything appeared to be as he remembered it. There was a rusting hot plate that he hadn't seen before; an unwashed frying pan resting on its lifeless burner; a paperback novel on the table, its worn cover a steamy illustration of two bosomy streetwalkers resting beneath a lamppost; an ashtray overflowing with lipstick-smeared cigarette butts; the crucifix . . .

There were papers on the dresser in the bedroom: unpaid bills, advertising brochures, a Spanish-language newspaper. Vince shifted them across the surface of the dresser with the eraser end of a pencil, careful not to add his prints to those Forensics would uncover. A year-old copy of the *New Yorker;* that didn't figure. It was too sophisticated a magazine for Charlene or Lucia to be reading. It opened easily, the pages held in place by paper clips attached top and bottom, revealing an advertisment spread across two adjoining pages. CASTANGA, the headline said simply in white letters on a stark, black background. PORTRAITS MACABRE. The name and address of the gallery had been carefully obliterated with a black marking pen.

Vince felt his blood run cold.

35

CASTANGA WAS THERE, somewhere in the hotel, and Charlene was with him. There was no logical explanation for the feeling, but Vince was as sure of it as anything he'd ever felt in his life. It was more than a hunch, more than the arousal of instincts he'd spent most of his life developing. It was the certainty of shared experience, the common strain of unspoken communication usually reserved for seasoned partners, for old married couples, for long-time lovers . . .

Was that what Castanga had been talking about? Was the monumental joust of life and death he'd spoken of no more than a twisted seduction? If that was true, it seemed he had succeeded. They were on the same wavelength now, lovers in the most perverted sense, the only kind of love Castanga could enjoy.

The thought came from an unfamiliar place, maybe a whisper from the growling abstractions Castanga had talked about in the plane. It angered him, embarrassed him; assaulted the core of everything he believed about being a cop . . . about being a man. Maybe Boyle had been right. Maybe he *had* been hanging out with the fags too long. He closed the magazine and turned to the young patrolman who'd accompanied him upstairs. "What's your name, Officer?"

"Donald Conlan, Detective," he answered.

"How old are you, Donald Conlan?"

"Twenty-four, sir."

Vince pointed to Conlan's holstered revolver. "Ever use that thing?"

"Only on the range."

He looked closely into the young officer's eyes and made an instant decision to trust him as a backup. It was the same as trusting Conlan with his life. "Okay. Keep that thing on your hip until I tell you otherwise, then remember what they taught you to do back at the academy. We're gonna get ourselves a murderer."

Vince led him to the stairwell and began a slow descent, watching carefully for fresh blood, pieces of torn clothing, anything that might tell him Castanga and Charlene had passed that way. There was blood, but the stains were already set on the walls and concrete steps, not recent enough to be of use. They were probably left by junkies who used the stairwell for shooting up, Vince decided, or crimes of another day. The Elsinor had seen more than its share of them.

Charlene's purse had been missing from the apartment. That meant she'd taken it with her, indicating she'd left without a struggle. Castanga had been able to coerce her in some way, either by persuasion or intimidation. Most likely the latter, he thought. Charlene must've been scared out of her wits after what he'd done to Lucia. But there was her gun . . . she carried it everywhere she went. Why hadn't she used it? There were no reports of gunshots.

He halted at the fifth-floor landing and debated whether or not to check out the rooms. There were at least fifty rooms on each floor, divided and subdivided by the greedy landlords. Checking them all would take forever and would

probably be a waste of time. Castanga had said he'd taken
pains to select a gallery as obscene as his subject. That
indicated a place he'd had access to before; somewhere he'd
been able to prepare his gruesome exhibition at a leisurely
pace. The rooms were too heavily traveled, too many
transient hookers and hoboes filtering through them every
day, to allow him the freedom he needed.

He continued slowly down the stairwell to the main-floor
landing where he waited while Conlan went for additional
backup. The only thing that made sense was the basement.
It fit all of the conditions: access, privacy; it *had* to be as
loathsome and disgusting as any place in the city. That
would fit right in. In another way, it would satisfy his
twisted sense of symbolism. The basement could represent
a tomb . . . a catacomb . . . the violent hell of Castanga's
fevered imagination. It was sheer guesswork, but Vince was
going all the way with it this time. There was the pervading
sense of Ronald Castanga leading him on . . . telling him
he was right on target.

Conlan returned and Vince led him down the remaining
stairs to the basement, accompanied by two additional
patrolmen he'd managed to enlist. It was go-for-broke time,
the time when the only choice remaining was to go ahead,
to suck up the flabby remnants of his faltering resolve, and
remember why the hell he wore a badge in the first place.
He could feel the exaggerated thumping of his heartbeat
echoing in his temples as he swung the heavy metal fire
door inward and stepped into the clammy blackness of the
cellar hall.

The place reeked of heating oil and decay, of rotting
wood and slime-encrusted concrete and a half century's
worth of accumulated trash, stacked in boxes and plastic
bags along every available wall. There was no sound, other
than the rasp of his own labored breathing and a single,
monotonous drip coming from someplace: thwap . . .
thwap . . . thwap; growing in intensity as the eerie silence

pressed in around him: *thwap . . . thwap . . . thwap . . .*

He groped along the wall, found a switch and flipped it, dimly illuminating the hallway with the light from a single bulb. It hung precariously from a frayed wire in the ceiling, seeming to sway with each forward step he took, animating the black shadows in his path like dancing specters mocking his progress. *Thwap . . . thwap . . . thwap . . .*

An unearthly squeal—a rat, the size of a dog, scampered for shelter amid the piles of garbage—then another, and another. Vince swallowed hard and drew his revolver as he approached the first of several doors lining the hallway. He waited while the backup officers positioned themselves, then reached across the door for the metal handle.

"That's far enough!" Castanga's disembodied voice barked from inside. Vince froze.

"Congratulations, Crowley," he went on through the closed door. "I never doubted for a moment that you'd show up. You've justified my faith in you."

Vince flattened himself against the wall. "Is Charlene in there with you?"

"Charlene? If you mean that misbegotten scum, that abomination of the human form you seem to have become enamored with, of course it's here. Why else would I have gone to all this trouble . . ."

Vince signaled for Conlan to go upstairs for reinforcements. "Why don't you come on out now, Ronald? We can talk about what it is you want me to do."

"Don't patronize me!" Castanga exploded. "We both know what's happening here!"

"No I don't, Ronald . . . I really don't understand, but I want to. I want you to tell me what my part is in all of this."

"Oh my, we have grown, haven't we?" Castanga's voice was a high, mimicking cackle. "At least we're willing to admit we have a part. That's certainly progress. Careful now, or we'll find ourselves admitting we really enjoy it."

Reinforcements clamored down the stairs, filling the

narrow hallway with police officers and firepower. Vince signaled for everyone to stay back and squared himself to the door. "I'm coming in, Ronald."

"By all means Crowley . . . but alone. You won't like what happens if your lackeys try to storm in here."

"It's just me . . ." Vince released the door latch, raised his revolver high over his head with both hands, and pushed the door slowly inward with his foot. "No surprises, Ronald . . . we can work this thing out . . ."

The door opened to total darkness. "That's fine, Crowley." Castanga's voice seemed to float out of the void. "I can see you perfectly, so it would be a big mistake on your part if you tried anything heroic. Come inside and shut the door behind you."

Vince stepped into the blackness and kicked the door with his trailing foot, leaning backward against it until it made contact. There was a brief, terrifying moment when nothing happened, then the lights went on.

"Welcome to my party, Crowley."

He squinted against the unaccustomed glare and felt his entire body stiffen as Castanga materialized before him, his head shaved, his naked body smeared with meandering crimson slashes glistening in the room's eerie glow. Charlene was beside him, suspended from a water pipe in the ceiling by both wrists, her legs spread-eagled and tethered to the floor. Castanga caressed her nude body, dappled with hundreds of tiny punctures, gathering her trickling blood on his fingertips, applying it to his skin like ritualistic warpaint. "I'm afraid I've gone and started without you."

Vince choked back a wave of revulsion, leveled the revolver in both shaking hands, and trained it on his target. Castanga was in his gunsights, shifting in and out of focus as beads of warm sweat ran down his forehead, into his eyes. He felt his index finger tighten on the cold metal of the trigger . . . heard the unfamiliar rasp of the unoiled hammer, the faint tick of the cylindrical bullet chamber as it began slowly to rotate . . .

"I wouldn't do that if I were you!" Castanga moved behind Charlene's dangling body. "Not yet, anyway. It would be a shame to spoil things now, after you've come this far . . ."

Vince stared into Charlene's pleading eyes, penetrating beneath the greasy shocks of matted hair that streamed across her face, covering the knotted gag stuffed in her mouth. The terror of what she had experienced was etched in every strained tendon of her face, the dread certainty of what was to come reflected in every trembling muscle. There was no clear shot . . . no way to get Castanga without hitting Charlene first.

Castanga produced a knife, reached around Charlene's body and began moving the blade sinuously across her abdomen. "You see Crowley, we're meant to be here, you and I . . . to partake in the final glorious moment of creation, the moment we were both born for . . ."

"What do you want from me?" Vince found himself saying in a choking voice. "We can work this out, Ronald . . . Just give me the knife and I'll do anything you say."

"You're already doing exactly what you're supposed to be doing." Castanga began laughing convulsively. "You still don't get it, do you Crowley? You still don't see that this is precisely the role I created for you. All you have to be is what you're trained to be. You don't need any instructions from me. That's the beauty of all of this . . . the sheer, uncluttered essence of it . . ." He pressed the tip of the knife deep enough to draw blood.

Vince took a step forward and sighted over the barrel of the revolver. "No more, Ronald. Just drop the knife and come out here where I can see you. We'll get this whole thing straightened out. I promise."

"It's almost time . . ." Castanga had begun to cry. "Up

until now, everything has been foreplay. Now, in just a few seconds, you and I will enter the infinite . . .''

Vince was walking steadily forward now. "It's all over, Ronald. I'm arresting you for the murder of Miguel Ramos . . .''

"Just think of it, Crowley. You, a dumb New York cop, and I've given you the chance to share my ultimate triumph!''

"You have the right to remain silent . . .''

"I've exposed myself . . . laid myself naked to you because I know you want it this way . . .''

"If you choose not to remain silent, anything you say can and will be used against you in a court of law . . .''

Castanga was sobbing now. "God, Crowley! This is our destiny . . . yours and mine. Neither of us has the right to deny it.''

"You have the right to be represented by an attorney . . .''

"Our lives have been the same life since the beginning of time . . . riveted in space . . . pointing toward this exact moment of fulfillment. All we have to do is take this final, glorious step together . . .''

"If you cannot afford an attorney, one will be appointed for you by the courts . . .''

"Live it, Crowley! Live it with me now! Breathe the infinite and you and I will live forever!'' He stepped out into the open and plunged the knife toward Charlene's motionless body.

Vince squeezed the trigger.

36

IF HE'D WANTED to feel sorry for himself, to shake, to cry . . . to simply close his eyes and get a handle on his runaway emotions, there wasn't time. The smoke had barely cleared before the department bureaucrats began descending on the scene, pencils poised, determined to defend the system and the reputation of the police who were paid to uphold it.

Everybody wanted a piece of him; an assistant Felony DA from Manhattan, the Borough Detective Supervisor, a union representative from the Detective's Endowment Association . . . Vince repeated his statement for each of them, and answered their questions mechanically, without passion. The discharge of an officer's firearm was a matter of extreme concern. No shooting was justified until the tribunals of the police department and the city of New York determined it was justified.

For the record, his interrogators were professional, non-committal, but privately they conceded it was an open-and-shut case. Castanga's final lunge had gone awry with the impact of Vince's bullet in his chest. Charlene would live and her testimony would support his version of the shooting. No investigation would be forthcoming, no panel of inquiry would be adjourned. The death of Ronald Castanga would be determined a righteous kill.

A righteous kill . . . for the first time in what seemed an eternity he found himself alone, standing on the periphery of the receding crowd as the final elements of the spectacle played themselves out. Paramedics toting IV bottles and emergency paraphernalia wheeled Charlene through the hotel lobby on a metal gurney and deposited her in a waiting ambulance. CSU detectives returned from the basement, along with the District Attorney's Videotape Unit, and proceeded to their respective vehicles, their individual records of the event packed away in manila envelopes and cardboard cartons . . . fodder for the downtown files, to be stored away and forgotten.

Tommy Ippollito arrived; it was the kind of news that traveled fast. "How you holding up, partner?"

"I'll make it . . . no big deal."

Tommy nodded. "Buy you a cup of coffee?"

Vince looked around the lobby. "I dunno, I guess they're finished with me."

"Better straighten your tie. The press is out there."

Outside, a technician from Channel 5 News trained a minicam on Chief Robert Shea as he answered questions from a female reporter. "If you want the real story, go to an expert, right?" Tommy quipped as they passed unnoticed.

Vince managed a grin. "Better believe it. I don't think the son of a bitch was ever inside the building."

They drove downtown in Tommy's car until they found a diner; parked and sat at the counter, surrounded by harried office workers who were trying to squeeze a leisurely brunch into a fifteen-minute coffee break. The clock over the grill said 10:35; almost five hours had passed since he'd gotten Castanga's call at the stationhouse. No wonder he was tired . . . so very tired. He rested against the counter and stirred the cup of murky coffee absently. "I shot a dog once," he said finally. "Back in Brownsville, the old seven-three. It'd just gone berserk for no reason, bit a couple of kids . . ."

"This was a good piece of work," Tommy said.

"Yeah, I know . . . righteous."

"You just gotta let it go, Vince. You did what you had to do."

"I wonder . . ."

"Hey . . . it was him or you, man. You know that."

"Was it?" Vince drained his cup. "I dunno, Tommy. I got this crazy feeling Castanga set the whole thing up . . . like I was just going through the motions; playing a part in his sick show."

"Well, he sure as hell didn't plan on a slab in the morgue," Tommy said.

"Why not? He didn't try to defend himself. They found Charlene's gun in his pocket. He didn't even try to use it."

Tommy paid the check and accompanied him out to the street. "Maybe guns just weren't his style. Maybe he forgot about it. Who the hell knows how a psychotic thinks? What you gotta do is cool it for now, man. You're gonna think yourself into a nervous breakdown."

Vince leaned against the fender of the car and inhaled the moist morning air. "You're right. I just need to get back to work, that's all."

"You coming back to the precinct?" Tommy asked.

"Why not? It's where I work, isn't it?"

They drove silently toward the FDR Drive, through the usual press of slow-moving vehicles, illegally parked trucks disgorging their cargo for the multitude of tiny shops lining the downtown streets: lacework, buttons, and millinery; desks, typewriters, office equipment; electrical supplies, restaurant supplies, plumbing supplies . . .

Vince was drifting . . . down the Bruckner Expressway

to the Triborough Bridge and across into Manhattan with Billy at the wheel, quoting poetry from his nimble brain.

> *. . . And rise O moon from yonder down*
> *till over down and over dale*
> *all night the shining vapor sail*
> *and pass the silent-lighted town . . .*

"That's Tennyson," Billy would tell him, and he would look out across the expanse of brilliantly lighted buildings and grin again. "Look at all of this and tell me he wasn't writing about this city of ours."

And Vince would look; first to the fading light of the South Bronx in the rear window of the car, shimmering like tiny Christmas bulbs through a canopy of angel's hair . . . then on to Harlem and downtown through the East Side, Sutton Place and Ward's Island . . . Gracie Mansion and the UN Building . . . the smells of the river penetrating . . . carrying him out onto the barges and tankers, across the bridges to Queens and Brooklyn.

God, what a city this is!

Tommy crept through the snarl of traffic, past sweating day laborers, barechested against the surge of spring warmth, crowding the sidewalk with hand trucks and dollys . . . a kinship of Spanish, Italian, Greek, black jive; the pandemonium of the street blend.

Tony's . . . a shoe store; Schein's Wigs and Bags; Blattstein's Jewelry; Action Radio and TV; The Power House Evangelical Mission of Christ and the Holy Trinity. They flanked the crowded sidewalks like sentries, a tapestry of mood and color highlighting the ceremonial of the street . . . the street dancers.

They were younger than he remembered, and more energetic; contorting their glistening bodies to the pulsating beat of ghetto rap, strutting like spastic toy soldiers, spinning like dervishes, breathing magnetic life into the decaying concrete.

"Do me a favor and let me out at the next light," he said to Tommy. "I feel like walking for a little bit."

Tommy pulled the car to the curb. "Want me to wait for you?"

"Uh-uh." Vince exited the car. "See you back at work."

The dancers paused as he approached, determined that he was no threat and continued. He stood at the edge of a gathering crowd of onlookers, absorbed in their rhythmic clapping and the throbbing tattoo of music. "Oh I'm never gonna dance again, guilty feet ain't got no rhythm . . ."

Billy knew where the truth was; where they could find open-air concerts and street fairs and jubilation . . . where young punks gathered on street corners, challenging them . . . defying them. We could take them if we had to, Billy; but for now, let's just cruise by and let them know we're onto them. That way, everybody knows where everybody else stands. We gotta let them know we're not afraid of them, Billy. That's where the respect comes. There's dignity in this job if you know where to look for it, eh partner?

"No I'm never gonna dance again, the way I danced with you . . ."

A burst of applause from the crowd snapped him out of his reverie. The show was over and the street dancers passed the hat among the diminishing onlookers seeking contributions. Vince reached for his wallet and felt the edges of the envelope in his jacket pocket—his letter to Jessy, dog-eared now from constant fingering. He dropped a dollar in the hat and headed for the corner where a red, white, and blue mailbox stood, surrounded by a pile of uncollected garbage. He deposited the letter and crossed the avenue. Behind him, the trailing sounds of music reap-

peared as the dancers began another performance, conse-
crating the narrow street with resonance and new life. He
walked uptown until the sound was lost in the melody of
traffic.

Bestselling Thrillers —
action-packed for a great read